Behind Picket Fences

Hend Hegazi

ISBN: 978-1-7340921-1-0

Cover Design by Reyhana Ismail

Interior Design by Scribe Freelance
www.scribefreelance.com

Author's Note

During the editing process of this novel, a family member fell ill and experienced events similar to those of one of the characters in this book. I just want to make it clear to all those who know me, to my family especially, that this novel had already been written for over a year when our beloved sister was diagnosed. Although the two stories run parallel, this was purely coincidental, by the will of God. I hope all of my readers will take a moment to pray for her; you may not know her name, but God is the All-Knowing.

Thank you to everyone reading this for your interest in my work. Kindly take note that there is a glossary of Arabic terms located at the end of the book to help you understand any foreign words. I hope you enjoy.

Acknowledgements

Any success that may come my way is by the Grace of God. I Praise God and thank Him for allowing me to fulfill my lifelong dream of becoming a published author. I pray for His continued guidance to help me put forth novels which provide not only entertainment, but also encourage compassion toward one-another, highlighting the truth that we are all more alike than different.

I will always be indebted to my parents for all they have done for me throughout my life. Your constant encouragement and support are the light that shines my path. I love you, Mama and Baba. God bless you both and reward you bountifully in this world and the next.

A huge thank you to the FB Publishing team. Gary Stevens and Chris Cornell, I cannot thank you enough for giving me a start and supporting my journey. Andrea Rubin, all of your hard work does not go unnoticed...thank you. And to my editor, Allison Lane, thank you for your guidance and suggestions.

To all my beta readers, your input was invaluable to me. I sincerely appreciate the time and support you gave me.

As it's not practical for me to list all of my family and friends and thank them individually, let me just say that each of you – those I've known since birth as well as those I've only known for a few years – have played some role in the person I am. Thank you all for always being there, for your honesty and your support. I love you all.

My wonderful children deserve so much more than a thank you. They keep putting up with my craziness, and miraculously, continue to love me and be my biggest fans. God blessed me so very much with all of you; thank you for the hugs and kisses and for always rooting for me. I pray it lasts forever. God bless you all, keep you safe and healthy, give you strength of faith, peace of mind, and always guide you to the Straight Path. Ameen.

Lastly, my loving husband, Ahmad. You rank first in my life, second only to my Creator. Having you by my side gives me a different level of strength. I pray that God continues to bless our union through this fleeting life so that we may be together in Eternal Paradise. From the bottom of my heart and soul, I love you.

CHAPTER 1:
The Families

Her neighbor's kids were playing outside again when Sidra pulled into her driveway. She rushed to gather her purse and briefcase so that she would not have to encounter their mother. Sidra liked Mariam; what she didn't like was chitchatting about those kids. Racing to the front door, she let out a sigh of relief as the door closed quietly behind her. With a few deliberate breaths, Sidra tried to erase all the tensions of her day. She tried to forget about the car that cut her off that morning, her boss who kept making inappropriate comments about how she dressed, and her work that always seemed to drain her. Taking in a deep breath, she tried to push it all out of her mind. Putting away her briefcase and purse, she went upstairs to get herself ready for dinner. James would be meeting her at the restaurant in just an hour, and, although part of her felt like she should cancel, she knew this date would get her out of her grumpy mood. It would be good to be out of the house. Although they had lived there happily for years, recently the house seemed uncongenial in its enormity. The walls seemed too hollow, the air inside too cool. At one point, Sidra's life had been everything she had wanted: a grand house with expensive cars in a beautiful neighborhood. Their money allowed them to afford lots of things, materialistic things. But the thing they craved most couldn't be bought by money, and it was completely out of their reach.

As Sidra stood in the bathroom rinsing her face, the sadness that she kept hidden in the innermost folds of her soul began to creep out and envelop her. She stood there, staring at the running water, wishing that just as it could cleanse the impurities from her body, it could also cleanse her heart of its anguish. "Stop it!" She tried to force the emotion away, proceeding to wash up. Face dripping, she stretched her hand to turn off the faucet, but froze mid-air as Sidra caught a glimpse of herself in the mirror. *How did I get so old?* she thought. Her hand went to her jet black ringlets, where her fingers traced more grey hairs than she remembered having. The wrinkles in her chocolate complexion, on the other hand, were few; hers was not an aging of years. Rather, it was marked by the despair of youth's abandoned hope.

Her heartache increased, seeing herself like this. *How sad is it that I can actually pity myself?* Sighing loudly, she turned off the water and dried her face and hands.

Sidra changed into a simple, sexy cocktail dress and stood at the mirror applying her make-up. As she finished up, she looked herself over and let out a shrug, "It'll have to do."

She switched purses and peeked at the mirror one last time. Just as she made it to the last step at the bottom of the stairs, the door opened and Farris walked in.

"Hey, Sidra. Wow, honey, you look great. Are we going out for dinner?" He leaned over and kissed his wife on the cheek as she rolled her eyes.

"I'm having dinner with friends. I won't be too late."

"Oh," Farris let out, managing to hide his disappointment. "What should I do for dinner, then?" he said softly, thinking out loud. Sidra purposely misinterpreted the question and retorted with as much animosity as she claimed to have heard, "I don't know, Farris. You're not a child, surely you can figure out something." The steam from her words lingered as she slammed the door behind her.

Farris let out an aggressive sigh as he stood staring at the door through which Sidra had just left. He thought of all the ways he could reciprocate her increasingly hostile behavior. He could be as negligent as she and come home late without calling. He could be as insulting as she and ignore her presence by spending all of his free time with his friends. Theoretically, he could. But he hung his head knowing that in reality, he had no such power; he was still very much in love with his wife. No matter how she acted, he could never be disrespectful.

"Soon, things will be more clear, Sidra," he said out loud as he loosened his tie and undid the top button on his shirt. "You'll probably hate me when you find out I'm having you followed, but I need this torture to end. One way or another, I will find out what's going on with you."

There had been a time when she had not been so guarded with him. The first four years of their marriage were filled with endless conversations about all types of issues. Sidra would talk jovially straight through dinner and it wouldn't be until they were snuggled under the sheets that she would ask about his day. And he loved it – he loved that she let him into every inch of her life and her mind. But now she was so distant… he would settle for any inch.

Lately she had been spending most of her time either at work or locked up in their room, alone. Her slouched shoulders and wilting eyes reflected pain and sadness. When Farris tried to discuss it with her, she would change the subject. As the weeks progressed, her sadness had morphed to belligerence. She would come home late, and, when Farris showed concern, would say, "My work comes first. Either accept that or move on." On the weekends, when he asked her where she was going, instead of giving an answer with a soft peck to his cheek – as she used to do just months before – she often replied, "That's none of your business." Sidra spread tension to all aspects of their life, even in the bedroom. It had been months since she would let Farris touch her. Over the past few weeks, he had become so disparaged that he had stopped trying. But Farris had vowed to himself that he would be patient with her. He kept telling himself to forgive her ugly behavior because he loved her. She was going through a difficult period, and he felt that it was his duty to be there for her. He told himself that despite her recent behavior, she still loved him.

Now, sitting alone on the couch, head in his hands, Farris recalled something she had said to him nearly a year before: "The only commitments we have to keep are to each other." Lately, however, he questioned her commitment to him. Her late night phone calls and frequent dinner meetings could only mean that her commitments were to someone else now.

~

Mariam let out a grunt as she peeled her fingers from the front door. *What in the world? This is so disgusting. Oh, I envy Sidra... I'll bet her doorknobs are never sticky.* Sighing heavily, she went to grab a sponge and clean up yet another mess made by her children.

Although Mariam couldn't deny that being a full time mother was exhausting, she also found great fulfillment in her job. She felt proud that she hadn't missed any of her children's milestones. She loved being the one they turned to for comfort and the one they chose to shower with hugs and kisses at various times throughout the day.

While their family had no shortage of emotions, there was no question that they had the most modest home in the neighborhood. The cozy three bedroom home, with its tiny kitchen and chipped paint revealing the graying wood beneath, had a moderate front yard decorated with bikes, balls, tricycles and an assortment of toys. When the children played outside, their shouting and laughter could be heard all the way around the block.

Every few minutes she peered out the window to check on the kids. Her eldest two, Adam and Dina, were only nine and eight years old, but they did a good job of keeping the younger two within the bounds of their yard. Mariam loved the chemistry they had with each other. Gabriel and Zain looked up to Adam and Dina and obeyed them as though they were a second set of parents. Watching them all play together, she wished she could drop everything and join them. She wanted to enjoy the warm weather with them. She wanted to chase and tickle them until their bellies hurt from laughter. She wanted to give them all horsy rides until she could no longer straighten her back. She wanted to, but she had dishes to wash, laundry to do, and bathrooms to clean. She looked forward to the day when her kids would take pride in keeping their living quarters neat, but part of her feared that day would never come.

Morgan pulled into their driveway about an hour later. Before gathering the troops he played with them for a few minutes outside. Mariam heard the energy level rise again and tried to finish up quickly, knowing that it was only a matter of minutes before they would attack. Laughing at the sounds she heard coming from outside, she pulled the leftovers from the fridge and quickly finished making the salad.

"All right you guys. I want you all showered, dressed in your PJs and sitting at the dinner table in twenty minutes. Adam and Dina, take care of your little brothers," Morgan commanded as he let the youngest down from his shoulders and ran his hand over his disheveled, dark brown hair. The kids raced up to do as they were told as Morgan went to greet his wife.

"Hey, gorgeous." He gave her a gentle kiss and wrapped his arms around her. He loved feeling her plump, soft body against his broad frame; he took pride in being her support, being the pillar from which she gained strength. "How was your day?"

Mariam answered without lifting her head from his chest. "Oh, you know... same old, same old. I cleaned cookie crumbs from under the beds, pulled out perfectly clean clothes that were shoved in the laundry basket, and had a super hard time wiping away some kind of gooeyness that was painted on the walls... I couldn't figure out what it is and now I just want to pretend like I never saw it. What about you? Anything fun and exciting happen with you?"

"The seniors started a food fight at lunch. When the principal turned his head, I chucked a bagel at this kid. Got him square in the face."

She pulled away from him softly, laughing. "It's so good that they have a role model like *you* to look up to."

As Morgan went to grab a piece of cucumber from the salad, Mariam slapped his hand away gently. "Uh, uh. Not with those disgusting fingers you don't! Go wash up while I finish this."

At the dinner table, the kids dominated the conversation with things that happened at school. Mariam and Morgan listened attentively as they heard that mean Robby made fun of little Suzy because she had to wear glasses. "But I stuck up for her because he made her feel bad. I said, 'You shouldn't make fun of people Robby. That's not nice. Plus, I think her glasses are pretty.' Then he left her alone after that."

"You really helped her confidence, Dina. Good for you!" Morgan encouraged.

The younger two loved hearing stories about school. They couldn't wait till they would be able to go, too.

"Mom! I want to go to school. I want to tell Robby to leave Suzy's glasses alone!"

"Don't worry, Gabe. It's really not that fun. Most of the time we just sit there listening to the teacher talk about capital letters and commas and addition and stuff. Trust me, it's not all fun." Adam wanted to make sure his little brothers didn't get the wrong idea about school.

"You'll get to go soon enough, honey," Mariam assured him, patting his head. "Now, everyone finish up. It's getting late."

Once all the teeth were brushed, the stories told, and the teddies tucked in tight, Mariam crept into bed and cuddled up to her husband as he watched TV. "The phone and credit card bills came today. But we don't have enough in the bank to cover them. We'll have to wait for your next paycheck."

"Really? We don't have enough?" The news made Morgan sit up straight. "How did that happen?"

"I know. I hadn't realized we'd been cutting it so close, either. I'm sure we'll start saving again within the next month or two."

Her attitude calmed him a bit, but he wasn't as sure as she was.

"Things always seem to pop up, though. And then what if there's an emergency, God forbid. We won't be able to handle it."

"Don't say that, Morgan. We can't worry about that kind of stuff. All we can do is try to save as much as we can and pray that things work out."

He lay back again, worry still on his face. "I guess you're right," he said, but even the words themselves knew that he did not believe them.

"Just make sure you give me that paycheck as soon as you get it."

Morgan's head barely moved as he clenched his jaw and nodded, unaware that the anticipated emergency was just around the corner.

Summer and Porter lived across the street from Mariam and Morgan. Porter left the house every morning at the same time his neighbors' kids were out waiting for the school bus. Every morning he smiled at them and gave them a warm hello, then silently thanked God that he and Summer had decided to wait a few years before having kids. They were always too loud, too full of energy. And although he never actually saw them pick their noses or eat dirt, those were the images he had in his mind.

Porter and Summer had only been married for two years, making them the newest couple to the neighborhood. They focused their lives on their careers. Porter owned a small import/export business and was doing moderately well. Summer was a struggling artist. She spent most of her days painting and the majority of her evenings trying to book herself into exhibitions and searching for customers to purchase her work. So far her paintings were costing her much more than they were making, but she was optimistic that one day her efforts would be well rewarded.

On the outside, Porter and Summer seemed very different. He was very serious all the time while she took things lightly. He always dressed formally while she felt her best in wide jeans and flowing tops with her layered, loose red waves framing her face. He was very organized, and she was very free. And that's exactly what attracted him to her.

He loved her energy, the way her hazel eyes beamed when she spoke. He loved the way her hair seemed to go in all sorts of directions, yet it never looked messy. He was captivated by her from the moment they met.

It took Summer a bit longer to warm up to Porter. She had never met anyone so structured. But he treated her with respect and kindness, and quickly she found herself growing more and more fond of him. In the two years they dated, she managed to get him to stop wearing ties and to grow his dirty-blond hair just long enough so that she could hold onto it when she ran her fingers through it. He didn't mind bending his ways for her.

Likewise, he enjoyed passing on his experience to her. From him she learned a little about time management and how structure and routine help make a person more productive. Before they were married, she was used to waking up after noon, working in her studio for a few hours while simultaneously answering her phone calls, then spending the rest of the day doing errands or reading at her leisure. Of course time always got away from her and before she knew it, it was too late to make any business calls or network.

Once they were married, however, Summer got into the routine of getting up early and working uninterrupted for a few hours. Sometimes she read or thumbed through magazines for inspiration, but she always kept one eye on the clock, making sure to leave herself enough time to make important phone calls.

Up until the past few months, that routine worked fine. But now, she felt stuck, bored, and more than just a little unsuccessful. Porter even noticed that her complexion looked more wan, her eyes more sunken. Her usually cheerful demeanor had been replaced by one marked with lassitude. Hating seeing her so, he made a recommendation.

"Maybe you should think about taking on a regular nine to five job."

With knitted eyebrows, Summer stared at her husband. "I'm not a nine to fiver, Porter. You know that."

"But even if it were doing what you love? I mean, you could be an artist for a magazine. Or even teach it. That would be fun."

"But I wouldn't be painting what I want. God, I can't believe you would even suggest that," she fumed.

He tried to convince her that a structured job in her field might provide her with the inspiration to make wonderful paintings on her own. He tried to tell her maybe a change from her routine to a different one would rid her of the ennui she felt. He tried, but she didn't listen. She was stuck, and none of his ideas would solve her problem.

"Can you believe he *actually* suggested that I get a nine to five job!" she confided to her therapist. "I mean, if he knew me *at all* he would never have said that. I love him – I really do – but sometimes he drives me crazy."

"Why do you think he made that suggestion?"

"I know his heart is in the right place. I know he just wants to help... to get me out of this rut. But it totally had the opposite effect. I felt like even my closest friend doesn't really know me. And that made me feel... even more unhappy. And completely alone." She shook her head slightly as she wrapped her arms around herself.

"Do you think that there was something you wished he would have suggested instead?"

Summer was quiet, staring off into space, searching for an answer. "I don't know," she whispered moments later.

The doctor let her sit in silence for a while. Some time later, she softly brought Summer out of her trance. "Have you been taking your medication?"

Summer let out an exhausted sigh. "Yeah," she lied.

The therapist nodded and made some notes on the clipboard in her hands.

"And you feel like your unhappiness and loneliness are always intense, or was it just this incident that escalated those feelings for you?"

The question seemed to echo in her mind: *Are you always unhappy and lonely? Are you always this miserable?* The words kept repeating themselves, causing her heartbeat to quicken and her breathing to increase. Her eyes began to well with tears as she started hyperventilating. Without saying another word, she snatched her purse to her chest and burst out of the office.

Once out on the street, Summer gasped deeply, as though her lungs had been deprived of air for hours. *What is wrong with everyone?* she thought. *Why do I keep coming up against brick walls everywhere I turn?* Summer was convinced that no one – not even the therapist she was paying – understood her. She worried that perhaps she didn't even understand herself. She racked her brain to think of a friend that she could turn to, someone who would help her feel less alone. But how could anyone relate to her when none of them were in her position? None of her friends were married and she didn't expect that they ever would marry. That was the type of commitment none of them felt they should make – they felt marriage would stifle not only the habits they had grown accustomed to, but even their personalities. Months before, when she was not yet so desperate, they had proven that their lack of marital experience meant their advice had to be taken with a grain of salt.

"We warned you about it, Summer. We warned you, but you didn't listen."

"I just think that... ahh, I don't know," she had sighed. "I don't want to believe that love, the most pure, most beautiful thing in this world, could be so fatal."

"It's not love that's fatal," her girlfriend had remarked. "It's all the sacrifices that are expected of you once you make those vows of forever. Those sacrifices slowly wear away at your essence, until one day you open your eyes to find you're standing in front of the oven wearing a hideous floral apron, stirring the pasta sauce with one hand and ironing your husband's dress shirts with the other."

Even though Summer didn't agree with her friend, she hadn't voiced her objection... she had just kept quiet.

"You need to get out," her friend had said. Now, considering the unruly state of her life, she thought that was perhaps the best idea. And the cleanest weapon she could use to 'get out' was sitting right in her medicine cabinet.

~

May and Hasan had moved to the neighborhood before any of the other families. Before she had given birth to Noor, May had been a rising editor at a literary magazine. When she decided to put her career on hold to raise her children, her work ethic and eye for perfection prompted the editor in chief to guarantee her a job at any time she decided to return. Now that her youngest was finally in school full time, she was looking forward to delving back into her work.

For the past week, however, May hadn't been feeling well. Hasan had been struggling to get the kids ready for school every morning so she could rest. He wasn't used to making lunches, helping his youngest to get dressed, and making sure they got some breakfast before leaving. These chores paled in comparison, however, with the stress of waking up Noor.

"Come on, *habibti*. You're going to be late if you don't get up right now. Deen's already washed up and dressed and he's downstairs having breakfast." Although he was frazzled by all the new duties to which he needed to attend, he managed to keep his voice firm but calm as he coaxed his daughter out of bed.

"Baba, I'm tired. I don't want to go to school today."

"Oh, come on. Do you want the rest of your classmates to get ahead of you? You'll end up being the worst in the class. You don't want that." He tried to entice her, but it failed.

"Yes, I want to be the worst."

It was the second time this morning he had gone to her room, and now he was running out of patience.

Standing up straight and raising his voice slightly he said, "Noor, get up. The school bus will be here soon and if you miss it, I don't have time to drive you. Get up."

Figuring he had made his point, he went down to check that his youngest was still on schedule.

"Did you finish your breakfast, Deen? Do you want anything else?" Hasan spoke as he cleared some empty glasses and a plate from the table.

"No, thank you, baba. I'm all done. *Alhamdu lillah.* And my bag's ready and I even put my lunch in my lunchbox."

"Good boy, *habibi.*" Hasan kissed his son on the top of the head and washed the items he had just placed in the sink. He finished up hurriedly then went back upstairs to check on the progress that Noor was making. His face became bright red when he saw that she was still in bed.

"Noor! If you don't get up this instant, you won't get any allowance for a week and you'll stay home to do homework when we go out to the park on Saturday!"

Noor knew her parents enough to know they did not make empty threats... if he said no allowance, he meant it! She jumped up.

"I'm up, baba. I'm up. I'll get washed up and be downstairs in a few minutes."

Once he watched his kids get on the bus and saw it pull away, Hasan went back upstairs to kiss his wife goodbye. He had woken her plenty of times already to ask her what Deen should wear, what he should make for their lunches, and where Noor's permission slip was. He knew she needed her rest and he hated to wake her again. But he couldn't leave without saying goodbye.

"Did Noor give you a hard time again?"

"A little, but I'm getting a bit better at it."

"If she does it again, splash some cold water on her. I forgot to tell you that trick; she hates it and it gets her right up."

Hasan laughed at his wife's technique.

"Don't laugh. She's in sixth grade and in all these years she hasn't missed the bus once. Trust me, it works."

"I'll try it tomorrow. But don't you worry about all this stuff; just concentrate on getting better. Is there anything in particular you want me to pick up on my way home today? Anything special you want to eat?"

"Whatever the kids want is fine."

"I'll try not to be late. I told them not to give me any patients past three. My regular two thirty takes about half-an-hour, so I should be home before three thirty. If I don't have any sessions just before or after lunch, I'll try to come back to check on you. I love you."

"I love you, too," May said to her husband as he kissed first her hands then her forehead. He tucked her in again, then made his way silently out the door.

May loved the quiet that came once the house was empty. She stayed in bed for a half hour more, then decided she needed a change of scenery. May was careful as she got out of bed. She sat up slowly. She started to stand up even more slowly, but her legs were too weak to hold her, so she quickly sat back down.

This had been going on for too long now and she was starting to get frustrated by it. She had just had her annual physical a few months before and the doctor said she was in perfect health. She knew this was just some temporary bug making her weak and queasy, but she wanted to be better. She felt weak and old and wished, for just a moment, that she could feel young again. She wished she could feel as young as her neighbor, Summer, looked.

"When did I become this old, disabled woman? I feel worse than

I did while I was pregnant," she said out loud to herself. Then, almost as soon as she had let the words out, she started to laugh. Sure, she was old... but not that old. How hadn't she thought of it before? That must be it! The weakness, the tiredness, the queasiness... all the symptoms pointed to her being pregnant.

Once she felt strong enough, she got up, had breakfast and showered. The drugstore was a short five minute drive away. Within 20 minutes, she was back at her house, sitting on the covered toilet seat, waiting for the stick to change color. Just to be sure, she had bought three different tests and peed on them all. Within a few minutes, they all came out negative.

May was both relieved and puzzled. They had never planned on having more than two kids and another now would mean putting her career on hold again. Not to mention she quite simply didn't have the energy to chase after another baby. But what else could all those symptoms mean?

Suddenly she felt exhausted again. Lying on the couch, she surrendered to sleep.

That night, after they had eaten dinner and the kids had finished their homework, they all sat together in the living room. May was reclined on the couch with her head resting in Hasan's lap, and the kids were both on their bellies watching TV.

"I think I need to go to the doctor."

"Yeah, I know. I called from work and made an appointment for tomorrow."

"I went out today and bought some pregnancy tests, but they were all negative."

"Were you feeling pregnant?" Hasan's eyebrows curled in surprise by what his wife had just said.

"Well, I was having all the same symptoms that I got when I was pregnant. And I couldn't think of what else it could be. But that wasn't it."

"*Alhamdu lillah* for everything."

"*Alhamdu lillah*, of course," May repeated. "But to be honest, I got more worried when pregnancy got ruled out."

"Don't be silly," her husband assured her, rubbing her head. "*In sha' Allah* it's just a bug. It'll run its course and go and you'll be back to your normal self before you know it. But just to be sure, we'll go get you checked out in the morning."

His words were comforting, but she knew him well enough to see beyond what he wanted her to – she knew him enough to see the worry in his eyes that he was desperately trying to hide.

The doctor's office was, surprisingly, not crowded. The nurse called May, and she and her husband went into the examination room to wait for the doctor. When the doctor came in, she asked May some general questions about her health, then she performed a general exam.

"Your weight today is less than it was when you were here for your physical. Have you been trying to lose weight?"

"No," May answered. "I just haven't had a very good appetite lately."

"Have you had any excessive bleeding or unexplained bruising?"

May thought for a minute. "Ummm, I usually have unexplained bruising... it's one of the perks of being a mom."

May laughed, but the doctor did not.

"But you haven't noticed that it's gotten worse lately?"

May shook her head, "I don't think so."

The doctor continued to poke and prod at her body for a few more minutes. When she finished, she pulled May's gown closed and patted her knee to indicate she should sit up. Smiling, the doctor said, "Well, let's do an abdominal ultrasound and some blood work so we can pinpoint what's making you feel like this."

The doctor obviously had her suspicions about May's symptoms. May and Hasan both wanted to stop her before she walked out of the room, to demand that she tell them what she thought might be going on. Hasan knew that he should speak up; he'd been a physical therapist for more than twelve years now and was familiar enough with the medical field to understand what questions to ask. He knew he should speak up, a voice inside him urged him to. But the feeling in his gut won the battle; he didn't dare open his mouth.

After the ultrasound, the nurse proceeded to take the blood samples. Her hands were icicles, even through the gloves, but May was too nervous to care. She stared, expressionless, as the needle entered her arm. She knew the doctor wouldn't have ordered all these tests unless she suspected something in particular. Powerless to gain instant knowledge, all she could do was pray that the feeling in her gut – the one sensing catastrophe – would prove to be wrong.

CHAPTER 2:
Sidra and Farris

Months before Farris had the idea of spying on Sidra – and before her sadness had turned to hostility – he thought of doing something to help them reconnect. After weeks of thinking and planning, Farris suggested that they take a vacation, go away somewhere to refresh their energy. He hoped it would be a start to bringing her back. Surprisingly, Sidra agreed willingly.

They only took a few days off from work, but linked with the already long weekend, Farris was confident that the time was enough to shed their negative spirits and return with a more positive vitality. Sidra was glad to get away, she wanted a change. She knew, of course, that she wouldn't find the change she was looking for on a short trip away; the change she yearned for was more permanent. Even still, she expected the sun and fresh beach air would help her decide the direction she should take at this point in her life.

After checking in at the hotel and grabbing a quick lunch, the couple changed into their beach clothes and headed out.

"Could you get my shoulders?" Farris asked his wife as he handed her the sunblock. She took the bottle without speaking, and applied the lotion rather methodically to her husband's back. When she finished, she hesitantly passed him the bottle. Farris gently rubbed the sunblock throughout her back and shoulders, messaging them as he went. He loved feeling her body beneath his fingers and didn't want it to end. Hesitantly finishing up, he laid a lingering kiss at the nape of her neck, taking in her sensual scent.

Stretched out under the warm sun, with kind breezes brushing against them, Sidra remained mostly quiet. After a short while, Farris invited her to take a dip, but she refused, claiming that she didn't want to get her hair wet.

Farris swam out a short distance then enjoyed just floating along on the small waves. There was a family playing on the sand, and he couldn't help but watch as they chased after one another, kicking up sand all over. The oldest daughter, who couldn't have been more than eight or nine, squealed with delight as her father rose from the sand pile she had buried him under and scooped her in his arms. Sprinting into the water as he carried her, he threw her up with all his might. She flew for a few seconds then landed in the sea. The young girl's laughter was louder than the crash which arose as her body hit the water.

Farris laughed out loud. Looking over at Sidra, he could tell that she was pretending not to have noticed the beautiful scene of the family playing together. She was pretending to be napping. Watching her as she lay there – her beautiful chocolate brown body contrasting with the white towel beneath, her huge brown eyes hiding behind dark shades, closing out the world – he wanted to pull her close to him, to unite with her in a way they had been addicted to not so long ago.

As quietly as he could, he snuck out to the shoreline, filled his cupped hands with as much water as they would carry, stealthily approached his wife, and soaked her.

"Farris! What are you doing?!"

"I'm getting you wet. You want to do something about it?" he teased with one eye cocked.

Her enraged shock quickly turned to a smirk as she tried to shake herself dry. "Do I want to do something about it?" she repeated playfully, her soul beginning to peer out from behind its solemnity. "Are you daring me to a water fight?"

"Maybe I am," Farris said as he walked gingerly back toward the water and refilled his hands. But before he could turn around, a slight force knocked him over.

"After five years of marriage, you still haven't learned that I will win every fight, even a water fight?" Sidra taunted as she stood over him.

Laughing with his whole body, he got up quickly and scooped his wife in his arms.

"Oh is that so? Well, we'll just have to see about that."

"Farris, don't you dare throw me into the water." Sidra tried to hide her desperation behind her firm tone. "Farris, I'm warning you!"

"Oh... you're warning me. Well in that case...." He lowered his arms slightly, tricking Sidra into thinking he would just put her down. Then suddenly, in one swift move, he lifted her and tossed her as far as he could.

"Ahhh!" she screamed. And in a second she became drenched from head to toe.

"Ugh! I can't believe you just did that! I'm going to get you for that." Her laughter was the only sound Farris could hear.

They splashed at each other for a while more, then Farris surrendered. He placed his hands on her waist and gave her a quick kiss on the lips.

"Does this mean you admit defeat?" Sidra joked, standing straight with her hands on her hips.

Farris lowered his head and nodded, feigning shame.

"I told you I'd always win!" Their smiles lit up at the sound of the other's laughter. Sidra knew that Farris had planned this trip to get her out of the mood she couldn't shed, and she appreciated his effort. But she loved that *he* was enjoying himself. As they stood holding each other in the water, enjoying the beautiful moment, it felt rehabilitating to Sidra to know that she was the reason for Farris' laughter.

The remainder of their trip passed by with just as much love and laughter. After hours of begging, Farris managed to get Sidra to agree to go to the small amusement park in town.

"But if you try to get me to ride a roller coaster, I will have to hurt you."

"Fair enough," said Farris, "no roller coasters."

Standing in line at the first ride, Sidra began to regret their decision.

"Farris... we should go. Look at us... we look like these kids' chaperones. They're all so young... and we aren't."

Turning his cap sideways, slouching his shoulders, and swaying from one leg to the other, he said, "I don't know about you, dude..." coming out of character just to clarify he continued, "or would you be dudette?... whatever... but I'm only 19. I snuck out of the house to come here today. My pops and moms think I'm at school."

"Oh yeah?" Sidra giggled, raising her eyebrows to emphasize her sarcasm. "And what school is that? The Academy for the Aged and, judging by your performance just now, Delusional?"

"Of course," Farris played along. "The Academy for the Aged and Delusional, where we all have perfect GPA's for acting as old as we feel."

The smile never faded from his face as he adjusted his cap and tucked his t-shirt back into his jeans.

"And you feel 19?" Sidra asked, still smiling but looking him straight in the eyes, expecting an answer.

"No, not 19. But not 34 either. I feel the same way I did ten years ago... so why not act like I'm ten years younger? I mean, do I look 34?"

Sidra examined the face she knew perfectly. "I guess not."

"And you don't look your age either. And even if we *did*, what's so bad about acting as young as we feel?"

He had a point. The only problem was that lately she felt much older. She felt like she was a middle aged woman with the beauty of life behind her, and no promise of a brighter tomorrow. She could feel on her soul the wrinkles that had not yet appeared on her face.

That was exactly why Farris had insisted they go to the amusement park – to revive their younger selves. And by the sounds of the shrieks of laughter coming from his wife as they rode the Rollin'

Rock n' Roll ride, Farris knew that it had been a good idea to come.

They spent a good hour at the game booths and arcade center, and they left with Farris carrying a medium sized stuffed pink rabbit which Sidra had won for him at the water gun horse race. Sidra walked along holding an enormous ball of cotton candy. Despite her efforts to the contrary, she was making a bright blue mess of her face and hands.

They spent the next couple of days enjoying the sun and the water and just being away. On Sunday morning Sidra insisted they find a nearby church. Farris thought they could enjoy a vacation break from services.

"I'm most at peace in church, Farris. It's important to me."

He watched her during the sermon, the intensity of her focus made him wish he had the power to soothe her soul. He closed his eyes, folded his hands before him, and with all his spirit, prayed to the Almighty to ease his wife's emotional struggle.

Later that day, as their retreat was coming to an end, Sidra was surprised to realize that she hadn't missed the sound of her phone ring nor had she been obsessed with checking her email constantly. It gave her a sense of relief to be free of all the constraints which held her captive. She enjoyed the peace so much that the thought of going back sent pains throughout her body. It wasn't going back to work that she dreaded; it was the idea that she would soon be back in that large, empty, quiet house.

Sidra napped through their car ride home. Farris drove, the whole way replaying in his mind all the beautiful moments they had shared that week. He was confident their vacation had served its purpose. Maybe everything wasn't completely back to the way it had been a few years ago, but he knew that his wife had not only enjoyed her time away, but she had started to reconnect with him and with herself. When he remembered seeing her lips and chin covered with blue cotton candy, he couldn't help but smile. All of her actions all week pointed to the fact that she had rediscovered in herself and in her life enough blessings to pull her from the sadness that had been slowly drowning her. He looked forward to walking into their home with the same woman he had carried over the threshold five years before.

With her eyes closed and making sure to keep her mouth open slightly – as Farris often mentioned she did while sleeping – Sidra prayed for guidance to solve her problems, just as she had done earlier at church, and just as she did every night. She silently repeated The Lord's Prayer, then ended with her own supplication. *Please God. Only you can ease my distress. Guide me, O Lord.*

Even as she prayed, a plan which was bound to repair the wounds in her life began to formulate in her mind. Surely it would not repair them all, as not all wounds can be healed, but for those that were within her power, she would start to mend. She knew her plan would end up breaking her own heart – and she wondered if her Lord would forgive her for bending the rules of morality – but these were things she would have no choice but to endure.

CHAPTER 3:
Mariam and Morgan

For the second consecutive month, Mariam couldn't pay the bills before Morgan's paycheck had been deposited. It worried her to think that they had become like so many families she had heard of, living from paycheck to paycheck. The insecurity of it made her nervous, but she tried hard to be hopeful and not let Morgan see her anxiety.

Her efforts, however, were for nothing; he was more concerned about the situation than she was. He spent hours awake at night trying to think of ways to cut back, trimming corners so they could manage to put something, anything away. He tried to think of how things would work if they sold one of their cars, but solving the logistics of a one car situation proved a failure.

He tried to find other solutions, ways to cut back on expenses. But his mind kept coming up against a wall. Much as he tried, he could think of no luxury expenses. All of their money went to food, clothes, doctor's visits, diapers, and utilities. They ordered pizza or take out very rarely, and that was a small but important treat he didn't want his family to give up. From every angle he examined it, there was no way out.

Morgan began to worry that the situation might be long-term; he was concerned that he wouldn't be able to provide properly for his family. In case of an emergency, they would be in debt. He felt suffocated by the weight of it, and the pressure began to manifest itself in his behavior.

Mariam noticed that for the past week he had stopped playing with the children. He would come inside as soon as he pulled in, give her a curt hello, and go wash up for dinner. He stopped asking about her day, and he seemed to be preoccupied even while they all sat together for dinner. An occasional nod or "uh-huh" was as much as he contributed to their conversations, and only if a question was specifically directed at him.

Each night she tried to comfort him. She enveloped him in her arms and squeezed tightly. "Don't worry so much. It will all work out," her soft voice tried to calm his anxieties. But each night he responded the same; gently unfolding her arms, he would give her a fake smile, an indifferent kiss on the lips, and turn on his side, away, pretending to fall asleep.

She tried not to be upset, she knew his change was not caused by a decrease in love for her. She knew that his behavior had changed because of the stress he was feeling. Her mind knew all of this, but still, she couldn't help being a little hurt. Maybe if they talked about it together, they could find some sort of solution. Maybe. But Morgan insisted on carrying the burden himself. Now, those pressures weren't only affecting their daily lives, but they were starting to disturb their emotional wellbeing as well. She wanted to try to find a solution.

Early one morning, before her six a.m. alarm went off, Mariam heard a strange noise. The hushed sound of a running river was what her mind immediately pictured. *But the closest river is hundreds of miles away.* She sat in bed for a while, trying to shake the half-sleep confusion away. The clock read four forty-five, and the rhythm of Morgan's deep breathing filled the room. Forcing herself to concentrate, she again heard the sound of the river.

Rain, maybe. Standing by the window, the pitter-patter of raindrops deceived her at first. Straining her ears again, she determined the location of the river sound... and it was not coming from outside. Following the gushing sound down the stairs, her bare foot found it before her eyes. Splashing through the kitchen to reach the light switch, her heart sank at the sight of the flood which extended throughout the entire first floor.

"Oh my God. Oh my God. I must still be sleeping. Wake up,

Mariam. Wake up!" She pinched herself hard, but the scene before her didn't change. Without thinking that she may wake up the kids, she called out to Morgan repeatedly until he finally woke and descended the stairs to join her in the nightmare. More than a few moments passed with the two of them standing silently in the midst of the indoor pond. Morgan finally snapped out of his shock and ran throughout the house searching for the cause of the water. Some moments later he reappeared.

"A pipe burst in the bathroom. I turned off the stop tap."

A few minutes later, he looked at Mariam, searching for an answer. "What now?"

Despite feeling overwhelmed by their situation, she knew there was no time to lose. "We need to... uh... take pictures for the insurance company. Yes, pictures. I'll grab the camera. You get the shop vac from the closet."

Mariam snapped photos of every inch that was covered in water, taking extra pictures of the pipe which had burst. Morgan worked diligently, vacuuming up the water and emptying it in the tub. The kitchen and bathroom didn't take much time, but the living room area, with its wall-to-wall carpeting, was proving a challenge.

"I've wiped up what was left in the kitchen and bathrooms. Let me take over for a while."

Morgan reluctantly handed Mariam the vacuum just as the alarm upstairs went off. "That's the third time it's gone off. What time does that make it now?"

"Probably about six twenty," Mariam replied. "You should go wake the kids up and get ready. I'll be up to help in a few minutes."

The day was already off to a bad start, but with this new catastrophe, there was no denying that their financial problems were becoming unsurmountable. Mariam knew that even if the insurance company covered the bulk of the water damage – and that was a very big 'if' – there would still be things that fell outside of the coverage.

After the kids had left for school, Mariam confronted Morgan, hoping to get him to share the burden which was becoming heavier by the day. She cleared her throat and swept a runaway strand of wavy brown hair behind her ear. "I think we have two options: our first is that we sell the house. We sell the house and rent a small apartment near the center of town. The kids will get to stay in the same school, and we'll be walking distance from the park."

Morgan hated the idea of having his four children grow up in an apartment. "What's our second option," he asked hesitantly, leaning forward, resting his hands against the kitchen sink.

"I get a job."

His eyes closed from the pain produced by her words. He hated that he needed his wife's help to provide for the family; he should be able to do it on his own. But what hurt him most was that he knew the enormity of the sacrifice Mariam was offering.

Since before they were married, she had said that she would not work outside of the home until her youngest was at least in first grade. "And even then," he remembered her saying, "I might still decide to stay at home."

She didn't want anybody else raising her children. She didn't want anyone changing them, feeding them, dressing them. Yes, it was hard on her, doing everything for them on her own, but she took pride in it. "They are my mark on this world," she had always said, "and I won't allow any strangers to play a part in how they're raised."

And now, here she was, taking it back. Morgan knew how hard it must have been for her to say the words and, because of that, it was just as hard to hear them.

Without saying a word, he grabbed his suitcase and headed for the door. He had already placed his hand on the doorknob when Mariam called out, "Wait! You're going to leave without saying anything? What do you think?"

He sighed heavily, then paused with his back still to her. After a few seconds he mumbled, "We'll talk about it later." He opened the door and left abruptly, without looking back at her.

As the days rolled by, Mariam was busy meeting with different contractors who assessed the damage caused by the broken pipe. The wall-to-wall carpeting would have to be completely replaced as it had not been dried thoroughly and mold had begun to grow beneath, causing a serious health hazard. But after all the estimates, after all the photos and explanations had been sent to the insurance, their final decision came: they would reimburse the family for fixing the burst water pipe, but none of the subsequent damage would be covered. "But the mold is a health hazard... we have to have it professionally cleaned or it will cause harm to my family! How can that not be covered??"

"I'm sorry ma'am," the young insurance representative on the phone sounded as sympathetic as a robot, "any damage directly caused by the water is not covered. If you'd like, we can offer you a new plan to include water damage. Shall I look into that for you?"

"No, I don't want you to look into that for me!" As her rage increased, her voice turned to a hiss. "I don't even have the money to make sure my kids aren't breathing deadly air, and you're trying to get me to purchase a more expensive insurance package? What is wrong with you people?!" Mariam slammed the phone down and let out an agitated huff.

Later that night she broke the news to Morgan that the insurance company would not pay for the bulk of the damages. "But we have to deal with the carpets and the mold now... this isn't something we can wait on." Her words were heavy, and they hit Morgan's ears with their full weight. He knew they were in a bad situation, but he couldn't see any way out... and his silence proved it. Minutes later, Mariam provided a short term solution.

"Let's borrow the money for the repairs from my parents for now. It won't really be a huge burden on them. And we can pay them back in installments, a little at a time."

Morgan looked up at her suddenly, with a new found urgency. "No, definitely not your parents. I'll borrow the money from my brother."

"Morgan," Mariam said calmly, "what's the difference?"

"The difference is that he's *my* brother, that's what. I'll get the money from him tomorrow."

Shrugging off the hurt, Mariam nodded and let the conversation end.

Some days later, after the mold had been cleared and the new carpets installed, Mariam again tried discussing with Morgan a long term solution to their financial problems, and again he refused. Mariam didn't like being out of sync with her husband, but she felt like she had no choice. His feelings of being an unfit provider were deepening and they were clouding his judgment about making the right decision for his family. The following day, she updated her resume and sent it out to more than two dozen places. She saw it as a necessary step to improve their situation; what she didn't see was how that step would cause a fatal crack in her marriage.

CHAPTER 4:
Summer and Porter

Looking at the run-down ghost that stared back at her from the mirror, Summer focused her thoughts on the medicine bottle which lay out of sight, just inches away. She took it from the cabinet and glared at it intently for several moments. The pills inside were sparkling with freedom, promising her a permanent escape. The offer seemed attractive, but instead of opening the bottle, she chucked it into the trash can.

"Get a grip on yourself, Summer," she said to her reflection. "That is not what you want. A change, yes. Just... not that change. Not yet. Oh, God. What is happening to me?"

Just as self-pity was about to tighten her reigns, the phone rang and brought Summer back to the present. The man on the other line was an art connoisseur who had seen a painting of hers at a friend's house.

"I'd be very interested to see more of your work, Mrs...."

"Oh, please call me Summer."

"And you can call me Roberto. Do you think I can stop by this evening?"

"Of course, of course. This evening would be great." The prospect of a new client erased her earlier sadness and she was almost screeching into the phone.

"Great," Roberto chuckled. "I'll be there at seven."

"I'll see you then. I look forward to meeting you."

Roberto's call had switched off her depression, at least temporarily. But her new found elation masked her ability to think rationally about the coming prospect. She had dealt with enough disappointment to know that just because someone seemed interested at first didn't necessarily mean a sale. In her experience, it usually meant, "I'm sorry, I was under the impression that your paintings were more modern" or "I expected something more classic," "more exotic," "less mysterious." There was always something her work was either lacking, or in excess of. But right then, none of those negative thoughts came to her and her hopes continued to soar.

Summer called her husband right away. "Porter, you'll never guess who I just got off the phone with. His name's Roberto and he's an art collector; he owns a gallery in the city. He's coming over tonight at seven to see my work."

"So, I guess this means you're standing me up?" Porter was only half pretending to be upset, but Summer didn't understand.

"What? What do you mean?"

"We had a date tonight. Remember? You were going to meet me at the restaurant at six, then we were going to catch a movie."

"Oh my God! Porter, I totally forgot. Do you mind if we...."

"Don't worry about it, sweetie. I'm just kidding. This is a great opportunity for you."

"So then you'll be here? You'll meet him with me?"

Porter didn't hear the desperation in Summer's voice. "Uh... I think that I might take advantage of the few extra hours at work. You'll be working anyway... I'll just be in your way if I'm there."

"That's not true... I want you...."

"Summer, sweetie... I'm late for a meeting. Good luck with this Roberto guy. I'll try to be home by eight thirty. Love you."

Summer was more than disappointed. She wished Porter would show more interest in her work. She understood that he wanted her to depend on herself. "You're not just an artist," he had told her a thousand times, "you're a businesswoman. You have to sell your product at the highest price while making your customer think he's gotten a deal." She knew that was his style, his way of supporting her. Nevertheless, she wished he could support her in the way she needed.

Summer spent a few minutes reviewing, in her head, all she had learned from Porter about business. She tried to recall all the pieces of advice her husband had passed to her over the years, but a quick glance at the clock made her jump up and begin preparing the house for the arrival of her guest.

~

Porter had been looking forward to the date with his wife all week, so despite being happy for Summer that an opportunity was making itself available to her, he was slightly discouraged when she cancelled. He had noticed the change that had come over her the past few months, but he didn't realize how severe it was. He had begun to feel distant from her lately... as though she wanted space from him. They had been spending less and less time together, and although he carried on as though nothing had changed, slowly he felt his heart breaking.

At about five o'clock, his secretary walked into his office.

"Is there anything else you need, Mr. Lawson?" his secretary asked.

"Yes, actually, Kara. Please have a seat."

Kara shut the door and took a seat across from her boss. She waited patiently for a few moments as he read through some papers, then nodded to himself and arranged the pile neatly on his desk.

"I've been meaning to ask you if you'd like to start training as a second assistant for me. Bill is really great; so great, in fact, that if he ever takes a personal day, I end up completely lost. I've seen how you greet the customers and I appreciate your professional yet friendly approach. I see potential in you. And... I'm hoping you'd like to learn the ropes so that you can fill in for Bill, if the need arises."

Kara raised her eyebrows in disbelief. She always felt like her boss never actually saw her.

"You look nervous," Porter said, misreading her expression.

Kara shook her head. "No, no... not at all. I'm a bit surprised is all. Surprised in a good way."

"So... does that mean you're interested?"

"Of course!"

"I just want to make a few things clear, though, so there's no misunderstanding. The position of assistant is much more time consuming than you'd think. Basically, Bill knows all the ins and outs of the business. He's the one who handles the clients most of the time. On business trips, he's got the schedules, the contacts, the prices. He points me in the direction and I move. Really, he's got all the info and I'm just the face. With you, you'll have even more to do because it will be in addition to your secretarial position. Do you think you'd like to take on that kind of responsibility? Can you handle that kind of time commitment? Work load?"

Kara didn't even pause before answering, "Definitely."

"Good answer. So, first thing I need you to do is to adjust all the reservations for our business trip next week so that you're included. When you file the invoices, make sure that your stuff goes under 'employee training.' Until you get the hang of everything, both of you will come on those trips, but after that, I'll only need one of you to accompany me."

"Sure."

With a list of new reservations to make, Kara got up and made her way to the door. Before she closed it behind her, she felt the need to show her gratitude. "I really want to thank you for this opportunity, Mr. Lawson. I know there were at least a few others you could have chosen. I really appreciate that you picked me."

Porter smiled. "Like I said, Kara, I see potential in you."

Roberto rang the doorbell at ten of seven. Summer had shed her sorrow-laden appearance and answered the door wearing a sleeveless white dress with her hair flowing.

"Wow! You sounded sexy over the phone, but this... I did not picture."

The compliment made her smile; the accent made her entire body blush. "Thank you, Roberto. Please come in."

He couldn't help but notice all the beauty around him as he walked through her home. Vases, decorative boxes, and all sorts of trinkets enhanced the coffee tables and china cabinet. Paintings and picture frames lined the walls. "Did you decorate your house yourself or did you have a professional do it?"

"I did it all myself. And actually these two paintings are mine."

Roberto examined them casually. "I see you and I have very similar taste."

"I'm glad you like them. Please follow me to the studio downstairs. The rest of the paintings are there."

He had a hard time keeping his eyes off of his hostess. Her beauty was so pure, so fresh. Even with minimal makeup, her face was the type of beauty musicians sang about, the lines of her body were femininity itself. She was, he thought, a work of art.

Summer didn't notice his distraction as she gave him a brief introduction to each piece. And he didn't hear anything until she had shown him all the pieces and turned to him, eyes sparkling with hope and ambition, to hear his opinion. He forced his eyes away from her body, from her face, and started with the task at hand. But once his eyes finally fell on the paintings, they too managed to capture his interest.

Summer stood in the background as Roberto examined the work. She wanted to give him enough space and time to investigate all aspects of her work, but Porter's voice in her head made her anxious. "Sell them," she heard him say, "tell him the story behind each one. Remember, these are not just your paintings... they are your work. Sell them!" Wringing her hands nervously, she tried to suppress that voice.

Sometime later, Roberto emerged from the sea of concentration he had been swimming in. "Can you take some constructive criticism?"

The words made Summer do a double take; he had been smiling and nodding to himself for the past twenty minutes – she had taken these gestures as signs of approval. She managed, however, to keep her voice steady and hide all traces of surprise. "Of course... it can only help me to improve."

He cupped his mouth with the side of his fist and stood there staring at one painting for a few moments.

"I think your work is a little... how do you say... amateur? Your lines are too clean and your colors too fresh for the emotions you want to express. But I definitely see your talent. I think with some tutelage, you can be very successful."

"Tutelage?" Summer wasn't sure if he meant she should take more art courses, or if she should spend time – one on one – with a particular artist.

"Sí. Tutelage. I can be your instructor. I can teach you a lot... not just about how to paint what you feel or how to get a specific emotion across, but also about the business side. Soon you may be able to open a gallery of your own."

"I would greatly appreciate that, Roberto, but it seems like a lot for me to ask of you."

"Don't be silly. It will be my pleasure to spend time with such a gifted, beautiful woman."

Again, his words had her body tingling. Somewhere inside, she wondered if maybe the out she had been searching for didn't lie in a medicine bottle after all. Perhaps it had finally arrived.

CHAPTER 5:
May and Hasan

Every day Hasan called the doctor's office to ask for the results, and every day the nurse told him the same thing: "Mr. AbdulShafi, the results haven't come in yet, but I promise you we'll call you as soon as they do."

"What's taking them so long?" His impatience was out of character.

"Lab results can take a while. They probably won't be ready for a week. But like I said, we'll call you as soon as they come in."

Hasan became more concerned about his wife's health with each passing day. Although he kept assuring her that it was just a bug which would eventually pass, he no longer believed that. His worry kept intensifying and every day it ate away at him more. His eyebrows were permanently furrowed over eyes which had turned from tender to stern. But he forced his lips to smile, hoping laughter with his family could ease their anxieties.

Four long days later, the phone finally rang. Instead of telling May the results, the nurse only said that they needed her to return to the doctor's office for more tests.

"What do you mean more tests? More blood work?"

"I'm not positive, Mrs. AbdulShafi. The doctor told me to have you come in as soon as you can. She said she would explain it to you here." The receptionist's tone was not insensitive, nor unkind, but May didn't have the patience for her lack of information. She quickly hung up and called Hasan to tell him the 'news.'

"So they didn't give you any indication as to what further tests they want to do?"

"No, she didn't sound like she had a clue. She said the doctor would explain."

"Okay," Hasan said, "well, I'll be right home, then. Call Mariam and...."

May cut him off, "Hasan, we don't have to go right now. We can go tomorrow or even next week. Don't leave work early for this."

Hasan sighed, "If you knew how much I cherish you... if you understood that nothing in my life – *nothing* – is as important to me as you are, you wouldn't say such foolish things.

"Now, call Mariam and ask her to watch the kids. *In sha' Allah*, I'll see you in about twenty minutes."

As soon as they arrived at the office, the nurse brought them in to sit with the doctor.

"May, your lab results came back today. They show an abnormally high white blood cell count. We want to do more tests to determine the cause of the elevated white blood cells and to make an accurate diagnosis."

"Does this mean there's something specific you guess could be the problem?" Hasan knew there was, and even though that feeling in his gut still told him not to question, his eagerness to put an end to the mystery was stronger.

"The elevated blood cell count, along with the slightly enlarged spleen we discovered from the ultrasound indicate that we may be looking at leukemia. I want to do a bone marrow aspiration and biopsy so we can know for sure. Basically it entails injecting a couple of needles into your hip bone to extract what we need. Then the samples will get sent to the lab. The procedure is slightly painful, but we'll ease it as much as we can with local anesthetics and pain relievers."

But neither May nor Hasan had heard anything the doctor had said after the word leukemia.

"Leukemia?" May whispered. "So... how long? How much longer do I have?" Her face had turned pale and her eyes bulged with shock.

"May, we don't want to get ahead of ourselves. That's exactly why we need more tests. It may turn out to be something totally different. Or it may be in an early enough stage that therapy could cure it. These tests will help us determine just that."

The nurse didn't give them time to sulk in shock; she ushered them into the biopsy room and asked May to undress. Hasan stood beside his wife, holding her hand as the doctor extracted the samples they needed from her hip bone. He wanted to be strong for his wife, he wanted to protect her and take away her pain. But he was powerless and felt weak. The best he could do was to control the anger and sadness erupting inside of him. The lump forming in his throat absorbed his emotions, but he knew that if he opened his mouth to speak, the flood would be uncontrollable.

May felt exhausted when they arrived home. She was so drained that she couldn't even sit with her kids in the living room. Hasan distracted his thoughts by focusing on the kids. He floundered through dinner preparations, but the meal ended up burning so badly that he finally gave up and ordered pizza. Then he helped the kids with their homework and got them ready for bed.

May had been immersed in her thoughts when a knock at the door interrupted her solitude. "Can we sit with you for a few minutes before bedtime, mama?" Deen stood in the doorway smiling, with his sister and father standing behind him.

May stared at them for a moment. Sensing that these moments with her family would be finite, she tried to cement the picture in her soul.

"Of course, *habaybi*. Come sit with me."

Spending time with her family helped heal her spirit. They talked and laughed and May tried to record their voices in her mind.

"I'm sorry I couldn't sit with you guys earlier. I was just so tired."

"Where were you today, mama? Why have we been spending so much time with Auntie Mariam lately?"

Neither May nor Hasan answered. They each tried to figure out what exactly to say, how exactly to say it. But the words would not be formed. It was still too early to make any definite statements anyway. May and Hasan both knew they shouldn't worry their kids prematurely. With the lump beginning to form again in his throat, Hasan was just able to say, "Mama and I had some errands to run. Now… it's past your bedtimes. Good night, Noor. Good night, Deen."

The couple kissed their kids good night. When they got to the door, May called out, "I love you, *habaybi.*" Despite her efforts to suppress thoughts that she may not get the chance to see her kids grow, her eyes welled up with tears. Hasan, still fighting back his own emotions, wrapped his arms lovingly around his wife. In his embrace, her eyes closed, her smile widened, and a tiny, imagined sense of security calmed her to sleep.

A few days later the receptionist called to inform them that the doctor wanted to see them regarding the results of the bone marrow tests.

As soon as he hung up the phone, Hasan washed up, laid the prayer rug out in their bedroom, and began to pray. On his last prostration, with forehead still against the floor, he made a personal supplication: "Oh God, please bless my wife with good health. Let the lab results bring good news of her health. Oh God, please let the lab results bring good news of her health. Oh God, you are The Sustainer, The Healer… cure my wife from any illness and sustain her good health. Keep away from her all evil and illness. Grant her a long, healthy, happy life."

It was basically the same prayer he had been making for his wife since the day they had been married, but this time his heart shook with uncertainty and his eyes glistened with tears. May hadn't heard the phone ring; she was sitting outside watching the kids play in the yard. As soon as she saw her husband's face, she knew the news was not good.

"I take it the doctor's office called?"

He shut the screen door carefully behind him and sat down next to her. "Yeah. They want us to go in for the results." He did a good job of keeping his voice steady, but the anxiety in his eyes, which had been there for weeks now, had become deeper. "I'll go ask Mariam if she wouldn't mind having the kids play over there for the next hour or so. I'll be right back."

About twenty minutes later, May and Hasan sat holding hands, both staring across the desk at the intensity and concern etched on the doctor's face. She, on the other hand, was having a difficult time looking at them. Her eyes alternated between the papers which her hands fidgeted with and the intensity in their eyes.

"May, the lab results show that you have a serious condition, but it can be controlled with the proper treatment plan. I've been in touch with a specialist and he recommends that you start treatment immediately." The doctor's voice was soft and apologetic, but unfaltering.

"What's the name of the condition? What's the diagnosis?" Hasan needed to know exactly what they were dealing with.

"May's condition is called acute myeloid leukemia."

The word made time stop. Any hope they had been clinging to, any shred of light they had been counting on to put an end to this nightmare crashed into nothingness as the doctor's words pierced their hearts.

After a short pause, Hasan spoke through a forced whisper. "What's the prognosis?"

"With proper treatment, we can control it, maybe even send it into remission. The oncologist I spoke with expects to see you within the next couple of days. He'll be able to tell you more than I can as well." The doctor held the oncologist's card out to May, but she sat frozen, staring at her hands in her lap, too engrossed in her thoughts to notice. Hasan placed one arm around his wife and forced the other to accept the card from the doctor.

CHAPTER 6:
Dinner at Sidra and Farris'

Their short vacation had been exactly what Farris had hoped, but once they got home, he worried that their regular routine would cause the gap between himself and his wife to re-emerge. He was determined not to let Sidra pull away again. He made a point of calling her at least once a day during work, and he insisted they have a date night each week.

His phone calls always made her smile, especially when she asked, "What's up? Why'd you call?" And he answered, "I just wanted to hear your voice. I just called to say I love you." Once he even broke out into song, making Sidra laugh out loud.

"I think you should leave the singing to Stevie Wonder, honey."

"What? You're trying to say I don't have the talent he does?" Farris joked.

"Oh no, no. It's not that at all. It's just that Stevie calls me around this time just to say he loves me, too."

It was Farris' turn to chuckle. "Well, if it was anyone else, I might get jealous. But I'll let it go... because it's Stevie."

"He'll be relieved to hear it."

On her end, Sidra had given herself a two month window. Two months to enjoy the beauty of their marriage. Two months to hear his laughter and hold him in her arms. Two months to perfect her plan and set it into action.

The only problem was that her plan became increasingly difficult with each day she spent with him. Sidra was falling more and more in love with her husband, and she knew that if she kept it up, by the time her self-imposed deadline arrived, she would be unable to go through with it. With a heavy heart, she kissed away the serenity and love that had become so strong, and decided she had to set things into motion immediately. "Lord, have mercy on us," she prayed, hoping her plan was rightly guided. The first step was putting an end to Farris' date night.

Sidra knew that if she tried to use the excuse of not feeling well, or having no desire to go out, Farris would simply ignore her attempts, and drag her out anyway. The only thing to do was to make it impossible for him to reach her.

Farris got home from work that Friday just before six. He found his wife dressed, but the dining room table was set... for eight people.

"What's going on?" Farris asked after he had kissed her.

"What do you mean 'what's going on?' Oh... don't tell me you forgot! Farris I told you I invited the neighbors over for dinner tonight. I told you."

He was quite sure he had never heard that before, but her insistence that she had informed him made him doubt himself.

"You told me? You told me when?"

"Oh, Farris," Sidra sighed, annoyed. "It doesn't matter. Just hurry and wash up. They'll be here any minute."

He did as he was told. In the confusion, he forgot about their date.

The evening was comprised of good food and laughter. It wasn't the first time Farris had met his neighbors, of course, but it was the first time they had spent an entire evening together. The dinner conversation varied from Mariam and May's anecdotes about their kids, to Porter describing the nature of his business, to the best meals and favorite restaurants. Summer, being the youngest and most removed from that world, felt slightly out of place, but all in all the group enjoyed each other's company.

After dessert, the women sat on the patio drinking coffee and tea.

"Thank you for taking care of the kids so often these past few weeks, Mariam. I know you have enough to deal with already. I really appreciate you being there for me."

"Don't be ridiculous, May. That's what neighbors – and more importantly, friends – are for." The women exchanged warm glances.

A few seconds passed then May replied, "I'm glad you feel that way because I may need your help more in the coming weeks."

Mariam heard the underlying severity in her friend's tone. "Why? What's going on?"

These women May was sitting with, they weren't family. They weren't even her closest friends. It made no sense, but she wanted to confide in them. Maybe she just needed to tell someone, anyone.

"I hadn't been feeling well for a while," May began. "So I went to the doctor. And, well, after lots of exams and blood tests, they've diagnosed me with a serious form of leukemia."

Someone let out a soft gasp. Summer covered her mouth and held her breath. Mariam and Sidra were fixed in shock.

"Oh, May," Mariam whispered a moment later as she embraced her friend.

Sidra and Summer gave her affectionate hugs as well. But no one knew what to say.

"So what now?" Mariam asked with tears filling her eyes.

"I have a long road ahead, filled with treatments and therapies. I just don't know if I'm strong enough."

Wrapping her arm around May's shoulder, Mariam said, "You *are* strong enough... you can beat this. And we'll do whatever we can to help."

Sidra's mouth started speaking before she had a chance to filter the words. "I'm not really a 'kid' person... I don't really like them. But I'm here in case you ever need someone to watch them. I can't guarantee that you'll receive them in the same state of cleanliness nor in a state of non-hunger – because quite frankly if they don't eat what I offer, I won't offer them anything else – but aside from that, I will return them safely."

Mariam and Summer stared at Sidra with their jaws wide open, but May smiled weakly at her unabashed honesty. "Sounds like you'd make a perfect mom, Sidra."

The sincerity in May's soft words struck a chord with Sidra, but she tamed the emotions before they had a chance to manifest into any kind of physical expression. Shrugging her shoulders, she claimed, "I'm much better with errands, and stuff like that. If you need someone to go grocery shopping or run your dry cleaning, or whatever, you know who to call."

The support in their voices was like a column for May, standing strong and exposed, inviting her to lean on. Their reaction touched her. She wanted to convey her appreciation, but all she could do was sink into their hugs.

Inside the house Morgan was pointing out all the expensive things around Farris' home.

"Is that painting an original? It must have cost a fortune."

A few minutes later, they turned on the game.

"Your big screen television is like a cinema. How much was it?"

Farris was uncomfortable with the questions about money, but he discreetly and politely avoided answering them.

"Hasan's not impressed; he's been so quiet cuz he'd rather be watching the game at his house."

When he heard his name, Hasan snapped out of his trance and forced a smile. "No, no. Not at all. I'm enjoying the company."

"You always this quiet?" Farris pushed.

His neighbor was just being polite, trying to engage him in conversation. Hasan felt he owed an explanation for his extreme silence all evening, but he didn't want to ruin everyone's mood.

"May's been having some health issues lately. I'm just preoccupied with that a little."

"Is it serious?" Hasan heard someone ask.

"Ah... Yeah... we just found out that it's quite serious. Leukemia."

The men were silent for a moment.

"If there's anything we can do, I hope you'll let us know," Farris said as he patted his neighbor on the shoulder.

Hasan nodded in appreciation of the offer and drifted back to his thoughts. The other men tried to end the awkwardness by commenting on the game.

About an hour had gone by when Mariam peeked in on the men. "Morgan, it's time for us to go. Thank you, Farris, for a great evening." All the men rose to their feet.

"Thank you guys for coming," Farris replied.

"We should get going, too," Hasan said, encouraging Porter to call it a night as well.

They all stood at the door, thanking their hosts for the evening.

Hasan felt he should apologize for bringing down the mood earlier. "I'm sorry for being such a downer tonight. It's just that the news is still very fresh for us and I.... "

Farris cut him off, "Please don't apologize, Hasan. We're neighbors, and we should be there for each other. Please just promise to let us know if there's anything we can do."

Hasan shook his neighbor's hand and gave him a warm smile. Sidra embraced May and reiterated the offer her husband had made. Sidra and Farris stood in the doorway, watching as their neighbors walked back to their homes.

After they had closed the door, Sidra began to clean up. Farris went to the stereo and put in his favorite CD. He caught his wife off guard, twirling her to face him, his arms binding her to him, and his gliding feet forcing her body to move in rhythm with his.

"Farris... I don't have time...."

"Shhh... no words."

His wide smile always enchanted her. Despite herself, she was lost in him. For a few moments she breathed in his scent and rested her head against his strong chest. For a few moments she fell deeper in love with him. But only for a few moments, until the alarm inside of her went off.

"I have to finish cleaning up, Farris." Her voice was only firm as she pulled away. But when he tried to pull her back, it became annoyed.

"If you don't want to help, that's fine, Farris. But don't get in my way."

She had ruined the mood, but he wouldn't let her irrationality get the satisfaction of knowing that. He simply began helping her, and started a conversation as though nothing unusual had just happened.

"I feel so bad for May and Hasan."

"Yeah, me too. I wish there was something we could do for them. I mean, I offered to run errands if they ever needed it, but that hardly seems enough."

"I know. It's such a load for them. And for their poor kids, too. It all just sucks."

It wasn't the most eloquent way to put it, but Sidra agreed: It *all* sucked.

Sidra avoided subsequent date nights in much the same manner. The last time Farris made an attempt, Sidra made sure that he would not try again. He called her around noon and asked where she would like to go that evening.

"Tonight? What do you mean?"

"Sidra, date night. Today's Friday."

"Oh, Farris. I'm really swamped with work today. I was actually just about to call you to let you know I won't be home for dinner."

"Sidra!"

"What do you want from me, Farris?! I have a lot of things I need to take care of before the weekend."

"Well... can't anyone else do that stuff?"

Annoyed, her voice retorted, "They're my cases, Farris. I need to deal with them myself."

Despite the tangible disappointment in his silence, she did not waver. "They need me for a meeting now. I'll try not to be too late. Bye."

Alone at home, Farris substituted dinner for a bag of chips and a soda. He tried to replay in his mind all the moments he had spent with Sidra over the past few weeks. Had he done anything to upset her? Had some incident reminded her of her past sadness? Was he losing her again?

"No... no... I won't," he said out loud. "I won't lose you, Sidra."

He racked his brain thinking of what more he could do to bring her back to the self she had rediscovered on their vacation. Phone calls? He was already doing that. Trying to be more loving, more sensitive? He was doing his best.

"I don't know what else I can do. Lord, help me to get her back. Don't let me lose her."

Then he began to doubt his feelings; he wondered if maybe he was making a big deal out of nothing. Maybe she wasn't pulling away again. He tried to blow it off, convince himself that maybe she really did have a lot to do at work. He tried to convince himself, but he simply could not.

At nine o'clock, Sidra walked into their room. Looking up from his book, Farris pushed aside his feelings of anger and dejection and greeted his wife with a smile.

"Welcome home. Long day?"

"Yes, it was pretty long." She spoke as she undressed and stepped into her pajamas.

"Did you get everything done?" Farris asked innocently.

"It seems like everything never gets done," Sidra shrugged. "They're changing the system, so I have to update all my cases... along with all the new cases I acquire weekly. It seems like I'm going to be working late for the next few months."

"For the next few months," Farris emphasized, raising his eyebrows as he nodded.

"Yes, Farris," Sidra sighed heavily, "that's what I said. For the next few months. Do you have a problem with that?" The defiance on her face and in her stance – legs apart, hands on her hips and shoulders back – had Farris staring.

Farris just grimaced as he shook his head. "No... no problem." He tore his eyes away from her and refocused on his book.

Letting out an audible huff, she continued to get changed. A few moments later, Sidra stared up at the ceiling, off into the distance, and forced a longing smile. "I'm so glad James was there with me tonight. Having the company was really...." She paused for a moment, thinking of the right word. As it came to her, the corner of her mouth went up subtly as did her eyebrow. "Satisfying," she let out in a hoarse whisper.

The words forced Farris to stare at his wife as his jaw fell open. The shock knocked from him the ability to speak, but his eyes remained glued to her as she gingerly moved around the room, then finally disappeared behind the bathroom door.

The ringing of the doorbell brought him out of his reminiscence and back to the present. He stood up from the couch and walked over to the door, knowing that in just a few minutes, his spy would give him information that would probably change his life.

CHAPTER 7:
We Have So Little

Some weeks and a few interviews passed before Mariam finally accepted a position at the same high school where Morgan worked. Although the job managed to alleviate some of the financial burden they had been under, it produced a completely different problem. Morgan became very aloof. He would come home, eat dinner in silence, sit with the children for a while, then retreat to the bedroom. Since they now worked together, they drove together to and from school, and much of these drives were spent in silence.

Morgan didn't know that every minute he ignored his wife felt like centuries to her. He didn't know that his frigid behavior was the heaviest weight she was carrying. She could handle the kids *and* the house *and* work... she couldn't handle being rejected by him, feeling like she had no one to turn to. Just a few weeks before they were a happy family – now he was always distant, and she felt all alone.

Mariam kept hoping that time would heal the fault that had sprung up between them. When he avoided making decisions with her, or answered in yes's and no's instead of substantial replies, she tried not to be heartbroken, hoping that soon things would go back to normal.

Quickly, however, her feelings turned from hurt to anger. How dare he treat her this way? She was the one sacrificing... she was the one who had put aside her desire to be a full time mother for the greater good of their family. She was the one who knew that her younger children needed her, and despite this agreed to be apart from them for most of the day. It was her own life that had been turned upside down when she began to work: how dare he treat her this way after all she had sacrificed for their family?

At first the manifestations of her anger were small, almost unnoticeable. She 'forgot' to pour his coffee at breakfast or iron his favorite shirt. She didn't pick up his shaving cream when she went grocery shopping. Then she stopped walking into the school with him. As soon as he stopped the car in the parking lot, she jumped out and nearly sprinted to the main entrance. Then one evening after dinner, she managed to make it to their bedroom before him. She grabbed his pillow and a blanket and set them outside of the locked room.

Morgan had noticed the change in her behavior, but he kept trying to convince himself that he was imagining it. Once he saw his pillow on the floor, he knew that things had gotten out of hand. He hadn't meant for them to grow so far apart. He hadn't meant to unnerve her; he was simply hurt that she had made such an important decision without him. But more than that, he was hurt that he had proven himself to be an inadequate provider. He was hurt that he needed her help. Of course he knew that he couldn't blame her, but it was easier to take it out on her than to admit it to himself. When she kicked him out of the room, he knew she'd had enough and he had to try to fix things between them.

A couple of days later Mariam awoke to a very peculiar sound: the sound of silence at ten a.m. on a Saturday. Usually her kids barely let her sleep until eight, so she knew something was awry. As she tried to orient herself, forcing her eyes to open and focus, she heard the kids' laughter coming from far away. She searched every room in the house failing to find them. When she entered the kitchen, she noticed the dishes stacked in the dish rack and a few empty juice glasses in the sink. The laughter drew her eyes to the window, and she saw something outside that she hadn't seen in many months: Morgan smiling and laughing, playing with his four kids. The sight was too beautiful to dismiss. Mariam watched her family play for a good half hour. When she realized that they had probably been out for a while and would return soon, she grabbed a quick breakfast and headed for the shower.

She fully expected to be interrupted in the bathroom as her kids always managed to do, and was more than just a little surprised when she had enough time to even get dressed. The laughter had subsided and become muffled noises coming from the living room.

"Good morning," she sang cheerfully to her kids.

They all dropped the crayons they had been drawing with and ran to give her hugs.

"Dad made us breakfast this morning then took us out to play so you could get some sleep. Did you sleep well? Huh? Huh? Did you? I hope you did because I wanted to wake you up so you could play with us but dad said no." Gabriel, in his best three year old jabber, excitedly recounted all the wonderful games they had played that morning while Zain clung to her legs, begging her to pick him up. After Gabe's report, she let Zain down so he could continue scribbling. Morgan spoke softly, "I know they usually get you up early, so I thought I would take them out to let you get some sleep."

She meant to say "Thank you," but something seemed to take over her body, forcing her face to a look that more nearly said, "Oh really? I doubt that very much!" But Mariam was glad that force wasn't strong enough to actually make her speak the words.

Did he really think he could just wash away his unforgivable behavior of the past few months in one morning of helping with the kids? Mariam couldn't get over his audacity as she pretended to read her book. She was relieved that he had finally come to his senses, but she deserved an apology. Pretending the past few months hadn't even happened was out of the question.

Morgan knew he hadn't done nearly enough to make up for his behavior and he continued to put in an extra effort over the next two weeks. He got the kids ready for school, helped with homework, made breakfast. To Mariam's surprise he even managed to cook them dinner on a couple of nights. She knew he was trying to make things right, and she was even beginning to soften up some, but she was intent on getting a verbal apology. She knew she deserved nothing less.

One evening, after the kids had gone to bed and Mariam was tidying around the house, Morgan leaned against the opening of the door and watched his wife silently without her noticing. Or maybe she was pretending not to notice... he couldn't tell anymore.

Her wavy brown hair was tied into a loose ponytail at the top of her head, and her rosy complexion contrasted with the gray and white sweats she was wearing.

"I miss you," he said.

The words took her by surprise but she didn't miss a beat.

"I've missed you for the past few months. So what?" She continued to gather the toys and place them in the bin. His silence betrayed his unmitigated lack of preparation for the conversation. But Mariam did not want to lose the opportunity. She dropped all the toys from her hands and faced him. Although she was a good four or five inches shorter than her average sized husband, standing there with her arms crossed, Mariam was a rock.

"What exactly did I do to make you act like such a jerk to me? Basically ignoring me? And not just for a few days... we're talking a couple of months now. What did I do?"

Morgan's voice was soft as he spoke, "Mariam, you know what you did."

"I know what I did?! You mean, I got a job."

"It's not that you got a job," he sighed hesitantly. "It's that you made that decision without me."

"I made that decision after I tried discussing it with you several times and you refused. I made that decision because it was the only option to get this family out of a tight spot.

"Your behavior towards me implies that I did something selfish, just for myself. When, in fact, I'm the one most affected by it. I didn't want to work yet, Morgan."

"I know."

"I wanted to be home for the kids until they were all in school full time, and maybe after that."

"I know," his words barely above a whisper.

"I sacrificed that. I changed my plan because our family needed it... not because I wanted to."

"I know."

"And you've been acting as though I did it on a whim or something."

"I was just... mad."

"Mad at me for trying to do my best for this family?!" Mariam's confusion was unmasked by her tone.

"Mad at myself for not doing better." He stood up straighter and stared at his feet, more ashamed that he had spoken the words than that they were true.

She was still hurt, but his honesty calmed her a bit. She dropped her arms to her sides in frustration. "Morgan, you were doing your best."

For the first time he raised his eyes to hers, "It wasn't good enough. I should be able to provide for you all without anyone's help."

"And I'm anyone?" Mariam's voice cracked slightly with pain at his words.

"You know what I mean, Mariam."

"No, I don't. We are a family: you, me, and those kids asleep upstairs. We are one unit. And we should work together like one unit. It's not shameful for us to help each other, Morgan. It's what makes us a team. And if you try to play the game all alone... you'll lose."

"I feel like I already have lost, though. We have so little... and we're in debt. Look at Farris and Sidra's place. It's gigantic, it's beautiful. They have everything I want... expensive cars, fancy furniture. What do we have? We have bills and loans that we're struggling to pay off. We can't even afford to have dinner at a nice restaurant."

"But life is about highs and lows," she replied, her voice now soothing. "We can't dwell on the fact that we're going through a rough time... we just have to work together to try to get back to a high."

"It doesn't bother you that we drive the crummiest cars in the whole neighborhood? Or that our house is the most simple?"

"Yes," she said matter-of-factly. "Yes, I want a luxurious car and a fancy house with a swimming pool and tennis court and a garden designed by one of those landscape architects." She paused for a second, and continued with a more unyielding expression, "But I'm happy with my crummy car and simple house because these things belong to me and my family now. I'm happy with them because of who rides in the car and who lives in the house. I'm happy with my family."

"And that's enough?"

"I hope that that will always be enough for all of us," Mariam replied sincerely.

Morgan took a few steps toward his wife, slowly and hesitantly wrapping his arms around her. He pressed his face against the nape of her neck. He didn't apologize verbally, but the conversation had softened Mariam's heart and made her forgive him. Still, there was an uneasiness inside of her, an unsettling feeling that told her the wounds Morgan's behavior had inflicted on their marriage would not heal so easily.

CHAPTER 8:
Propositions

"So he wasn't interested in any of your paintings?" Porter wasn't quite sure what Summer was saying.

"No, he was. He just thinks I need more training. He thinks if I study with an instructor my style will improve, making it easier to sell my work."

"And he seemed sincere?"

She shrugged, "I don't see why he would lie. I mean, what's he got to gain?" She paused for a few seconds. "I think he was being sincere."

"Well... good then." Porter put the papers he had been working on back in his briefcase and set it beside his night stand, turning off the lamp.

"I think I'm going to take him up on his offer," Summer said decidedly. Although she knew that was what she wanted, she also wanted to hear Porter's opinion on the matter. When he didn't respond, she prodded, "Don't you think so?"

"Don't I think what?" he mumbled from somewhere just shy of sleep.

She knew it had been a long day for him, but she needed his support... the fact that he was so uninterested annoyed and angered her. Rolling her eyes, she exhaled a huff as she turned away from him and switched off the lights.

A couple of days passed, but Summer continued to be short with Porter, still upset by his complete lack of interest in her work. As he had been drifting in and out of sleep during the incident, Porter didn't understand Summer's irritation.

"Kara, please arrange to have two dozen red roses sent to my wife.

She's been pissed at me lately and I have no idea why... maybe flowers will get her to talk to me."

"Sure thing, Mr. Lawson."

"I have a few errands I need to run, then I'll meet you and Bill at that restaurant up the street. We have a bunch of new prospective clients we need to discuss, as well as the details for our next trip. I'll meet you guys there at about one."

"Sounds good. I'll let Bill know."

About an hour later, Porter entered the restaurant to find Kara sitting alone at the table.

"Where's Bill?"

"His wife called just as we were leaving and said something about his mother not feeling well."

"That's too bad." Porter's disappointment was obvious even as he tried to distract himself with the menu.

"We can postpone this lunch till tomorrow if you'd prefer, Mr. Lawson."

With eyebrows still furrowed, Porter looked up at Kara. "It's just that we have so much that needs to get done before next week."

Kara nodded and placed her purse on her lap, preparing to get up.

"But... " Porter paused for a moment. Relaxing his face, he continued. "You know, we're already here. We might as well have lunch. I guess we can put the business stuff off one more day. And if Bill still can't make it, then you and I will just have to manage." He gave her a tired smile, not picking up on the air of relief that overcame her.

They made small talk until their food had been served. As they ate, the conversation shifted from the general, non-intrusive topics, to the somewhat more private.

"I grew up with two older sisters," Kara answered. "The oldest is a doctor and the middle is a pharmacist. My parents were disappointed that I didn't even apply to any four year colleges. But school was just not my thing. I hated studying and taking tests... I wanted to get out and experience life. And now that I've been in the work force for about a year, I see that I really had a point. Life isn't about what you learn in the classroom. Even just the very fundamentals of business administration... what we learn in the classroom is not exactly how it's done on the job. So in order to learn – to really learn – you have to live it.

"And that's what I plan on doing: living. Seeing the world. I'm working now to save enough money to tour Europe. I'm going to pick five or six countries and spend about six days in each. Then I'll come back, start saving again so I can tour South America. Then Africa, then Asia and Australia. Within the next five or so years, I want to have traveled to all the places I want to see. Then I'll pick one country, and spend a year there."

"Doing what?" Her chatter had lifted his mood and Porter was feeling entertained.

Kara shrugged, answering candidly, "Working. Living the life of a local. I want to experience what it's like to be a resident of a different country. I think not only will I learn about another culture, but it'll make me appreciate my own culture more."

She paused for a few seconds. "Or less, I guess, if I end up having a really great time and come to the conclusion that life here sucks. But in that case, I can just stay abroad."

"You wouldn't mind being away from your family?"

"No, I don't think so. I mean, don't get me wrong, I love my family. But they drive me insane. I think some distance would do more good than harm."

Porter nodded in understanding. "I see what you mean, but I couldn't be away from my family for so long. They drive me crazy sometimes, but I find comfort with them."

"And by 'family' you mean your wife?" Kara pried.

"No, actually I was referring to my brother and sister." Porter paused and Kara nodded.

"Summer is not my family... she's my life. I don't think I could make it out of the state without her.

"The only thing is," he continued, looking down at his plate as he poked at the meal with his fork, "that lately she's been so... distant. I know that she's sad, but I think more than that, she's bored. But I'm not sure of what... she won't open up to me. Is she bored with our routine? Is she bored of me? I don't know."

"That's too bad," Kara sympathized.

"Lately I just feel like..." his voice became softer, as though there was a confession he was being forced to make, "she hasn't been there for me."

The disappointment in his voice seemed to envelop him; he simply sat there, frozen, staring at his plate.

Kara remained silent, hating to see him in such a state. She had grown fond of him since she began working at his company. He was always professional, never vain. Kind and gentle, but not soft. Seeing him in pain made her long to comfort him. She wasn't sure whether she wanted him to understand or not, but, after a brief moment, she managed to utter, "I can be there for you."

Summer had been spending part of every day with Roberto at his studio. He had kept to his word and devoted his full attention to her for the couple of hours they were together. She felt more than lucky to be getting such special attention and advice from him.

They spent a good part of their sessions studying Roberto's own works that he kept in various places around his home. He explained why he had used specific colors and brush strokes, although he always gave her a chance to analyze first. For the second part of their sessions she had to complete an assignment while he was the watchful critic.

"Focus on the shade, Summer. Make sure you can find the emotion in the shade you use," he would say. Or, "Softer brush strokes might be better here. Don't forget, every detail counts." She appreciated all the comments, and his encouragement gave her hope that her next piece would be successful – that finding a buyer wouldn't be an unbearable obstacle.

That rainy day, as Summer stood in front of the easel working on one of Roberto's assignments, she saw him from the corner of her eye, shaking his head.

"No... No... No, Summer!" He paced angrily back and forth, thinking of how to word it. This was the first time he had shown outright disapproval of her work. His disappointment was not only surprising, but it made her feel as though the past couple of weeks had been for nothing.

"When you go to start a piece, what do you bring with you?"

Summer's eyes raced back and forth across the easel as she tried to unmask his words. A moment later, unable to figure it out, she simply answered, "My brushes, my paints, all of my...."

"No... no," Roberto said, shaking his head and brushing her words away with his hand. "What do you *bring* with you?!" he emphasized, softly beating a fisted hand to her chest. Standing directly behind her, he continued, "Your painting should be less about what's up here..." pointing to her head, "and more about you. You should bring with you the feeling of warmth you got as a child playing with a puppy," he said, wrapping his arms around her tightly from behind. "You should bring the anger you felt when you last fought with your sister... the passion you felt when you last made love. It should all come from within...." The palms of his hands beat her hips once, then pulling her body firmly against his, his hands traveled up her abdomen, between her breasts, and pulling her arms out to the sides, continued all the way to her fingertips. The act was so sensual that even after he had moved away from her, it took her a minute to regain her composure. "It should all come from your soul to your fingertips," he continued. "Right now you're painting with your head, not with your emotion."

His face remained red, eyebrows furrowed, as he lit a cigarette and paced before the easel. Summer stood still in front of her painting, scanning every inch, every stroke, every color, trying to identify the exact source of Roberto's disapproval.

By the time he had finished his cigarette, he had calmed down enough to continue with the session.

"We have to start from the beginning. You have to stop this mind painting of yours. I thought it would just come naturally in time, but you haven't improved at all since we've begun. Come sit down... watch me."

He changed the canvas and began. "When I am angry, red and black color my eyes... they are bold and frightening." He was almost yelling, acting out what he had just described, painting furiously, colors flying all over the place. He worked swiftly and resolutely, his gaze never falling from the canvas. Time passed by quickly as she watched him. It seemed like he had only been at it for a few moments, but when he stepped back, away from the easel, Summer found herself staring at a masterpiece that not only captivated her sight, but also sang to her soul.

He had helped her with her own brush strokes before, but this was the first time she had seen him compose an entire piece. He turned even the physical act of painting into an art form. Standing beside him, studying the canvas, the sigh she exhaled was as much a symbol of adoration of the piece as it was a proclamation of her own inadequacy.

He turned toward her so that their bodies were touching and again began to teach. "When you find your emotions, you have to display them. You have to find them. I will help you find your passion." With his hands on her hips, he slowly pulled her even closer, gently nearing his face to hers. He lingered in that position, breathing in her breath, causing her heartrate to accelerate. They stood there for several moments, until Roberto finally kissed her firmly on the lips.

CHAPTER 9:
Passing By

Hasan had insisted they get a second opinion and was only satisfied with the diagnosis when four different oncologists concurred. May had been content to start therapy after meeting with only one.

"He did go to medical school, you know, Hasan. He's not a grocer... he's a physician. He knows what he's talking about."

"They are only human, May. They can make mistakes, misdiagnosis. I just want us to be as sure as possible of the diagnosis and treatment plan before we begin."

She was too exhausted to argue with him, so she let her husband make all the appointments and do all the talking. When he finally felt comfortable with an oncologist, and his treatment plan, May began right away.

It was excruciatingly hard on her physically, but it was even harder to see the concern in her children's eyes and not be able to appease it. She could see their fear, their worry, and all she could do was try to smile and tell them she was fine, hoping they weren't yet old enough to see through her lie.

"How much longer will you have to stay in the hospital?" Her daughter tried to suppress her tears, but their need to be shed was more powerful and they rolled down her cheeks anyway.

"*Habibti,*" Hasan wrapped his arms around her, "mama has to stay here a little while because the medicine they give her is very strong. It can have some serious side-effects, so they want mama here to keep an eye on her. But, *in sha' Allah*, if all goes well, she'll be back home in no time."

"How's *Sitto* doing? You guys have to be extra nice to her, you know. She's your only grandparent and she was good enough to travel all this way to stay with you. Noor, you'd better not be giving her a hard time in the mornings."

"No, mama. I get right up. I try to help Deen get ready. I offered to help with the chores but she said, 'Your only chore is to do your homework without having me watch over you. And help your brother.' She seemed kind of disgusted when I showed her how to clean the cat's litter box. Then when Poppy came sprinting into the kitchen searching for his food, she sort of freaked out, threw the towel she'd been holding, and ran out of there. It was her first time seeing him."

May imagined her mother-in-law's reaction to seeing the crazy cat and couldn't hold back her laughter. Hasan smiled at the music coming from his wife's lips.

"Try to help out with Poppy, Deen. Let him stay out as long as you can so he's out of *Sitto*'s way."

"Okay, baba, I'll try. But it's not just Poppy. *Sitto* screams at everything. The other day the school bus honked for us, she ran around screaming, 'The truck is headed right for the house! It's headed right for us!' "

They all giggled at Deen's imitation of *Sitto's* very on-edge behavior, but then it was time for Hasan to drive the kids back home.

"I love you, *habaybi.* Be extra good."

"I love you too, mama," the kids said in unison. After hugging her tightly, they followed their dad out of the room.

When Hasan returned to May, about a half-hour later, she was sleeping. He washed up, changed into his pajamas and prayed. He spent five extra minutes on his last prostration, making supplication for his family, especially his wife.

"Oh God, let the treatment be easy on her and let her body get the most benefit from it. Oh God, you are the Only Healer, cure my wife from this disease quickly. Oh God, The Sustainer of Mankind, remove the illness, cure the disease. You are the One Who cures.

There is no cure except Your cure. Grant us a cure that leaves no illness. Let her regain her health so we can return home. Bless her, God, and bless our entire family. Let it all be for our good and pass easily. God, give us all the strength to endure."

Not wanting to wake her, he picked up his book and began reading. A few minutes later she began to stir and opened her eyes. "Can I get you anything, *habibti*?" He bent down beside her bed.

"Have you had dinner?" she asked him, wrapping one arm around his shoulder, and stretching with the other, still trying to fully awaken.

"Mama tried feeding me when I took the kids back, but I wasn't hungry."

"You have to eat, Hasan. Go get yourself something from the cafeteria."

"I'm not hungry."

"Hasan, do I look like I'm in the mood to argue? Now, I'm your wife, which means when I tell you to do something, you do it."

"Oh, is that right?" Hasan laughed at his wife's banter.

"Of course," she giggled. It was an exhausted giggle, but a giggle nonetheless. "Now, put your robe on and go get something to eat."

"Yes, ma'am," Hasan joked, standing up and saluting her.

"Now that's more like it."

As he ate, May continued to tease him. "See how good things come your way when you listen to your wife."

"Of course. Next time I won't put up a fight."

"Glad you learned your lesson."

A few minutes later, as Hasan was finishing up his dinner, May asked about her mother-in-law. "Have the kids driven mama Hanaan insane, yet?"

Hasan chuckled loudly, "I don't think she had very far to go to begin with, but I'm sure they've pushed her over the edge. She said to me, 'Deen thinks it's okay to let Poopy sit on the counter.' So I said, 'Mama, his name's *Poppy*, not Poopy.' 'What? Poppy? What's Poppy?

He should be named Poopy; he stinks and he's stinking up the whole house.'"

May giggled, "God, I love that woman. God bless her for all she's putting up with."

They continued to talk about the kids for a while, then May felt her head getting heavy.

"That's enough. You need to sleep."

"But I want to stay with you."

"I'm right here," he said from across the room.

"That's too far. I want to sleep in your arms."

"Done."

Hasan squeezed next to his wife and wrapped his arms around her. She laid her head against his chest and fell asleep almost instantly.

He held her for some time, then once he was sure she was sleeping soundly enough, he snuck out from beside her. Making sure she was comfortable, he pulled the covers up snugly around her neck so she wouldn't feel any draft. When he got into the other bed, from those few feet away, he watched his beautiful wife sleep. He could feel the agony he had been suppressing building in his throat, until finally the knot became too strong, and had to escape. He sobbed silently for a few minutes, thinking of how much pain she must be in, thinking of how he wouldn't be able to live if she didn't make it. She was what made his life make sense... without her it would just be a big, ugly, lonely mess. "Please God, cure her of this disease. Please... Please... I need her. Please cure her." Repeating the same prayer, over and over, he drifted off to sleep.

The next morning a peculiar sound awoke him. Rubbing his eyes, trying to adjust to the morning light, he tried to make sense of it. Moments later, looking all around, he finally understood the noise – it was May's sniffling.

Rolling quickly out of bed he ran to her. Without saying a word he took her in his arms.

She let him hold her for a few minutes, then she pulled away slowly.

"They brought my breakfast this morning and there was a small cup of Jell-O. I remembered how in pre-school, that was the only snack Noor ever wanted. Then I started to think about all their favorite things that I'll never know. All their important moments... graduations, weddings, children... all their lives... it's all just going to pass me by."

Hasan concentrated on keeping his voice steady, "Don't think like that, May. You have to have faith that God will cure you of this. You have to. I do."

"You do?"

The doubt in her voice almost caused his to waver, but he managed to remain firm. "Very much. And I need you to have faith, too. Your body needs positive energy."

"I just... I've been trying to be positive... I don't think it's gotten us anywhere."

"May, how can you say that? Do you know how much of a difference your attitude makes for the kids? On the way home yesterday, Deen said, 'Baba, are the doctors sure mama's sick? She seems fine to me.' Your joking and laughing gives them hope."

"I'm not talking about the kids, Hasan. What I mean is.... "

"I know what you mean. But if it makes such a difference with the kids, it must be making a difference with you."

"That doesn't make sense, Hasan."

Just as he was about to convince her of a theory he had only just formulated and only half-believed, the doctor entered.

"Mr. and Mrs. AbdulShafi, I would like to talk to you about where we are with your treatment plan."

CHAPTER 10:
Betrayal Begins

Once Sidra finally put an end to date night she continued to mention James enough times to finally evoke some questions from her husband.

"Is James new? I've never heard you mention the name before."

"Actually, James just got transferred to another office, but sometimes stays late to wrap up some old cases. He's really cool. Drives a motorcycle. You'd like him."

"I doubt that," Farris muttered under his breath.

He tried not to get too worked up about it, although on the inside he couldn't stop the doubts from jumping around his head. Still, he kept any further comments to himself.

He couldn't help but notice, however, that Sidra had replaced her simple morning routine – jumping out of the shower, getting dressed, brushing her hair and heading out the door – for one which was more time consuming. She spent extra time styling her hair, applying foundation, then eyeliner, then blush, then lipstick. She had always chosen what to wear rather quickly in the mornings, not giving it a second thought; now she dawdled in front of her open closet, and tried on several outfits before deciding on just the right one. He hated what this change could mean, but he never mentioned anything to Sidra.

As though that weren't enough, Sidra got in the habit of making late night phone calls. Each night just before going to bed, she took the phone to the living room and closed the door behind her. She was close enough for Farris to hear what she said, but far enough away that he had to pretend he hadn't heard anything.

"I don't think we have to worry about that with this case," she said into the receiver one night. "But we can look at it more closely in the morning."

Pause.

"Don't be silly, it's not urgent. Plus, it's just a few hours away."

Pause.

"I miss you, too, but we can make it to the morning."

Pause.

Sidra laughed faintly and said, in a jovially sarcastic tone, "I never would have guessed you thought I looked hot in that dress... with the way your eyes were glued to me all day."

Pause.

"So we're already at the point where you make requests about what I wear?!?"

Hearing her chuckle like that made Farris want to get up and grab the receiver. He wanted to send his fist through it, and strangle whoever was on the other end. But the heartbreak left him paralyzed; he had no choice but to sit and listen.

"You, too. Sweet dreams."

Sidra hung up and went back to the bedroom where Farris tried to keep cool, pretending to watch television.

"What was so important you had to deal with it at eleven o'clock at night?" he asked, his clenched jaw betraying his anger.

"Just some details about work we had to work out."

"And it couldn't wait 'til morning?" Farris asked softly despite the fire that was building inside of him.

"No, Farris, it couldn't," Sidra snapped. "I don't get on your case when you bring work home. Why is this such a big deal? You do it all the time."

Farris turned off the television, turned away from his wife, and closed his eyes. Sidra let out an agitated sigh and followed suit.

The following night at dinner, Sidra informed Farris that, similar to the previous few weeks, she would continue to work late for the next few.

Farris shrugged, "It's not like you're with me even when you are here."

Sidra slammed down her fork, "Farris, you always supported my career before. I don't know what's going on with you lately! I mean, do you want me to stop working... is that it?"

"Sidra, don't be ridiculous."

"Then, what? What?! I can have a career but I can't excel at it?! Is that it? I can have a career but I can't care about it?! Farris, I'm only doing what's being asked of me at work. I'm not trying to be a hero. I just don't want anyone to say that my work is less than acceptable. And right now, that means spending more time at the office. So that's what I'm going to do."

"Good," Farris replied nonchalantly as he cleared his plate, leaving Sidra fuming by herself at the dining room table.

Sidra managed to keep herself productively busy during her extra work hours. She caught up on phone calls and paperwork, even managed to update some house calls and interviews.

After about a week, the exhaustion from the extra work load began to settle in. One night as she filled out some paperwork at her desk, she caught herself dozing off. *I'll rest for just a minute*, she thought. Laying her head on the desk, she was fast asleep within seconds. Before her a beautiful dream began to unravel: Farris was in the yard of a house foreign to her, chasing two young children. She could see him catch the little boy, who was simply a smaller, younger version of Farris, pinning him to the ground and tickling him until the boy could no longer breathe. Her mind's eye tried to focus on the woman standing with them, the mother of these beautiful children, but she would not come into focus. When Sidra woke, tears were streaming down her face. Needing someone to talk to, she called the one friend she confided everything to; she called James.

CHAPTER 11:
The Closest Envy

The tension had finally lifted in Mariam's home and for the next few weeks she enjoyed a peaceful daily routine. The younger kids had gotten used to daycare, somewhat easing the stress and guilt she felt each day as she dropped them off. Afterwards, Morgan and Mariam enjoyed each other's company on their way to school. He had continued to help around the house even after they had made up, increasing Mariam's appreciation for him and lending to a stronger relationship between them.

"What do you say about a date night?" Morgan asked one day on their way to work.

"I say, date? What's a date? If it doesn't involve sticky fingers, runny noses, making lunches and reading bedtime stories, then I have no idea what it is!"

"I'm serious! We can ask May and Hasan to take care of the kids for a few hours while we go have dinner... just the two of us."

"We can't really ask May and Hasan, though. She's still in the hospital, and I can't do that to Hasan."

"Oh... you're right. I forgot." Morgan thought for a moment. "Then we can ask Sidra and Farris."

Mariam let out a sigh, revealing her real hesitation. "Morgan, we've barely caught up on our debts, and our income is just covering our expenses. My entire paycheck goes to day care and paying your brother back for the money he lent us. It's not really wise for us to do any spending now."

How could it be that even now, with both of them working, they still couldn't afford one dinner out? Morgan's familiar feeling of inadequacy began to slowly creep back. Dinner out seemed like such a simple request. How was it that he could not provide it?

Mariam sensed the change in Morgan's mood, and quickly tried to alleviate it.

"What about a date night at home? After the kids go to bed, we can get dressed as though we're going out, then I'll cook you a gourmet meal unlike any restaurant can make."

But it was too late; Morgan was beyond the point where words could soothe.

That night, after Morgan had washed the dishes and Mariam came down from putting the kids to bed, she turned the music on, took hold of her husband, and forced him to a slow dance. He held her closely against his body, knowing she was only trying to comfort him. But his mood wasn't changing. Before the song had finished, he kissed her forehead, told her he was exhausted, and went up to bed. An hour later, when Mariam went into the bedroom, Morgan was already sound asleep.

Luckily, Morgan had just needed a good night's rest. The following morning he woke up in his usual good spirits. Mariam was thankful that his mood hadn't lasted, and enjoyed listening to his morning jokes.

The sound of his laughter stayed with her all day until suddenly the school secretary informed her that the principal wanted to speak with her. Getting called to the principal's office as an adult gave her the same queasy feeling it had given her a lifetime before as a student. She actually considered hanging out in the bathroom for a few hours to evade him.

"Get a grip, woman!" she yelled at herself. Her eyes quickly darted around the room to make sure no one had heard her. Shaking her head, she rolled her eyes at her own foolish behavior and headed to the principal's office. As soon as she entered, the frown lines burrowed into his face told her that she was in trouble.

"Sit down, please, Mariam. I'm just going to get to the point.

Many of the students you've been counseling have shown a dramatic change in their grades. The adjusted classes along with your advice have really made a difference.

"So although you've only been with us for a short while, we would like to put you in charge of the Beyond Graduation Office. You'll have at least two counselors who will report directly to you. The purpose of the BGO is to help students decide what to do after graduation – whether it be go to college, find a job, enlist in the military – then help them fulfill that goal. You will be helping juniors and seniors pick which colleges they are best suited to, as well as follow up on their applications, and the like.

"This is definitely a promotion in position as well as in salary, but before you accept you also have to be aware that the work load is going to more than triple. I'm confident, however, from your performance over the past few months, that you're more than capable."

Pleasantly flustered by the words of praise, Mariam managed, "Thank you. That's very flattering."

"Do you have any questions?"

"Ummm..." Shaking her head to shake away the surprise and make her mind function, she finally asked, "But it's all still during school hours?"

"Yes, for the most part. As the college application deadlines approach some students end up needing more help after or before school, but scheduling that will be up to you."

He fidgeted with some papers on his desk as Mariam thought quietly. A moment later he asked, "Would you like some time to think it over?"

Mariam slowly shook her head. "I have nothing to think about. I'll gladly accept."

She left the principal's office feeling elated, and couldn't wait for the ride home so she could share the good news with Morgan.

As soon as they were in the car, Mariam leaned over, kissed her husband and almost shouted, "They gave me a promotion today!"

Morgan was more than surprised. "What? A promotion?"

"Yes, a promotion. They're making me the head of the Beyond Graduation Office. There will be two counselors answering to me, and I help the juniors and seniors sort of plan what they want to do after graduation."

"Wow," Morgan said with a straight face.

"He said it's a lot more work, but it's more money, too!" In her excitement she hadn't noticed Morgan's frigidity.

After a moment, Morgan asked plainly, "And you accepted?"

The absurdity of the question made Mariam stare at her husband, and for the first time she noticed that his face was rigid with disappointment.

"Of course I accepted, Morgan. Why wouldn't I?"

"Oh! Why wouldn't you?! Okay."

"What does that mean?" Mariam's forehead wrinkled in confusion. She adjusted her position in the seat, inching away from her husband.

"You don't see any reason why you shouldn't have accepted?"

Her patience was running thin, but she kept her tone low, speaking through clenched teeth, "If I had seen a reason, Morgan, then I wouldn't have accepted it."

He had killed her joy, and wouldn't even give her the satisfaction of knowing why. Morgan simply continued driving, focusing his stern brown eyes on the road before him, as though no exchange of words or emotions had occurred between them.

That night, as he lay with his back to her, she tried softly again to get him to point out her mistake.

"Morgan, please... please just explain to me what I did wrong."

"I'm tired. Good night."

His harshness stung. She turned off the light and let her mind recount and rethink everything. Over and over she thought... how could taking this promotion not be in their best interest? What could Morgan see that she couldn't? And why wouldn't he help take off her blinders? Again, here they were, sleeping in the same bed, and yet somehow, further apart than they had ever been.

She was determined not to let that chasm between them persist. Once the alarm clock went off in the morning and she was sure he was awake, she sat up in bed.

"Morgan, I'm going to go in today and tell them I can't accept the promotion. But just tell me why? I've tried all night to see how this could have a negative effect on us, and I've failed. So please just spell it out for me."

"You want the job, take it, Mariam. I don't see why you care what I think today. Yesterday you didn't."

He had meant to just say his piece and get up, but Mariam, who was now kneeling on the bed facing his direction, quickly grabbed his arm.

"What are you talking about? Since when do I not care what you think?"

Morgan let out an agitated, impatient sigh. But the moment was long enough for the light to go off in Mariam's head. And although she finally got it, she could not believe it.

Letting go of his arm she said, "Morgan, you do know that my work hours won't change, right?"

"Yeah."

"And any extra load is for me to deal with at school… it won't affect my time at home."

"I know."

"So what exactly was there for me to discuss with you before I accepted? It's a higher paying job in the same building, the same hours as before. Physically, nothing's changing. So… what was there to think about… talk about?"

"Wasn't it you who said we're a team and we have to play the game together?"

"Once you've strategized with your team, and everyone's in position, you don't stop before you take a shot to ask if you should score... you just do."

"You still should have asked for my permission."

He had meant to say opinion, but it was too late to take it back.

"Permission?! I should have asked for your permission?! And that's because I'm a senseless woman who can't make any competent decisions on her own?! I'll keep that in mind next time." She took one giant step forward, down off of the bed and stormed out of the room.

"Please do," Morgan called out after her.

He was still too angry at her lack of regard for him to understand the severity of their exchange.

CHAPTER 12:
Unsatisfying Affairs

Summer answered the door wearing a short, skintight black dress which hung much lower in the front than anything else she owned. Her wavy red hair covered the straps of the dress that could have easily been mistaken for a nightgown.

She was at first surprised not to see Roberto standing in front of her, then embarrassed at herself for how she looked in front of the person who was standing there. Anxiously, she tried covering herself with her arms and half-hiding behind the open door.

"Hi, Summer. How are you?" Hasan's gaze was lowered, as usual, allowing him to notice neither her overdone appearance, nor her embarrassment.

"Ah... fine thanks, Hasan."

"I just wanted to invite you and Porter to dinner Friday evening. We're celebrating May's return home."

"Oh, so she's doing better then?" Summer asked optimistically.

"Yes, thank God she's better. The doctors have us hopeful. I know the road may still be long ahead of us, but for now we're Praising God and celebrating this tiny victory."

"That's wonderful."

"I think May really needs to be around family and friends now, so please make sure you can both come."

"Of course we'll be there."

He walked away, leaving her peering out from behind the front door. As she watched him walk back toward his house, her eyes grew sad and her heart sank. She stood there for some moments, marinating in a guilt born of disparagement for all the important blessings in her life.

Hours later, as Roberto caressed all the curves of her body and expressed passions which screamed from every inch of his, she couldn't stop focusing on the image of a man thanking God despite his hardships and celebrating a blessing which was so much less than all of her own. May's illness had stripped her of her health and was obviously having a toll on Hasan as well. Yet there he was, praising God... thanking Him. It made her doubt so much about the way she had been living her life. Here she was young, healthy, living an unburdened life where she was not in need of anything. And despite all of that, she had never thanked God. Instead, she had entered into an affair, betraying her husband and her morals, and was sinking into a version of herself which shamed her.

As Roberto rolled off of her, lightly kissing her cheek, he whispered, "*That* was even better than our first time. That's the passion you need in your work." He lit a cigarette and continued to be oblivious to her inner turmoil. With the first puff of smoke that reached her, Summer turned away and shut her eyes tightly, wishing desperately to take it all back. She hated what she had done. She had thought that the affair with Roberto would provide her with the attention for which she yearned. She had thought that bringing passion into her life would help her feel more alive. It had done none of that. In fact it had done the opposite; losing her way had caused the black hole to reappear and eat away even further at her spirit. Tears flowed silently onto her pillow.

Despite the distance that had grown between them over the past three months, she knew that reprieve would only be complete by melting into Porter's arms. He was her comfort. Realizing that now, with Roberto beside her in bed, she felt like she couldn't breathe. And as if karma could be premeditative, thinking ahead for the best punishment to suit her now, Porter wasn't scheduled to return for another two days. And even then, what kind of comfort would her conscience allow her? The desolation she felt brought to her mind an image of the pills she had thrown away months before.

Once Roberto had finally left, she pulled herself out of bed and threw on her denim overalls. Walking into her therapist's office disheveled and unnerved, she announced, "Okay, I'm ready for the meds."

~

On his business trip, Porter often found himself occupied with thoughts of his wife and the health of his marriage. He knew Summer was struggling with her art, and he knew she had high expectations of how Roberto's instruction would pay off. Porter wanted to be supportive of her, he wanted her to learn and grow. When chances for business trips arrived, he took them unhesitatingly, falsely sensing that in his absence she would be less distracted. Over the past few months, this was his fourth trip, and the first one with only Kara as his assistant.

She had tagged along on the previous trips, learning and collaborating where she could, and when Porter informed her that she would finally have her chance to be his 'right hand man,' she was ecstatic.

"Oh, thank you so much, Mr. Lawson. You won't be disappointed."

"I know," Porter chuckled.

And she kept her word; she very professionally set his schedules, booked his meetings, and made all the necessary arrangements. She prepared him with all the materials he needed and kept one step ahead of him at all times.

"The rest of your day is very full so I'm putting a call through now so you can check in with Mrs. Lawson." He appreciated her diligence, and he felt refreshed to be in her company.

On his final evening away, after a long day of meetings and business dinners, he sat with his tie unfastened and head resting against the back of the couch. Closing his eyes, the only image before him was that of Summer. After trying unsuccessfully to reach her a few times, he finally put the phone down and consoled himself with the knowledge that in less than twenty-four hours, he would get to see her beautiful face and hold her in his arms.

Although that was what he yearned for most, he knew that it would be a bitter-sweet reunion. They had grown too distant lately, and any intimacy they shared always felt superficial, forced; it no longer brought him solace. He hated being so far removed from her, but he knew she needed to focus on her work. And he was convinced that she needed to do it on her own if she was to ever become a successful businesswoman.

The soft knock at the door brought him back to the empty hotel room.

"Sorry if I disturbed you, Mr. Lawson. I just thought that it's still early... you might be up for a drink?"

"I don't drink, Kara. But you're welcome to come in for some coffee, if you like." He walked toward the electric kettle and started preparing two mugs.

"Sure... thanks, Mr. Lawson. I just didn't feel like being alone." She walked in and closed the door behind her.

"No problem. And Kara, we're all done with work for the day. So... it's Porter." Her slight embarrassment showed more through her smile than her flushed cheeks.

"I think everything went well this trip, don't you?" she fished as they took their seats on the couch.

"It did. And it wouldn't have if it weren't for you. I really appreciate all your hard work. You did a great job. I know you put in a lot of extra hours to get everything right. I hope it didn't affect your personal life."

"Um... it sort of did, but in a good way, I think. My boyfriend – ex-boyfriend – was the type who sort of... " she looked away, moving her opened palms in a rolling manner, animating her struggle to get the right word, "suffocated? Yeah, suffocated. He was the type who suffocated you with his love. You know, the type who wants to be with you *all* the time and needs to be involved in *every* part of your life.

"Don't get me wrong... it's endearing. But only to a point. And although we've been together for three years, I've been far past that point for a while now."

"That's too bad."

"He took it really hard, but I think it's for the best."

The kettle behind them began to screech. Porter got up and poured their coffee, then went back to the couch. As he handed her the mug she said, "Now I can focus on my career... where I want to go from here."

"And you think doing it alone – whatever 'it' ends up being – will be satisfying?"

"I don't plan to be alone. I'm certain I can find someone who appreciates me and at the same time gives me space to live."

Porter murmured under his breath, "Don't be so sure that will cure you of loneliness."

He hadn't really meant for Kara to hear, but she pushed, "What do you mean?"

Her question forced his eyes to hers, and an exhausted smile appeared on his lips. "I mean, maybe it's that space that we think we need that leads us to loneliness. Maybe we're meant to live in less space... shared space."

"It surprises me somewhat to hear you say that," she said, the look of wonder plain on her face.

Porter chuckled at his own hypocrisy. "I know. I always tell Summer, 'you need to sell your work on your own because you are the only one who knows all its ins and outs.' But maybe that's what led to where we are now."

"You just wanted to encourage her... to support her to be a good businesswoman," Kara let out frankly, slightly shrugging her shoulders.

"Exactly. But maybe my physical support would have done her

better... us better. I don't know." He threw his free hand into the air and leaned back against the couch. Holding his coffee mug with two hands, he kept his eyes glued to its contents.

Kara set her mug on the coffee table and inched towards him so that their thighs were touching.

"Don't be so hard on yourself," she said, softly laying her hand on his knee. "I've seen how you treat your wife, Porter. You don't just tell her to be independent and leave her... you send flowers, plan dinners out... she's lucky to have you. Any girl would be. She should be there for *you*."

He nodded slowly, taking in all that Kara had said. It was sweet of her to try to comfort him. But she misunderstood his smile and the light tap on her back. Kara held her breath, and leaning in closer to him whispered, "Let me be there for you."

Just as her eyes were closing and her lips barely brushed his, Porter pushed her shoulders back gently and pulled away.

"Kara, what are you doing? I appreciate your compassion, but I didn't...."

Touching her fingers to his lips, she cut him off, still whispering, "I don't want anything. All I want is to be there for you. I won't tell anyone. Let me be the cure for your loneliness."

"I think you should go now, Kara." He stood up and took a step back.

Some seconds passed, then Kara rose and walked to the door reluctantly, taking small, slow steps, with her head hanging low. Just before stepping out, she turned to him and made one last attempt, "My offer stands. Any time you need someone, I'm here." She walked out and closed the door softly behind her.

It took him some moments to sober up from the shock of Kara's behavior. But a few minutes later, as he played the scene over and over in his mind, Porter found himself torn between the image of a wife now far removed from him, and the tenderness of a woman right next door, who simply wanted to love him.

CHAPTER 13:
A Party for May

She was still pale, weak and continued to move around slowly, but May's spirits had gradually lifted since the day she returned home.

"Can I help you with your homework, *habibti*?" She couldn't help panting softly as she sat down next to her daughter.

"No, thanks, mama. I got it covered. But you can keep me company until I finish... I'm almost done." Noor wanted to make up for all the time she had lost while her mom had been away. She tried spending every free minute she had with her. Noor had even begun to sneak into her parents' bed during the middle of the night just so she could wrap her arms around her mother.

"Good, *habibti.* But don't rush for me. I won't go anywhere until you finish."

May knew her hospital stay had been the hardest on Noor, so she tried to make it up to her. Deen, on the other hand, had grown very attached to his grandmother. Although May loved her mother-in-law and appreciated all she had done for May's family, she couldn't help but feel slightly jealous. At meal times, May would offer to cut up his food or pour his juice, but Deen always preferred that *Sitto* do it. At bed time, Deen wanted *Sitto* to read him a story. In the morning, he wanted *Sitto* to get him dressed.

Hasan noticed how these actions hurt his wife. He tried to comfort her, "*Habibti,* soon you'll be back to your normal self again and mama will leave, and you'll be the one doing all that stuff for him. It's sort of better this way; you still need to rest to regain your strength."

"It's *not* better, Hasan. It's not about who does those things for him, it's about who he *wants* to do them. Once your mom leaves I'll end up doing them by default, but he'll still rather she could be here for him. He'll be so upset when she leaves."

"He's just a little kid, *habibti.* Of course he'll be upset, but quicker than you know he'll re-attach himself to you and you'll be wishing my mom could come back to give you a break."

Hasan held her in his arms. She knew he was right, but that didn't help to alleviate how much she missed her little boy.

As she sat silently beside her daughter, May thanked God for the second chance He had blessed her with. *Maybe I will get to see Noor in her wedding gown. Alhamdu lillah. To a good man, God... let her marry a good man who will treat her like a queen, honor her, and never hurt her in any way. Someone who will consider her his partner, and know that her happiness is the key to his own. Please, God, bless her with that and save her from being with a man who does not respect her. Ameen.*

Maybe I will get to attend Deen's college graduation. Alhamdu lillah. Oh God... let him, and Noor... let them both be successful in this life and in the hereafter. Let them understand that doing their best in this life is more than studying and working hard, but it's about being kind, forgiving, and keeping You as close as possible. Oh God, please let them always be conscious of You, and they will succeed, by Your will. Ameen.

Maybe I will get to hold my grandkids. Alhamdu lillah. Oh God, bless my kids and all of their offspring. Ameen.

Maybe I will get to watch Hasan grow older and fatter. She couldn't help but giggle silently at the image of her husband which appeared in her mind's eye. She smiled at the beautiful images in her head and repeated to herself, *Alhamdu lillah. Alhamdu lillah.*

"I'm all done, mama. What are you laughing at?" The question forced small giggles from both mother and daughter. "Oh, nothing, *habibti.* Come on, let's go see what the rest of the clan is up to."

"Well, actually... you're not allowed to see."

May laughed aloud. "What do you mean, 'I'm not allowed to see?'"

"Some of the party preparations are a surprise."

"Ah. I see. Well, then, what shall we do?"

Noor didn't hesitate, "You can help me pick out what I should wear tonight?"

"Oh, that's perfect. Show me... what do you have in mind?"

Mother and daughter shopped in their closets for the perfect outfits to wear to the party. Noor was elated when her mother gave her permission to wear lip gloss that evening. The girls talked and laughed, and enjoyed being together for a couple of hours.

When she sensed that maybe her mom had had enough, she decided to let her off the hook.

"They're probably done with the surprise now. I know you want to spend time with Deen. You can probably go to him now."

May knew what a big step that was for her daughter to take. She held her close, rubbed her back warmly, and said, "I pray your wisdom and selflessness remain with you forever. You are something special, Noor."

In the kitchen she found *Sitto* and Deen having a snack. Her mother-in-law gave her a warm smile as she entered, and as May sat down said, "I'm just going to run to the bathroom. I'll be right back."

As she walked past, May squeezed her mother-in-law's hand tenderly in appreciation.

"Those carrots look really good. Can I have one?"

"Sure, *Sitto's* plate is full. You can take one."

"Oh, Deen." May feigned shock, letting out a soft gasp and putting one hand to her chest and the other to her mouth. "How would that look if *Sitto* came back and found me eating her food? She would think I was stealing it from her. But... maybe you could give me one of yours?"

Deen shrugged and held a carrot out to his mom.

"So... Noor tells me you guys are planning a surprise?"

"Yeah," he laughed. "It's really funny."

"Do you think you can tell me what it is?"

"Mama! Then it wouldn't be a surprise!" Deen was floored by his mom's irrational request.

"Oh... of course. Sorry." She pretended to be apologetic, swimming in the sound of his laughter.

"So, has *Sitto* gotten used to Poppy, yet?"

"I think so. But she still calls him Poopy." Again, Deen could not contain himself.

"Maybe we need to keep his litter box more clean."

"I don't think it matters, mama," he said matter-of-factly, shaking his head.

As they ate their snack, May continued to ask him all sorts of questions about school and his friends. She purposely chose topics she knew he would get a kick out of. His laughter was medicine for her soul.

Hours later, as Hasan, Noor and Deen were doing some last minute cleaning around the house, May sat with her mother-in-law drinking tea.

"May, I don't want to leave you if you still need me around, but I also don't want to stick around if you're feeling up to doing everything again. So, when you've had enough of me, just let me know."

"Mama... I'll never get enough of you. I know we have exhausted you these past months, but I wish you would stay even once I'm feeling better. All of us love having you around. And you only have an empty house to get back to... I know we give you a headache, but we keep you company, too."

"I have my routine. I like the comfort of my home. I know it's empty, but... you know what I mean. No place is like your own home."

"I think it's still too early to talk about this anyway. I still have to get my strength back and the kids need you. So, I'm afraid, you're our prisoner for a while more."

Her mother-in-law smiled, then after a short pause, said, "May... if I overstep my bounds with the kids... I mean, I know you can't do everything, but there may be things that you would rather do yourself, or you would rather I do differ...."

But May cut her off. "Mama, this is your home and these are your grandchildren. You have always done what's best... I trust your judgment." May appreciated how sensitive her mother-in-law was to her feelings. She knew that most people wouldn't be and would expect her to appreciate any help they gave her and in whatever form. That sensitivity helped assuage some of the jealousy May had been feeling about her relationship with the kids. May hugged her mother-in-law sincerely and said, "Thank you. Thank you for everything. God bless you always and reward you for all you've done for us."

After dinner and dessert, Noor and Deen were allowed to stay up for one last part of the evening. Hanaan, Mariam, Morgan, Summer, Porter, Sidra, and Farris all sat around an untidy dinner table. Mariam and the other women had volunteered to clean up, but Hasan and Hanaan insisted that the night was for celebrating and the cleaning up could wait till the morning. May sat semi-reclined on the couch with her legs covered by a thin blanket. They were all enjoying the evening.

Noor stood in front of the guests and announced, "Ladies and gentlemen, this portion of the entertainment is entitled, 'While Mom Was Away.' Please enjoy."

The young girl disappeared down the hallway for a few seconds. When she reappeared, she was wearing a scarf around her head and an apron around her waist. She knelt at the coffee table and pretended to be working in the kitchen, chopping and stirring with plastic utensils. Then suddenly Deen came running into the living room on all fours. Noor jumped up with a scream, throwing the plastic spoons into the air.

"Poopy! Poopy!" she screamed, imitating her grandmother's accent as Deen acted like the wacky cat, attacking her and running all over the living room.

"Stop Poopy! Deen! Deen, where are you? Come get this crazy cat!"

Hasan walked in on his knees wearing a baseball cap and a t-shirt.

"*Sitto*. He's not listening to you because you're calling his name wrong."

The pretend Poppy continued to terrorize "*Sitto*."

"You deal with him then! Stop that! Get off!"

So Hasan, still imitating his son's soft immature voice, called out, "Poppy. Come on. Come here, Poppy."

Slowly the fake Poppy walked over to his owner, and he picked him up.

"See, *Sitto*."

But "*Sitto*" was not impressed. "If that cat gets in my way again, I'm going to put him outside and call the neighborhood dogs to chase him into the next state!"

The actors bowed as the audience laughed and clapped. Hasan walked over to his mother, who sat with her arms crossed and a forced grimace on her face. As her son kissed her forehead, her hand shooed him away, her eyes smiled and a loud chuckle escaped her lips despite her pitiful attempts to contain it. The mood of the evening did not lend itself to feeling insulted.

"Okay, kids, time for bed now...." But Noor interrupted him.

"Baba, we actually have one more skit planned, but it was a surprise for you, too. It'll only take a few minutes."

"Okay, let me just pull up a seat next to one of my leading ladies." He lifted May's legs slightly, slid next to her on the couch, and laid her legs lovingly on his lap.

"Okay. Go ahead."

Again, Noor and Deen disappeared down the hall. When they reappeared, Noor was in the same costume, but Deen was sporting his father's shoes, necktie, and blazer. Everybody burst out laughing at the sight of the little boy who seemed to have been swallowed by his father's wardrobe. He sat down on the chair and Noor paced back and forth in front of him.

"Now Hasan," the pretend *Sitto* said, "just because the doctors are letting May come home soon does *not* mean you can just count on her to deal with everything around here, again."

"Mama, I help whenever..." Deen lowered his voice to get it to sound like his father's.

"Shhhhhh! When I'm speaking you don't interrupt me."

"Yes, mama." The audience giggled.

"She needs rest, and I'm happy to help out, but you and your kids should really be putting more in. You better tell Noor to get herself and her brother up and ready in the morning. She's old enough to use an alarm clock."

"Yes, mama."

"And tell Deen to clean his room. If I walk in there one more time and trip on the toys spread out all over the floor, I will fall and break my hip. Do you want that?"

"Of course not, mama."

"You say of course not, but I think that's what the kids have planned! If I find his toys all over the place again, I will throw them right out the window."

Deen giggled.

"Don't even think I won't!" Noor fought back the urge to laugh and managed to stay in character.

Lowering his head again, the pretend Hasan said, "Yes, mama."

"These kids need more responsibility, Hasan."

"They're good kids, mama."

"Did I say they weren't?! I know they're good kids, but you all have to help May."

"Yes, mama."

"And Hasan..." Noor paused dramatically, building up anger, her face even became flushed. "If I go into the bathroom and find the seat up one more time, I will beat you! You are my son; I don't care how old you are, you will always be old enough for a spanking!"

The crowd erupted with laughter. As they all clapped, May leaned over to her husband. He was flushed with embarrassment, smiling and shaking his head. May whispered, "Did she really say that?"

"Oh, the kids gave you the clean version of the story." May couldn't stop laughing.

The kids bowed, kissed their parents and grandmother goodnight, and said goodbye to their guests.

"They're really great," Farris said to Hasan after the kids had gone off to bed. Farris didn't notice the disappointment that came over his wife's face as she thought she heard something more in the words he had spoken.

"Yeah. Don't get me wrong," Hasan said, "they drive us insane sometimes. But they're pretty good."

While Hasan and his mother got up to make coffee and tea, Mariam sat down next to May. "As soon as you start feeling tired, just kick us out."

May patted her friend's hand. "I'm fine. The company's good for me."

"Well, if at any time – tonight or anytime – you need anything – someone to stay with the kids, go food shopping, pick up dry cleaning, whatever – I hope you'll let me know. I said the same thing to Hasan, but I just wanted to make sure you know you can count on me."

May hugged her friend. "I appreciate that, Mariam. Thank you."

"Same goes for us, too, you know, May," Sidra said. "Please let us know if there's anything we can do."

"I will. Thank you. You've all been really supportive. I really appreciate it."

Hasan and his mom came out with trays of coffee and tea. As everyone adjusted their sugar, the neighbors talked about school, work, recipes, and restaurants.

"I had a business lunch at this new restaurant downtown and it was so delicious. You'll have to try it," Sidra said to no one in particular.

This, however, was news to Farris. He smiled and at the most appropriate time he approached her and asked, "When was that business lunch? With who?"

"Last week... remember. I told you."

"Who were you with?"

She giggled and waved the question away with her hand, "It doesn't matter." Farris, clenching his jaws in an attempt to keep his tone soft and steady, asked again, "Who?"

"It was a business lunch with James, Farris. I don't know why it matters." Her familiar annoyed tone had returned and all Farris could do was nod his head.

May had noticed the tension in their conversation, but when her eyes met Farris', she politely looked away.

Summer sat with her hands tucked beneath her, staring blankly at the floor. Hanaan noticed her reservation and tried to get her to join in, "These people are too old for you?"

Hearing the comment motivated May to gaze intensely at Summer. She really was very young... at least ten years younger than May. And her youth just accentuated her beauty – her fair, smooth, unblemished skin, shiny soft curls, sensuous bosom, perfectly smooth legs. *She's more attractive than many of those lingerie models,* May thought. But before jealousy could step in, May smiled to herself and looked away. *Masha' Allah. May God bless her with beauty, safety, health and faith. I was that age once,* she told herself. *Not as beautiful, of course, but I've had my time. This is a much better time in my life.* She thanked God for the innumerable blessings He had granted her. *And thank you, God, for my health,* she prayed silently, *because so many people are far worse than I.*

Politely, Summer laughed at the elder woman's question, "No... of course not. We're all probably around the same ages."

"Then why're you so quiet? You're bored."

"Not at all. I just have a lot of work to do when I get home. I have a lesson and I'm preoccupied with all I need to finish before it."

"What type of lesson? Are you back in school?" Morgan had overheard and was curious.

"No, no. Nothing like that. My mentor has been helping me with my art, that's all. He sort of tutors me."

"Wow! That must be expensive."

For the second time in only a few minutes, Morgan felt like he was much less than his neighbors. They were going to fancy restaurants, getting private tutoring... he needed his wife's help just to get by. For one second he looked up and made eye contact with Mariam, then shamefully looked back down and fiddled with his coffee mug. He didn't even hear Porter's answer to his question.

"No, he tutors her for free. He really just wants her to better herself." Summer's heart broke hearing those words. Her smile faded and her eyes shamefully fell back to her feet. It was the first time she had consciously realized that this tutelage had cost her more than anything she had ever paid for. It had taken from her one of the most priceless things in her life: her honor.

Feeling ashamed and alone, Summer sank into the background and sat there looking around her. Replaying her affair in her mind, she wished she could pause the tape and avoid making the mistake. She wished she could cut that chapter out of her life. Guilt overpowered her, bringing a sting to her eyes and making her feel nauseated. Her red eyes quickly scanned the room, hoping to find an exit or bathroom to escape to where she could collect herself. A few seconds later, her eyes fell on the most remarkable image, and she sat frozen. In awe, she watched as Hasan handed his wife some pills and a glass of water. After May had taken her medicine, he kissed her cheek lightly. Summer couldn't help but feel envious at the contentment in May's eyes.

CHAPTER 14:
Deception Lies

It hadn't been an easy decision to spy on Sidra. A large part of Farris hadn't really believed her act, but what choice did he have? He had no other explanation for Sidra's increasingly hateful behavior. He wanted to believe that she would never cheat on him... both her love for him and her God fearing, Christian principles were against it. But despite this inner certainty, doubt had dug a shallow hole in his mind. He had tried hard not to let that doubt lead him to feeling betrayed. He had considered talking to her, asking her why the change of attitude, why the neglect, why the curt conversations and tense dinners. But he knew Sidra would just accuse him of not supporting her career again. He knew that talking to her would provide no real answers. But the days had gotten longer and harder to endure, and the pit in his stomach at the thought of his wife with another man kept growing heavier. He had needed any way to end the agony, and it seemed like having his wife tailed had been the only option which might possibly provide relief.

"I need you to keep an eye on Sidra for me," Farris had told his brother, Faruq.

"What do you mean 'keep an eye on'? Are you going somewhere?"

"No, no, Faruq. You don't get what I mean. I want you to watch her... follow her."

His brother raised his eyebrows, took a step back, and stared at Farris for a moment. His tone made no hesitation to his shock, "You mean you want me to spy on her?!"

"Exactly. For about a week. That should be enough time to figure this out."

"Figure out what?!" demanded Faruq.

"It's not important. Your job is just to follow her around and tell me who she meets and where. That's your job. And obviously, don't let her see you."

Having explained what he wanted from Faruq, Farris had left his brother's apartment in a rush as Faruq shouted out more questions. Farris couldn't tell him any more than he already had; more words would mean that the confusion and rage which had been building up inside of him might explode. He just kept walking, ignoring his brother and trying to tune out the two voices in his head. The first one said, "Are you really going to have her watched? How could you do that to her? Is this what your life has become?" The other voice countered, "At least now it won't be long before you get some answers. All the mystery will come to an end soon." The debate had him pushing at his temples to offset the pain.

Later that day he had walked into his house to find Sidra sitting at the dinner table eating.

"When you were late I just went ahead. But all the food's still warm."

Once upon a time she wouldn't have taken even one bite without him. Once upon a time it was their being together that gave flavor to the meal. But that was before the late night calls and secret lunches. Now the distance between them drained him of any appetite. "That's fine. I'm not hungry, anyway."

As he had turned away, he heard her say stoically, "Good thing I didn't wait, then."

They had become two strangers, both yearning for peace. While Farris wished for the simple love they had shared only months before, Sidra simply wanted it over with.

Now, sitting beside his brother on the couch, Farris listened attentively to the results of Faruq's detective work. He listened as Faruq explained how he had tracked Sidra from the moment she left the house in the morning to the moment she arrived again in the evening. Faruq made sure to stay far enough behind so that she wouldn't notice him.

Farris learned that on three of the five work days, her movements simply consisted of going to and from work. On Monday she went out to lunch, meeting a woman at the restaurant. On Friday she stayed late at work, then went out to dinner with the same woman and an unfamiliar man.

"So that's him! That must be him! Did you see him when you followed her to work? Entering the building in the morning, or leaving in the afternoon?"

"No. And even the car he drove to dinner that night wasn't one I'd seen at all in the parking lot at Sidra's work. There were never more than a few cars parked there, and his was definitely *not* one of them. You know, Farris," Faruq continued, "I didn't understand why you wanted me to spy on her at first, but after seeing the way those two were chummy-chummy, I get it. At one time the other woman got up to use the bathroom, and I could almost see the drool coming out of his mouth. I couldn't get close enough to hear what they said, but the flirting was out of control."

"That bastard," Farris muttered through clenched teeth. "What did he look like?" He stood there frozen, needing to concentrate on the description he was about to receive, needing to see, if only in his mind, this man who had ruined his life.

"Tall, skinny white guy with light brown hair and brown eyes."

"A skinny white guy? Really, Sidra?!"

"Yeah, and when they got up to leave, the dude hugged her forever."

"I'm going to break every bone in his body! Urgh!" Farris threw the mug he had been holding against the wall. It broke into several pieces and the tea stains bled down the wall.

"Hey, man. You hired me to be a spy, not a maid. You know you have to clean that up?" But Faruq's remarks were beyond Farris' perception. His mind was busy playing out the inevitable fight with James. Clenching his fists, his knuckles turned red with the sting of punches soon to come.

A few moments later, as Faruq reluctantly crouched down cleaning up the mess his brother had made, Farris shook his head to return to the present. "So what's our next move? How do we find out who this James guy is?"

Faruq sighed heavily, "I don't know, Farris." The annoyance in his voice was more due to the broken glass and wet paper towels in his hand than to the topic of discussion.

Farris stood cemented in place, arms crossed, his eyes searching the floor for answers. When he had finished clearing up all the traces of Farris' outrage, Faruq stood beside his brother, eyes squinting in concentration at the movement of Farris' eyes, swaying back and forth. As the moments passed, Farris' eyes moved faster and more intensely. Faruq nodded in anticipation of the verdict.

Finally, Farris spoke; "Watch her again. Watch her for another week. When you see him this time, follow him... follow him wherever he goes. That way we'll find out where he lives."

Faruq did as he was told, but as the week began to wind down, he thought his efforts would be in vain; he hadn't seen James all week. Sidra followed the same routine as the week before, basically going just to and from work. She went out to lunch only twice – once alone, the other time with the same woman he had seen her with the previous week. Faruq's only hope was an auspicious Friday evening.

He was not disappointed; when Sidra arrived at the restaurant, James was already seated at the farthest table from the entrance. He was alone. Faruq watched from his car as James greeted Sidra with a warm hug. He remained in his car, watching from afar and waiting for the table nearest to them to be free. Just a few minutes later, the couple which had been partly blocking his view got up. Without waiting for them to exit, Faruq swiftly entered the restaurant and motioned to the hostess toward the table which had not yet been cleared. When she began to object, he grabbed a menu to disappear behind, and took the liberty of seating himself. Luckily, Sidra herself was pre-occupied with the menu, so she didn't notice that her brother-in-law had sat down at the cluttered table beside her.

It took the two waiters some time to clean up, eliciting deadly stares from Faruq. They made such a racket that no matter how far back in his chair he leaned, he couldn't hear anything happening in the table behind him. Once the table was finally clean and Faruq had ordered, he didn't really have to strain to catch every word of Sidra's conversation.

"You look great in that outfit, James."

"I'd say hot was a better description," the man said, and they both giggled.

"I signed up for that training seminar today." It was a woman's voice that spoke, but not Sidra's.

What?! When did she *get here?* Faruq thought.

"*We* should do that," James said. "I've heard a lot of great stories about that, both with respect to business and personal relationships."

"Maybe we should do it together?" Sidra offered.

"I think so," James replied. "I think it'll be really rewarding."

"Done. I'll sign up tomorrow, then."

They were quiet for a while. *Probably just eating*, Faruq thought. Pricking up his ears he could hear whispers, but he couldn't make out what the couple was saying. A few minutes later he heard James excuse himself, saying he needed the rest room.

"So what are you up to on the weekend?" the woman asked.

"Tomorrow I have a date with the gym," Sidra replied, her voice slightly louder and firmer with triumph. "Then on Sunday, just church."

"So are you gonna go with him?"

Sidra's voice, which had been so upbeat just a second ago, fell to a hush. "No... you know I won't." Faruq didn't understand the sadness in Sidra's voice now.

"You know I think that what you're doing is wrong, right? I'm sitting here, happy to get you out of your head for just a few hours, but that doesn't change the fact that I think this is all wrong."

"It's what will make us both happy in the end. I think it will." She paused for a moment then raised her voice with more determination and reiterated, "It will."

Just then James came back. Noticing the change in Sidra's mood he inquired, "What's going on? Sidra, are you okay?"

"She's fine," the woman replied. "We were just finishing up. I think we should get going."

Faruq took advantage of the slow moving waiters to pay his bill at the hostess' station. He walked out quickly and sat in his car, eyes glued to the door of the restaurant. Things were taking much longer than usual. More than twenty minutes had gone by, and still neither Sidra nor James had appeared. The restaurant had become extra crowded and their table was no longer visible from where Faruq sat. He turned off the ignition and walked back inside. Straining his neck to look over and around people's heads, Faruq huffed in annoyance, but he couldn't risk approaching the table and being seen. Finally, some heads moved out of the way and he made visual. His eyes grew wide with disbelief as he saw another group of people were already seated and checking out their menus.

He forced his way through the line to the hostess' station. "Excuse me, where did the people who were sitting at that table go?"

She looked over to where he was pointing. "They left about 15 minutes ago."

"Ah... no they didn't. I've been sitting outside waiting for them – they're friends of mine – and I'm sure they didn't come out of these doors."

"No... they left through the rear exit."

Faruq's eyes followed her finger as it pointed to a discreet back door which he had never before noticed.

"Are you shitting me?!" he yelled out. Pushing back through the crowd to the door, he didn't care about the frowns, annoyed glances and whispers directed his way; he was too caught up in the image of his own body in place of the mug which Farris had destroyed a few days before.

CHAPTER 15:
Not Working Out

Morgan had been sleeping on the couch again for some weeks now, but this time he hadn't waited to get kicked out of the bedroom. He had collected his pillow and things and left more than willingly. He forced himself to be cordial to his wife around the kids, but it was easy for him to ignore her when they weren't around. Her accepting that position without first having his blessing was the utmost form of disrespect, and this time he would make sure it would not pass easily.

Even if he had wanted to let it pass, to try to forget about it, it would have been impossible for him to do so. The praise Mariam was receiving from both students and faculty at the school seemed ubiquitous. Whichever way he turned, he heard comments like, "She's really transforming some of these kids. After adjusting some class levels, one of my D students is pulling off B+ work." He overheard one student say, "I never thought I was smart enough, but the BGO counselors keep encouraging me. I'm actually thinking of applying to college. I'd be the first in my family."

Very quickly her popularity had skyrocketed, and he couldn't help but feel like she had taken his place as the 'cool teacher' that students could talk to. The jump in her salary was of course another factor making him feel inferior to her. It caused him to hate every minute that she worked. So when the time was right, he decided, he would tell her that their working at the same place was not working out. Soon she would start to slip up on some of her motherly duties and that would be the perfect time to end his agony. It was only a matter of time, he told himself.

As for Mariam, she was dealing with a reality that she had been trying to deny for the past eleven years. She had seen signs of his jealousy before, but they had been only glimpses... nothing significant. And they had never before been directed at her. Years before, she had seen him get so jealous as to lose a friend over a promotion he'd been denied. Morgan had once been embarrassingly rude to his own brother when the man came over to show him the new car he had bought. She knew he was envious of their neighbors' large houses and expensive cars. He always seemed to want what wasn't his. But all of that stuff was apart from their family, Mariam had thought. She never imagined that she could be the object of his envy. How could she be? Wasn't her success really their success? Wasn't any good that was coming to her, also coming to him? Whether it was reputation, money, class, anything... she saw it as being theirs, something shared between them. It broke her heart that his cruel behavior towards her stemmed from her success. They shared a life together – years of laughter, tears, raising children. She could not distinguish between his life and her own; they were intertwined. So how could he not find joy in her happiness? How could he hate her success? His reaction to her promotion had broken something between them, and Mariam knew that it could not be fixed. She only hoped the break would not continue to spread.

At work she managed to put away her personal issues and focus on the tasks at hand. The two counselors in her office were hard workers, always dedicated, which helped keep her own focus on the work. The fact that she rarely ran into Morgan, even accidentally, also helped.

There was no way of knowing how long the tension between them would last, but Mariam made an effort to not let it affect her duties towards her household. Morgan always found his clothes clean and ironed, dinner was always at the usual time, and if he wasn't nearby once the table had been set, she would send their son to get him.

"Dad," Adam called all over the house until he found Morgan. "Dad! Dad, dinner's ready and mom says we can't eat till you come down."

And although it had taken her a few days to get to that point, she had also decided not to object if he tried to come back into their bed. Maybe if she went through the motions, she could put this whole experience behind her. Maybe if they just continued to go through their daily routine they could get past this. But despite her efforts, she had not yet reached the point where she could just start a conversation with him.

Morgan didn't understand that she was fulfilling her household duties out of a sense of responsibility; he thought she was doing it to soften him up, to take that first step toward reconciliation. He assumed, from her actions, that she felt sorry for taking that position without consulting him first. For that reason, he didn't consider it a blow to his pride to be the first to speak.

"How was your day?" he asked on their way to pick up the younger kids from daycare.

"Fine. Tiring. I feel like I didn't get a break all day. What about you?"

"Same."

A few minutes later he started again. "I heard they're doing something different with graduation this year?"

"Different?" Mariam thought for a moment. "Oh... it's not a big difference, really. When the students get called to receive their diplomas, the announcer is also going to add where they're headed to. So, for example, if Jane Smith is going to go to college, the announcer will say, 'Jane Smith – Boston University' or wherever."

"That's cool. Sort of a way for them to show off in front of their families and friends."

"I wouldn't really call it showing off. I think it's just another way for them to share their accomplishments."

Morgan forced out a thunderous laugh and shook his head slightly. "It's showing off. Trust me."

Mariam pretended not to notice his patronizing tone. She was glad he was trying for a truce and didn't want to do anything to test the new found peace.

But the days proved to her that his peace treaty was based on the condition that she endure much more mocking and ridicule. He found something wrong with everything she said. When she told the kids to clean up and get ready for bed, he said, "Mariam, let them play for fifteen more minutes. It won't make a difference."

"They get up early, Morgan. They need their sleep."

"Fifteen minutes won't make a difference."

She knew, of course, that fifteen minutes would actually end up being thirty or maybe even forty-five minutes, which would definitely make a difference. But she hated disagreeing with him in front of the kids, so, despite her better judgment, she let it go.

The following morning the kids gave their mom an exceptionally hard time getting up. "Come on, Adam. I've already been in here three times! You'll be late if you don't get up now. Let's go. You don't want to miss the bus."

She had managed to get the rest of the kids up, but they were all cranky and crying. "Morgan, please get Adam up. I need to deal with these kids, and if he doesn't get up now he'll miss the bus." Not only did she have her hands full with the younger kids, but she wanted to make sure that Morgan understood that their current state of chaos was directly caused by his undermining her judgment the night before.

Only Morgan wouldn't give her the satisfaction. "I'm about to jump in the shower. You deal with him."

Unsurprised, she rolled her eyes, left the younger ones crying at the breakfast table, and went to deal with Adam for the fifth time.

Twenty minutes later, they were all sitting at the table. Adam and Morgan were eating breakfast, the other kids were coloring, and Mariam sat with her head in her hands trying to force the headache away. The crying had stopped, but Mariam felt like she could call it a day. Unfortunately, she knew that was not an option.

She looked around the room casually, making sure everyone's face was clean and they were each wearing matching socks.

"Finish up, Adam. Then go wash your hands and your face. The bus will be here soon.

"And kids, it looks like it's going to rain, so absolutely no jumping in puddles. I don't want to deal with musty, gushy shoes and smelly, wet feet when I get home today." She knew the warning was as good as telling them the opposite, but this way at least when she scolded them later she wouldn't feel guilty.

As Adam and Dina gathered their bags to get on the bus and kissed their parents goodbye, Morgan and Mariam stood at the doorway waving to them. "It doesn't look like rain. I think it'll be a beautiful day." His insistence on disagreeing with every comment she made had started off being annoying, but now it was the norm to Mariam. She thought it must be exhausting for him, especially since he usually ended up being wrong.

Mariam had been swallowing her pride for a couple of months, each day telling herself she just needed to be patient. *He's a good man deep down. He'll go back to being himself,* she told herself. *He loves you. This behavior can't last much longer.*

But her love for him had begun to dwindle since the day of her promotion. With each word of ridicule, another piece of that love died. How could she continue to love him when he showed her so little respect? She convinced herself that she would be able to tolerate a marriage with much less love than she had been used to, but without respect, there was no chance. And because she figured Morgan was intelligent enough to understand that, he would surely stop putting her down without reason.

Enough time had passed, and Morgan, too, wanted things between them to go back to normal. One Thursday night, after the kids had gone to bed, he decided it was time. He sat in the living room watching television as Mariam folded the laundry. "Did you wash my beige pants?"

"The ones you were wearing today? No, you took them off after I'd already started the machine."

He let out an annoyed huff, and turned off the television. "Mariam, we have to talk. I've noticed lately that you haven't been able to keep up with the housework; the kids' rooms are always messy, dinner the past couple of nights was almost burnt, and now the dirty laundry is just piling up and I can't wear what I want to because it's not clean...."

He was about to continue, but she managed to cut him off. "When exactly did you see the kids' rooms messy?"

"Every morning, Mariam. They get up and you just stopped making the beds...."

"I didn't stop making the beds, Morgan. You just see the rooms two seconds after the kids get up. I make the beds just after breakfast, before we leave for school.

"And the meals that you said were 'almost burnt'... it's called caramelization... they're supposed to be a little brown. It's what gives the food flavor.

"And about the laundry...." First she pointed around her at the folded clothes, then she walked away and came back with the hamper. "This is all the dirty laundry in the house; your pants and some underwear. That's it."

But Morgan had a plan, and nothing Mariam said would change it.

"I just think... I mean, it's obvious that work is getting in the way of your household responsibilities. This is just not working out," he said apologetically as he shook his head.

Mariam internalized the shock at his words. Rubbing her lips, she thought quietly for a moment, nodding her head the whole time. "You're absolutely right, Morgan," she said, taking deep breaths and a few steps away from him.

He smiled at how easy it had been. But that smile disappeared when he heard the rest of what she had to say. "This isn't working out. I think we need to separate."

CHAPTER 16:
Moments of Truth

Roberto's appearance in her life had only complicated it. Summer realized that now, but her affair had been going on for a few months, and it had become just another attribute of her life which entrapped her. What she had originally thought would give her a sense of freedom had instead imprisoned her in a cycle of betrayal and guilt. Her painting hadn't gained anything from this new relationship, but she kept thinking that maybe there was something more, something better to come. It never came.

She felt suffocated by her own actions, by her own life. Sitting on the floor of her studio, her mind found its focus on the medicine bottle upstairs. Pressing her fingertips to her temples, trying to force the thoughts away, she rocked herself back and forth. But it was no use: the image of her escape was fixed before her. She jumped up suddenly and ran up to the main level of the house. Just as she was about to climb the second set of stairs, her eyes landed on the keys hanging beside the front door. She grabbed them and ran outside.

Standing in the middle of her driveway, hands on her knees, she tried to control her breathing. Once it had returned to a normal pace, she straightened her back, and her eyes instantly landed on a sight across the lawn.

May was sitting on a plastic chair in her yard, listening to the sound of her kids shooting hoops in their driveway and enjoying the sun. Summer could see that May was consumed by the brightness of the day, so she tried not to startle her.

"Hello, May," Summer said in a tone barely above a whisper.

May's eyes popped open and her smile illuminated her face.

"Summer! How are you? It's so funny because I was just thinking of you."

Though her smile didn't fade, the look on her face betrayed Summer's confusion. "Oh?"

"I was wondering why you do your painting indoors. The weather is so beautiful, it's inspiring."

Summer forced a chuckle, "Good point."

"How are you?"

It was such a simple, common question. Yet Summer couldn't reply; neither answer would have been truthful. "I just wanted to see how you're doing. You look well."

"I am well, Praise God. My energy level is gradually rising... I'm even helping around the house now. Never thought I'd be excited to do housework, but it makes me feel useful and a bit like my old self. And the kids have taken my illness as an excuse to listen to me... so I can't complain!" May's laughter was sincere.

So was Summer's surprise. There she stood – young and healthy – caught up in an affair that was destroying her. It was showing blatant insolence for the blessings of her health and marriage, and here was this other woman – who had experienced painful, life altering illness – that was thanking God and laughing. Summer's face became serious, "How do you do that?"

"Do what?" May asked, still smiling.

"Thank God."

May giggled and sighed. "Noor," she called to her daughter, "please bring a chair from the backyard for Mrs. Lawson." Once Summer had taken a seat, May answered her question. "Don't misunderstand, Summer. I am in no way a saint. I have my share of angry moments, hating all that's happened. I've been through emotional periods of... well... blackness, really.

"But then something brings me back – my kids' voices, or something my husband does, or even just biting into a piece of something delicious – and I wake up again. God has blessed me with bounties that are innumerable: I have a kind, loving husband who always gives and never expects anything in return. I have two children who I hear at night pray for me to get better. We have enough money to shield our bodies from the cold and our stomachs from hunger.

"So how can I not thank God? Because He's thrown me some sickness? He doesn't give a hundred percent to anyone, but that's what will separate people on the Day of Judgment. I want to be one of the people to whom He says, 'You endured the hardships I gave you, and you continued to believe in Me, to thank Me. Here is your garden in Paradise.'"

Summer listened attentively to her neighbor and tried to absorb all she heard.

"You're nodding your head," May said a few moments later, "but I can see that you're not really convinced."

Summer looked up with a faint smile and shook her head. "What would you say to someone – to a friend – who when they caught themselves in that moment of unhappiness, instead of remembering their blessings, turned to a vice which put all that they had at stake?"

May could see that her friend's internal battle was not only causing her stress, but it was also wearing away at her spirit. May wanted to help ease her pain without giving her a false sense of security. Her face became more serious, but she leaned over and put her hand on Summer's knee. "We are only human, Summer. We all make mistakes, and sometimes those mistakes are almost unforgivable. But I believe that God is the Most Forgiving. He forgives all sins... all but associating partners with Him. Except for that, God forgives everything. All we have to do is recognize our offenses, put an end to them, and ask for forgiveness... and we'll find it. Also, it will lift the load from our shoulders."

Summer sat there quietly for some moments, nodding at May's advice. The words should have reassured her, but Summer kept seeing images of her affair flash before her. With every nightmare-painted flash, Summer cringed and folded in on herself. She felt like her mistake would be the shroud which would bury her, and she could not forgive herself for ruining her own once-blessed life. The guilt had her doubled over as the tears began to fill her eyes. "I don't know if we humans are as forgiving as that."

She sat there quietly, holding herself tightly, staring at the same spot on the ground. When she spoke, it was barely above a whisper. "What if he sees the sin as unforgivable?" she managed to whisper.

"That's not for you to say. All you can do is ask for it... the rest is out of your hands. If you're forgiven, then you'll get a new start. And if you're not, you'll still be lighter. That secret which was weighing you down will at least be free and unable to cause you pain again."

Summer was desperate to be free of her secret. She tried to picture Porter's face, to imagine his reaction to her terrible betrayal. She tried to see him forgive her, but that image never came to focus. Clearly, she saw him shun her, leave her, and take with him all that remained of life. She could not control her weeping, and for those few minutes, May held her close and rubbed her back.

As she tried to compose herself, Summer managed, "I'm sorry, May. You must think I'm so superficial. Here you are dealing with cancer and recovery... and here I am, crying about my own problems."

May's smile lit up her face once again, "Don't ever apologize for your feelings, Summer. Our burdens may be shaped differently, but they are all heavy."

Summer couldn't understand how this woman could be so sympathetic. She knew her hug was inadequate, but it was the only token she could give to show her appreciation.

A few hours later, Porter entered his home to a sight he hadn't seen in months: Summer stood, wearing her worn, paint stained overalls, with her easel before her in the middle of the living room. He noticed that her face was paler, her eyes heavier. "I haven't seen you paint in here in months. I thought you didn't want to risk messing up the furniture?"

"I don't," she said taking a few steps towards him to give him a quick kiss, "but it's more important for me that you see my work."

"But I always see it when you've finished," he replied, half-shrugging his shoulders.

"That's not what I mean." She shook her head lightly as she thought of how to re-word it. "It's more important for me that you see *me* work. That you see the actual process. That in, even a tiny way, you are involved in it."

He stood there for a moment, smiling softly and nodding his head; they had both come to the same conclusion. *Things are going to be fine*, he assured himself.

Summer had already re-focused on her work. "I'm just going to go change and wash up," Porter called back as he walked up the stairs.

An hour later they sat eating at the kitchen table. Summer decided that it was time to drop the weight. "I went over to see May today."

"Really? That was nice of you."

"I actually had just stepped out for a walk when I saw her sitting there. We had a good conversation."

"Mostly about her health... or what?" Porter furrowed his eyebrows inquisitively.

"Not really. Mostly about... I don't know... I guess you'd call it... our spiritual health."

"Our what? What does that mean?" The wrinkles in his forehead deepened for a moment. Then suddenly he raised his eyebrows in shock. "Oh, Summer! Did she try to convert you?! You have to be very wary of those Muslims. One minute they seem totally normal, the next they're trying to get you to read their Koran."

Summer was taken aback by Porter's reaction. "It wasn't like that, Porter. Wow, I never knew you felt that way.

"Our talk was about forgiveness. She told me that God forgives almost all sins. I think it's really comforting, actually. I think she's one of the most peaceful people I know."

Porter shook his head at Summer's naivety. "Don't take my word for it; just turn on the television. All over the place there are news stories about Muslim terrorists. I mean, I have nothing against May and Hasan, but I don't want you getting too close to them, either. Safer to keep our distance."

Summer was blown away by her husband's words. "Porter, we've only ever seen goodness and kindness from these people... how can you say that? Don't you remember last year when you caught that bug and were basically bed ridden for a whole week? May stopped by every day to ask about you. *Every day*."

"That may be so, but still... better safe than sorry."

The conversation had gotten completely off track. Her intention had been to start confessing to him by first talking to him about forgiveness. She wanted to tell him how May had said that even people who've done seemingly unforgivable deeds can find forgiveness if they were sincere. But now he had killed her entry point. She pushed aside the conversation about May and Hasan, intent that they would continue it later, and sat quietly eating, thinking of another way to word her confession. Realizing that she had no choice but to come out and say it, she began, "Porter, there's something I need to tell you."

"Let me guess," her husband said, "You have a lesson with Roberto this evening?"

Hearing the man she loved utter the name of her lover made her choke on the bite she had just swallowed. Her coughing lasted for several moments. She took a few sips of water to clear her throat. "No... ah... just the opposite, really. We're pretty much done."

"Done? You mean your lessons are finished?"

She nodded. She was about to continue when he said, "I hope you got out of them what you needed."

She stared at her plate for a moment. How could she respond to that? But this was her chance. "Not really."

"No? But you spent so much time with him?"

After a short pause she replied, "Well, I thought what I needed was freedom. Freedom to feel and express, and I guess I thought he could teach me that. But that's not what I needed. What I needed was..." she paused. "What I needed was you."

"Me? I don't understand, Summer. You have me."

"But I didn't... I guess I didn't realize it, or maybe... I didn't think that was enough." Her voice had started to shake.

She put down her knife and fork and laid her arms in her lap. She hated what she had done, she hated her lies, her cheating. She knew that her confession would change her world forever. The guilt and fear had been weighing down on her, and she needed to breathe again. Tears began to flow from her eyes, releasing with them just an ounce of the pressure within her soul.

When he noticed his wife's tears, Porter put down his knife and fork and stared at her down-turned eyes. He knew the paleness of her face must mean something serious, and the mere sight of it made the blood drain from his face as well. Unable to blink, Porter held his breath in suspense of the words to come.

"I didn't realize that it would happen. I didn't intend for it to. I thought he really wanted to help my work. But he kept saying I needed more passion in my painting. 'More passion,' he kept saying, 'we need to explore your passion.'

"And I felt like I needed a break from my routine. I had started to feel suffocated, and he seemed to be offering me a way to breathe again. Just being there, encouraging me, showing interest in my work – in me – made me feel... I don't know... special, I guess.

"He kept paying more and more attention to me, not just to my work, but to me. And the flattery... I don't know. Somehow...."

Her voice trailed off into a whisper, "I don't even know how I let it get that far."

She wept until her eyes were swollen and her nose was runny. She couldn't say anymore, but Porter couldn't grasp the words that were coming from her mouth. He squinted his eyes and shook his head.

"I... what? I don't understand. Summer, what are you saying?"

Her weeping and inability to answer him affirmed his fears.

"How far did you let it get, Summer?"

She just sat there, hugging herself, sobbing loudly. But this time he needed to hear it. "HOW FAR, SUMMER?!" he demanded.

"Too far. I'm so sorry." She didn't look up, she just kept rocking herself back and forth. "I never intended to. I'm so sorry."

"Too far doesn't answer my question. How far is too far?" Porter paused to let her answer, but when she didn't, he put it to her bluntly, "Did you sleep with him?" He stared at his wife and held his breath, waiting for an answer, knowing that he didn't want to hear it.

Summer's sobbing became louder and more intense. Although Porter knew that that was his answer, he didn't want to leave any room for suspicion... he needed to hear it. "Yes or no, Summer?! Did you sleep with him?!"

It was muffled through her sobs, but he heard it distinctly. "Yes."

CHAPTER 17:
Mothers and Daughters

"Thank you, mama," May said as her mother-in-law brought her breakfast in bed. "I don't know, some days I'm perfectly fine, and others I feel like I can't even open my eyes."

"May, I really think you should see the doctor. With your health, we can't risk it. What if, God forbid, it's worse than just a cold or the flu?" Hanaan pleaded with her daughter-in-law.

May sighed, "Ah, mama. Now you sound like Hasan. I just can't go running to the doctor every time I sneeze. I mean, who does that? No one does that."

"People in your condition do that. Yes, they do. If they're serious about getting better, they don't take any risks with their health."

May smiled, "I'm sure it's nothing. Just leave it in God's hands. He will do what's best for us all.

"But I just wanted to tell you... I know you had planned on leaving a while ago. I really appreciate that you stayed."

"Don't be ridiculous, May." The older woman sat down on the edge of the bed. "I'm glad to help out. I wish there was something more I could do."

"God give you health and strength always, and reward you for your intentions."

"You just eat your food and focus on getting better. If you're up to it, Noor wanted your help with some homework later."

"Of course. Tell her to come now."

Hanaan got up and walked towards the door, "Will do. If you need anything just call out; I'll be able to hear you. I have to go beat your husband for leaving dirty dishes in the sink. And it's funny... no matter how many times I tell him, he still leaves the toilet seat up! You're an angel for putting up with him."

May laughed, "He's not that bad, mama. I think he just got used to you carrying more than your load."

"Well if he doesn't start shaping up, I'm going to dump that load right smack on his head."

May continued to laugh as her mother-in-law left the room.

The kids had been trying to keep their distance somewhat from their mom, following their dad's instructions. "Your mom's body isn't yet as strong as ours," he had told them. "So we don't want to expose her to any more germs than necessary. I'm not saying don't spend any time with her at all, but try to limit going into the room. And please, please make sure you wash your hands very well before going in there."

They tried to do as he said, even though Deen didn't understand. "What's germs?" he had asked his sister after their dad's speech.

"Germs are tiny bugs that are so small you can't see them with your eyes. And they can make you sick. But when you wash your hands, that gets rid of them."

"They can make us sick like mama? That's what made her sick to begin with?" Deen had asked nervously.

"No. They can make you sick like give you a cold. Not like how mama's sick... that's different."

Relief came over his face despite the fact that he didn't understand why it was such a concern if his mom caught a cold. She'd had colds before – what was the big deal? But he had just walked away, not asking anyone for an explanation.

Noor knocked softly on the door and entered.

"Hey, *habibti*. How are you?" May's face lit up at the sight of her daughter.

"*Alhamdu lillah*, mama. How are you feeling today?"

"Much better now that I've seen you. Come sit next to me." May knew that Noor didn't really need help with her homework, but it was, of course, the best excuse to get permission from *Sitto* to enter her mother's room. "What's up?" May asked.

"Not much. I don't really need help with my homework. I mean, here is my spelling list if you want to quiz me, but I think I've got them down."

May took the paper from her daughter, but she could see that something was on her mind.

"And you're okay with the rest of your subjects?"

"Yeah," Noor answered as she nodded vigorously.

May quizzed her on the spelling words, and when she had finished said, "Very good. Just be careful of the difference between 'conscious' and 'conscience.'"

Noor nodded and sat quietly for a moment. May could sense that her daughter was trying to build up the courage to ask about something. So as not to add pressure to her, May went back to eating her breakfast.

"Mama," Noor began with an apparent hesitation, "I want to ask you something, but I'm worried you're going to get mad." She was fiddling with her fingertips and biting her lip nervously.

May could see how hard this was for her daughter and that in and of itself made her anxious as to what was to come. While her instinct was to scream out and demand to know what was going on, May nodded once to the side to let her daughter's words and actions register. She breathed in deeply and said, "Well, I'm not going to lie and promise you that I won't get mad. But I will promise to hear you to the end and *try* not to get mad."

Noor nodded repeatedly as she took in a deep breath. "Sarah and Kim are going to hang out at the mall on Saturday night, and they asked me to go along."

May's eyes wrinkled in confusion. "Why would I get mad about that? You know you're allowed to go out with your friends, as long as you're back home by eight. Baba should be able to drive you."

"No, it's not that I need a ride." She paused for a moment and ran her fingers over the pattern on the bed cover. But when she was unable to find a gentle way to put it, Noor just blurted it out, "They're going to meet three boys from our class there."

May looked down, quickly yet casually, and started fidgeting with the tray in front of her. She made sure that Noor did not see the shock which had come over her. *Noor is only eleven, and already her friends are going out in coed groups and double dating?! When did I become old enough to have a daughter who is already talking about boys?* She knew this was a defining moment in their lives as mother and daughter, and she needed for it to pass successfully. This could be the beginning of a close, open relationship between them, or the end to the innocence they shared and the start of lies and half-truths.

May smiled sincerely, put aside her breakfast tray, and drew her daughter to her warmly. "Noor, I'm so proud of you."

The young girl giggled in slight embarrassment, but that didn't affect the confusion which remained on her face.

"You could have just told me you were going with your friends. Why didn't you?"

The girl became nervous again. "Well, I thought you might not like it if we were meeting boys there."

"But I wouldn't have known. And that is why I am so very proud of you. It takes courage to be so open and honest, and I hope you hold on to that always.

"Now about your request...." May cleared her throat to bide a few seconds. "You were right to think that I won't approve of you meeting boys. I know that this is going to be an issue for you for years to come, and I pray you continue to be honest with me.

"You know that our religion doesn't allow that. It's one thing to be polite with guy friends at school, but that's where your relationship with them has to end. You know that having a boyfriend is forbidden...."

"But, mama," Noor cut her off just to clarify, not to beg, "they're not boyfriends. They're just some of our guy friends."

"I know, *habibti*. But even hanging out with guy friends isn't acceptable... because that's what leads to having a boyfriend. And those girlfriend/boyfriend relationships usually lead to sex outside of marriage – which leads to so many serious health problems, babies born to unwed, unprepared mothers, and a lot of other negative social consequences. Neither our religion nor our culture allow that. So in order to keep you safe from going down that path, we have to cut it off before it even begins."

Noor nodded, with dissatisfaction all over her face.

"Are you disappointed?"

Noor barely shrugged.

"I would be, too. Actually, I was all the time when I was your age. All my friends were going out, and I wasn't. They were always doing things I wasn't allowed to do, and it was frustrating. I used to get mad at my parents for always being the reason why I never fit in."

Noor just sat there. After a moment, May asked, "Are you mad at me?"

"No, mama," she said quietly.

"Do you understand why you can't go... even if you don't agree?"

Noor half-shrugged, "I guess so."

May pulled her daughter to her again. "I'm sorry I upset you, *habibti*. I think that one day you'll appreciate that these rules protect you and help you to maintain a strong connection to God."

Noor was quiet. She could understand the reasoning behind the rules, but in the end it meant that she would get left out. It would mean her friends would get to do things that she wasn't allowed to do. And she hated that feeling.

Because May had been familiar with that feeling as well, she tried to offer an alternative. One which, she knew, was not as attractive, but she hoped it would be enough. "Maybe we could do something together?"

Almost immediately, Noor snapped back to her usual, cheery mood.

"That would be great, mama! Can we really?"

May giggled, "Of course. We can have a girls' night. What do you want to do?"

May was content with how she had handled that first hurdle as the mother of a pre-teen. But she knew the hurdles would be getting higher and higher, and she prayed that God would give her the support she would need to leap them successfully.

Hasan was shocked when May told him about her conversation with Noor.

"She's not even twelve, yet!" he exclaimed. "Already there are boys in the picture?! This is not good."

"But it's normal, Hasan. And we can't freak out every time she comes to us with stuff like this. If we freak out, she'll stop talking to us, and that's when disasters happen."

"You're right. I know you're right. I just... I can't believe it. I can't wrap my head around the fact that she is already old enough to be talking about boys."

"Tell me about it. I feel like just yesterday she was learning to ride a bike. When did we become old enough to have kids this old?" With a sigh she continued, "Look at Summer – *ma sha' Allah*, she's so young and beautiful. Ahhh. Time is simply unmerciful."

Hasan came up behind his wife and wrapped her in a loving embrace. "You are young and beautiful. Summer's got nothing on you."

May laughed out loud and turned to kiss him. "I'm glad you feel that way. Will you still feel that way when I'm eighty?"

"I will feel that way for the rest of my life." He held her for a few moments then he pulled away gently saying, "I'm not sure it's such a good idea for you to go out with Noor Saturday night, May. Your health isn't really one hundred percent, and we don't want to risk it getting worse."

"I can't break my promise, Hasan. She'll be devastated. Plus, she'll never trust me again."

"But your health is more important."

May smiled and tenderly patted her husband's shoulder. "God will do what's best."

When Saturday finally arrived, Noor couldn't stop talking about the girls' night they had planned. "We can do dinner and a movie, mama. Or would you rather we do dinner then walk around the mall? But it'll probably be really crowded." She rambled on, not giving her mother a chance to reply. "We could probably walk around the outlets – they'll probably be less crowded. Or maybe we can go to that new arts and crafts place. What do you think, mama?"

Her daughter's excitement warmed May's heart. She laughed, "Whatever you want to do, *habibti*."

"Can I come?" Deen asked.

May hated that she had to deny him, but she smiled and assured him, "Once I get over this cold, we'll have a day, just you and me. But tonight it's Noor's turn. Okay?"

"But I want to come, too."

Her mother-in-law knew how to save the situation. "But Deen, I need you here with me. After dinner I can make popcorn and we can watch that cartoon you like... the one with the green monster and his talking donkey."

"He's not a monster, *Sitto*. He's an ogre," Deen puffed impatiently as he rolled his eyes.

"Oh. Of course. Sorry," Hanaan replied, putting her hand to her throat, and bowing her head slightly in a show of sincere regret. Her strategy was enough to temporarily distract him.

As May got ready in her bedroom, again Hasan tried to dissuade her. "*Habibti*, I have a bad feeling about this."

"You have to stop worrying so much, Hasan." Her attention was focused on her reflection as she pinned her scarf into place.

Hasan was getting agitated by her indifference. "May, you need to take things more seriously." He paused for a moment, pacing away from his wife. Standing at the window with his back to her, he announced, "I forbid you from going out tonight."

May froze with her hands adjusting her scarf. When the words finally registered, she turned away from the mirror, her mouth agape, and stared at her husband's back. "What? What do you mean 'you forbid me?'"

"Exactly what you think I mean. I won't allow you to go."

"Hasan, are you really going to play tyrant now? Now?! We're getting ready to leave... and your daughter has been looking forward to tonight all week!"

Hasan crossed his arms and remained standing there with his back to his wife. "Leading my family doesn't make me a tyrant. It's my responsibility as the head of this household to steer you to safety. As a husband and father, it's my responsibility... and it's your obligation to obey."

May raised her eyebrows in disbelief and sighed heavily. More than a few minutes passed before she was able to speak. "I don't even know what to say." She shook her head slightly and shrugged. "Noor is downstairs waiting and I don't want her to miss the movie." Without saying goodbye, May took her purse and left the room.

At the bottom of the stairs, she breathed in deeply and forced a smile. "Hey, *habibti*," she said to her daughter. "Are you ready?"

"Yes, mama. Look, I put on some lip gloss." Noor was beaming.

"Well, I hate to burst your bubble, but you're going to have to wipe that off. Since when do I let you wear lip gloss?"

Wiping at her lips with a tissue, Noor replied with a sly smile, "I thought, since it's a special occasion, you'd let me get away with it."

"But this isn't a special occasion."

"It sort of is, though," Noor rebuffed. "We've never had a girl's night before."

"Well, maybe we'll just have to make sure that it becomes a regular thing."

Noor gasped. A second later she ran to her mom and squeezed her lovingly. Just before she let go, the young girl said, "But even then... it'll still be a special occasion to me."

May kissed the top of her daughter's head, and prayed that they would remain that close forever. She knew that, just as had happened with herself and her mom, it was only a matter of time before Noor would prefer spending time with her friends instead of her family. May prayed that somehow miraculously that would never happen and that Noor would always enjoy her company.

They had just enough time to grab dinner before the movie started. Although Hasan's words kept ringing in May's ears, she forced them away, not wanting to ruin her daughter's night. Halfway through the meal May started feeling off, lightheaded. She ignored it, thinking that it was just due to low blood sugar, hoping the food would make her feel better.

Noor noticed her mom dozing off during the movie. When it was done she said, "Sorry you were so bored with it, mama. Next time you should pick the movie."

"No... it was fine. This bug just has me really tired all the time, that's all."

Noor continued to chatter on their way home, but by then May was feeling very ill. She thought of pulling over and calling Hasan to get them, but she didn't want to ruin her daughter's good mood, nor did she want to deal with Hasan's gloating. She focused all her energy on the road.

Somewhere in the background she heard Noor say, "What do you think, mama? Mama? Mama!"

But May couldn't answer. And she could no longer see the road.

"Stop, mama! It's a red light! MAMA!"

The blue car crossing the intersection let out an ear-piercing screech. The crash was deafening.

CHAPTER 18:
Defeated

"I'm coming! I'm coming! Hold on!" The incessant ringing of the doorbell and forceful knocking at the door could only mean catastrophe. Farris was tripping over his feet as he all but ran to the door. Sidra was two steps behind him.

"I need your help." Hasan was wearing a jacket over his pajamas and sneakers on his feet. "May and Noor were in a car accident. I need to get to the hospital right away, and I need someone to stay at home... Deen's sleeping."

"Of course, Hasan." Farris grabbed his coat and fumbled for his keys.

"The front door's open. My mom is already in the car...."

"You go ahead. I'll be in your house in less than sixty seconds."

Hasan would have thanked him, but he was too flustered to think properly.

"Go ahead, Farris. I'll get the keys and meet you over there," Sidra said hurriedly.

He nodded to his wife and closed the door behind him. From the window Sidra watched him run across the street and enter May and Hasan's home.

A few minutes later, after she had put on a heavy robe, some sneakers and grabbed a set of keys, she stood behind Farris as he checked that Deen was still sleeping.

"I hope they're going to be okay," Sidra said after they had settled down in the living room.

"Me, too. God, they've already been through so much."

Farris found a couple of the AbdulShafi's photo albums on the coffee table and began flipping through them. Sidra sat quietly, watching him laugh and smile at all the snapshots of the children.

A couple of hours later, Farris noticed Sidra dozing off as she sat upright in the wooden rocking chair.

"Sidra... Sidra." He tapped her shoulder lightly. "Rest on the couch. We may be here for a while. Go ahead and sleep on the couch."

She got up from her chair and lay down on the oversized, supple couch which was undoubtedly the heart of the living room. But the move was enough to awaken her.

"What about you? Where will you sleep?"

"I don't think sleep's going to come tonight. But if I get tired I'll just grab one of these throw pillows and spread out on the floor."

They were quiet for a few moments.

"It's been enough time; do you think we should call the hospital? You know, to find out what's going on?" Sidra asked hesitantly.

She found the same hesitation in Farris' response. "I don't know. I think I'm afraid to."

Sidra nodded in agreement, but their curiosity didn't last long. The sound of the phone ringing sent them both flying to their feet.

"Quick! Answer before it wakes up Deen!" Sidra screamed in a whisper.

Farris held the receiver to his ear, for a second only hearing the pounding of his own heart.

"Hello, Farris? It's me, Hasan. I just wanted to let you know I'm sending my mom home with Mariam. She was at the scene of the accident and she's been with us since then. I'm sending them both home."

There was a finality in Hasan's voice which made Farris even more nervous.

"Hasan, it's really no problem. If you need us to stay till the morning, that's fine."

"No, no. Thank you, Farris. It'll be better for Deen to see his grandmother when he wakes up."

To see his grandmother? What did that mean exactly? Did that mean he wouldn't get to see anyone else? Farris hated to ask, but he had to.

"Hasan, how are May and Noor? I hope they're okay."

"*Alhamdu lillah*. Some cuts and bruises, but they're both awake now. *Alhamdu lillah*." He was thanking God, but Farris could hear something more in his neighbor's voice. It didn't carry the relief that his words were meant to.

"Thank God. Look, Hasan, please don't hesitate if there's anything I can do."

"I really appreciate that, Farris. You've already been very helpful."

As they adjusted the cushions and put the photo albums back in place, Sidra looked over at her husband and thought she saw disappointment that they had to leave this comfortable home, with photo albums overstuffed with family snapshots, and the laughter of children almost seeping from the walls.

"Maybe you should go check on Deen once more," she offered.

"I don't think that's necessary. His grandmother will be home in a few minutes."

The key turning at the front door prompted them both to stand. Hanaan walked in followed by Mariam. Hanaan's eyes were sagging and her steps were heavy with exhaustion, but a faint smile assured Sidra that May and Noor were okay.

"Thank you very much for staying with Deen. We all really appreciate it. Even May sends her thanks."

Hanaan grabbed Sidra and squeezed her affectionately. The woman's sincerity and warmth touched Sidra considerably. "Oh, it was nothing, really. We're more than happy to stay if you'd like to go back to the hospital."

"That's nice of you... but the girls are okay, *alhamdu lillah*. I have to take care of some things around the house before Hasan comes back for us later."

"Is there anything I can do for you now before I leave, Hanaan?" Mariam asked.

"Thank you, Mariam. It was good of you to stay with us at the hospital. Thank you."

The neighbors left right away to let the older woman get some sleep before she had to begin her day.

As they walked together across a moon-less, silent street, shadows painted by the light of just a few lamp posts, Farris asked Mariam about the severity of the accident.

"It was so bizarre. You know how in the movies they can show you all the details in slow motion? That's what it was like for me. I was about to get into my car when I just happened to look up. I don't even know why I did. And even though the whole thing happened in just a few seconds, it was as though I was watching it in slow motion. May ran the red light and the oncoming car tried to stop. The screeching of the brakes was so intense, it's still ringing in my ears. Seconds later... not even seconds, milliseconds later, the cars crashed into each other, sending May's into a tail spin until it finally stopped on the opposite side of the street. I called 911 and the ambulance arrived within minutes. I followed them and called Hasan from the hospital. The girls came to shortly after they arrived there."

"Were they seriously injured?"

"Hasan said no, but I don't know... something about how he looked after he met with the doctors makes me think there's something more. I don't know. The man from the other car is okay."

"But you didn't see them... May and Noor, I mean?"

"The nurse said only immediate family, but Hanaan snuck me in for a few seconds just before we left. May was, as you can expect, pale and shaken up. She kept asking the nurses to bring Noor so she could see her. They tried to assure her that Noor was fine, but she kept saying, 'Please bring her to me. I need to see her for myself. I need to tell her I'm sorry.' It broke my heart. Especially since Hasan said Noor couldn't stop crying... not from any pain, just from the shock of it."

"Do you know if they're going to keep them long in the hospital?" Sidra asked.

"I think they're only keeping them in the hospital overnight. They should be released tomorrow."

They all agreed that a quick release was definitely good news. Mariam said good night and crossed her lawn to the front door. Just before entering her house, she looked up and caught a glimpse of Farris holding the door open for his wife. The sight brought a sad smile to her face and a knot to her gut; she couldn't help but wish that things were still that way between her and Morgan.

She tried to enter the house quietly, but despite her efforts, she needed to force the door shut. The sound awakened Morgan, who had been sleeping on the couch.

"Sorry," she said. "I didn't mean to wake you, but you know how this door sticks."

"I wasn't asleep. I was waiting for you. Are they okay? How's the car? Was it totaled?"

Mariam pretended to hear his concern for the neighbors. "Yeah, they're okay. They're bruised up, but they're going to be okay. They should be home sometime tomorrow."

"And the car? What about the car? Was it totaled?"

Part of her couldn't believe that he could be so superficial even in these circumstances. The other part said, *And this is why things have changed between us. This is why we need to separate.* He didn't notice her exhausted sigh and slight head shake.

"It was banged up, but I think it's fixable."

"Good," Morgan seemed more relieved about the car's condition than his neighbors'. "It would have been such a shame."

Mariam stared at him with one eyebrow raised. When she couldn't find any words, she simply climbed the stairs and went into her room.

Technically, they were living under the same roof, but in all their dealings with each other, they acted like a separated couple. They never sat together in private, nor spoke of anything unrelated to the children. They made a point to eat meals together as a family, but even when they went out on the weekends it was either with Mariam or Morgan, never both together. And the reasons were always the same: "Oh, mom's tired, kids. Let's let her rest." Or "Dad doesn't feel well. Maybe he can come next time."

The little ones were too young to catch on, but one day Dina had asked her mom, "How come you and dad never spend time together anymore?"

Mariam had stared openmouthed at her daughter. She wasn't ready for the question. She thought when the time was right, she and Morgan would decide exactly how to break it to their kids. But they didn't get the chance to plan it, and there she was, unprepared, and facing her kids with a truth that she knew would turn their lives upside down.

Mariam blinked rapidly, trying to think of how best to escape the question. "We do. We always eat our meals together as a family."

"But that's all. We used to spend an hour or two together before bed time… we don't anymore. When we go out, it's never with both of you." The young girl gulped visibly and crinkled her forehead. "Are you guys getting a divorce?"

Mariam saw tears begin to form in her daughter's eyes, and quickly she pulled her close. She hugged her warmly and rubbed her back. When she spoke, Mariam was careful of her words, wanting neither to lie nor give false hope.

"We're a little bit upset with each other. And we're trying to see if we can work it out."

"But it doesn't seem like you're trying."

As Mariam stood alone in the room now, her daughter's words echoed repeatedly in her ears. *But how can I try when he doesn't even see the blessings he has.* This thought, however, was not enough to diminish the guilt which Dina's remark had etched on her soul. She sat down on the bed, shoulders slouched, and rested her burdened head in her hands.

The following morning, as she was preparing breakfast for her family, Mariam caught a glimpse of something outside of the window. Pulling the curtain to the side, she saw Sidra and Summer speaking with Hasan in his driveway.

"I'll be right back," she said, dropping everything at hand and walking out of the door.

Mariam jogged across the street and arrived just in time to hear Sidra say, "We'll swing by the hospital later to check on her, then. Our prayers are with you."

"Thank you," he said, smiling weakly and giving Mariam a feeble nod as she arrived, only meeting her eyes for a second before they were focused on the ground again. "I really have to go now."

The women stepped aside so his car could back out of the driveway. As they watched him drive away, Sidra gave Mariam the update. "It appears that May's leukemia has taken a turn for the worse. The doctors think it's put her in severe anemia, which is what caused her to black out while she was driving."

"Oh, God." Mariam paused for a moment. "It's really bad, isn't it?"

"Hasan didn't really give specifics, and we didn't want to push, but this is the first time I've seen him like this. He seems almost...." Sidra paused, searching for the right word, but it came from Summer. "Defeated."

The three women stood together in silence. A few minutes later Sidra turned to Summer asking, "When did he say visiting hours were?"

"After six. Should we all go together?"

"Yes, I think that's a good idea. She needs to see friends. And it may be easier on us as well to be together," Mariam replied.

"I can drive. Let's meet in my driveway?" Summer offered.

The women nodded in agreement, then they walked out of their neighbor's yard together, and each one went silently back to her home.

Not wanting to enter the empty house, Summer hesitated at her front door. The temptations of the pills in her medicine cabinet were growing louder and harder to ignore. *Well if you would just take them as your therapist prescribed, you'd probably feel better*, she reasoned with herself numerous times. But it was the voice of fear that held her back; Summer didn't trust that she would have the strength to take just one pill from an open bottle. She turned around, lifted her head to the sky and breathed in deeply to take in the sun's warmth. *I guess I should go see my therapist.* But as the crisp morning freshness entered her soul, that thought was replaced by the memory of her visit with May from some weeks before. She recalled how May, despite her hardships, despite her illness and pain, continued not only to believe in God, but to praise Him, too. Despite her strong religious beliefs about right and wrong and sin and virtue, she spoke of forgiveness as though it were the rule, not the exception. May's attitude was truly admirable. For the first time since Porter had moved out, Summer felt inspired.

She set up her paints and easel outside, and began. She became so engrossed in her work that – even though the front door was wide open – she didn't hear the phone ring three different times over the span of two hours. She didn't hear the school buses or the kindergarten kids as they ran to greet their moms. She didn't even notice the car that pulled in right beside her, until Porter got out and closed the car door behind him.

"I tried calling to let you know that I was coming by. I just need to pick up a few things."

"Sorry, I didn't hear the phone. I've been out here."

Summer pulled the brush from the easel and rested it against her palette. Her eyes focused on the colors in her hands as the butterflies swam all through her stomach. She wanted to throw herself in his arms and cry. She wanted to explain how very sorry she was, how much she regretted what she had done. She wanted to beg him for forgiveness. But the only thing she had the ability to do was to stand there, holding her breath, and lift her eyes just in time to see him turn away and climb the few short steps to the front door. With his hand on the doorknob, he turned back around to face her. "I've never seen you work outside."

"I never did before. I don't know why. It was May's idea... she inspired me. Oh... did you hear that they were in an accident... May and her daughter?"

"No, I didn't know. Are they okay?"

"Some cuts and bruises, but they found out that May's leukemia has gotten worse. I'm going to the hospital later to visit her."

"I'll try to remember to call Hasan and ask about them."

Summer nodded, and Porter turned around and walked into the house. He walked up the stairs, and let out a loud sigh as he entered the bedroom. At his closet, he took out the few items he had gone for. As he turned to put the things on the bed, his arm knocked a picture frame to the floor. He picked it up and held onto it with both hands as he sat on the bed.

They had been so young. It was only two years old, but their faces were brighter. It was the happiness in their eyes, the love in their embrace, which made the difference. He felt his heart break again thinking about their current state. But despite her unfaithfulness, he missed her. He had been missing her for months even before he had moved out, but it hadn't changed... he still missed her. He hated it, and it confused him. How could he miss her after what she had done? How could he still love her? It tore him apart, but he did.

When she had admitted her affair to him, he was too hurt to do anything else but leave. He had needed to get away from her, to not see her. He had taken his most essential possessions and left that same night. And since then, he had been staying with his brother.

"You're more than welcome to stay as long as you want. But if you want my opinion, you just have to move on. Betrayal is unforgivable. You can't apologize for it or take it back... it will always be in your past, and you'll never be able to forget it."

At the time, Porter hadn't weighed his brother's comments. Now, however, sitting on his bed, staring at his wife in their wedding picture, the words rang in his ears: "It will always be in your past, and you'll never be able to forget it."

CHAPTER 19:
At the Hospital

"May AbdulShafi's room, please?" Mariam asked at the nurses' station.

"104. Down the hall, past the waiting area, and to your right."

The three women walked quietly down to the room, each carrying her own get well gift: Sidra clutched a bouquet of flowers, Mariam held a small potted plant, and Summer carried a large square shaped object wrapped in plain white paper.

At the door, Mariam placed her hand on the doorknob, and the three women stood looking in the window. The doctor, in his white coat with clipboard in hand, stood at the foot of May's bed. Hasan sat on the edge of the bed, holding his wife's hand and looking up at the doctor's somber expression.

"Maybe we should give them a few minutes?" Summer suggested.

"Definitely," answered Sidra.

In the waiting area, the three women sat down next to each other. Each one was anxious about the visit. Mariam kept fidgeting in her seat, unable to get comfortable. Summer bit her nails. Sidra kept looking for things in her purse unsuccessfully.

A few moments later Sidra asked, "What's your gift, Summer?"

"It's a painting I just finished this morning. May gave me some good advice a few weeks back. She inspired me; I thought it just made sense that she get it."

"That's nice of you."

"God, I hate situations like this. I never know what to say. And what to ask, what not to ask, how much is too much to ask. I hate it," Mariam admitted.

"Me, too," both Sidra and Summer chimed.

"You, too? Sidra, you always look like you have everything together," Mariam accused.

"Me?!" Sidra abruptly uncrossed her beige, trouser clad legs and her brown low-cut boot came down with a thud.

"Yes, you. You have this... air about you."

"I have an 'air about me'? You mean I act like a snob?"

Mariam chuckled, "No, not like that. You're just... self-assured. Not arrogant... confident."

Sidra huffed in disbelief. "Well, it's a good thing I look like that on the outside, because trust me, most of the time I feel... lost."

"Like you should talk, Mariam," Summer added.

"What?" Mariam snapped her head back in Summer's direction.

"Yes!" Sidra took over. "You're like... I don't know... super woman. You're raising perfect, adorable kids who are always happy and polite. You've got a great marriage, which we all know takes work, and, to top it all off, you're juggling a career! And even though you're always smiling, you've got this determination in your eyes. You never seem to miss a beat."

Mariam laughed, shaking her head and pulling the loose brown curls out of her face. "Trust me... I've missed more than just a beat. You could say I've screwed up entire songs!"

"Oh, I don't believe it," Sidra said, brushing aside her friend's words.

Mariam paused for a few moments, mustering up the courage to open up to her companions. Right as she was about to confide in them about the troubles her marriage was facing, however, she saw Noor and Deen coming down the hallway accompanied by their grandmother. The three women stood to greet Hanaan and the kids.

As she hugged the women, Hanaan thanked them for their support. "It's so good of you all to come. Have you been here long?"

"No, not really. The doctor's talking with May and Hasan so we actually haven't been in to see her, yet.

"Noor, we're all so thankful you're okay." Mariam, Sidra and

Summer each hugged the young girl.

But she was not the same little girl that had entertained them just a couple of months before. It was clear that her pale appearance indicated not only lack of color in her complexion, but also lack of energy in her spirit. Her now reserved nature had less to do with recovering from the accident and more to do with how she was dealing with her mother's illness.

"Thank you," she whispered, putting her arm around her younger brother and pulling him close.

"So that doctor is still in there? We left them over an hour ago. Maybe if we go in he'll wrap it up. Come on, ladies."

"Hanaan, we don't want to impose. It's more important that they speak with the doctor. We don't mind waiting." Sidra and Summer, nodding in agreement, were relieved that Mariam kept stepping up as their spokesperson.

Just as Hanaan was about to object, she looked up to see the door to May's room open and the doctor step out.

"Oh, there he goes. Finally." Hanaan held Deen's hand and led the kids towards their mother's door as she motioned for the women to follow.

They lingered for some time, slowly picking up their purses and gifts, hoping to give Hanaan and the children a chance to spend a few moments with May.

Reaching the door, again Mariam placed her hand on the knob, and the three women again peered in the window.

Although Hasan had his back to them, it was clear that he was wiping away tears. May's trickled down her face as she smiled and cuddled her children.

"I don't think this is a good time," Sidra commented.

"I agree," Mariam said, "But something tells me there may never be a good time." And with that thought she forced herself to open the door.

May wiped her cheeks dry as she greeted the visitors. "My

favorite neighbors. Mariam, Sidra, Summer. It's so good of you to come by."

They each hugged her and greeted Hasan with kind words and a smile. On his worn face was a meek smile contradicting the sadness in his bloodshot eyes.

Trying to give the women some privacy with May, he pulled his mother to the corner of the room and explained what the doctor had said. Although she sat there with her head tilted back for a moment, ears pricked up, trying to catch just the gist of what was being said, Mariam could only decipher the words coming from the women in front of her.

"We're all so sorry you're back in the hospital, May. We're praying for you to get well and come home soon." The sincerity in Sidra's words touched May; she hoped she could get well, too.

"Oh, I'll probably get to come home soon, *in sha' Allah*."

"Really, mama?! You're already better so you can come home?" Deen's excitement brought the tears back to May's eyes. They hadn't had a chance to explain it to the kids. "No, *habibi*. I'm not really better. But this time they're not going to keep me here. I'll get to come home soon so I can be with you guys." She held her son for a moment, knowing that his happiness to the news would be very short lived.

Noor, on the other hand, heard the discrepancy in her mom's words and wouldn't let it go. With knitted eyebrows she demanded, "Why? That doesn't make sense."

"We'll let you be with your family, now, May," Summer interrupted in a loud whisper. "But before we leave, I wanted you to open my gift."

"Summer, you really shouldn't have." The children got down from their mom's lap so that she could take the large, square shaped object from her friend. May wiped her face dry with her hands, then carefully tore away the wrapping on the gift. She laid the picture face up against her bent knees, and gazed at the beautiful, soft simplicity of the colors. She did not understand art. She didn't know if this would be considered a great painting, but for reasons she could not articulate, it gave her a sense of peace. As she clutched her hands to her chest, her smile let out a soft sigh.

"What you said to me – that day we spoke in your yard – about forgiveness, and just everything about how you carry yourself, how you continue to thank God for your blessings despite all the hardships you face, it inspired me. Everything about you inspired me. So I want you to have it."

May was quiet for some time as she stared at the painting. This time the tears that trickled down May's face were not about her disease. And, despite what everyone there must have assumed, they did not stem from a feeling of gratefulness or humility at those words of praise. Instead, they came from May's overwhelming feeling of shame. Shame that at that moment, lying in the hospital just after the doctor had told them there was nothing more that could be done, that her leukemia was too far gone now for any treatment to be effective, she could not see any blessings. All she could see were more moments in the lives of everyone she loved that she would not have the chance to be a part of.

CHAPTER 20:
End of Love

As she had been used to for months now, Sidra arrived home late one night and found Farris flipping aimlessly through television channels.

"Farris, I need to talk to you."

He looked up at her, knowing what was to come, not wanting to hear it. Sidra walked across the room, turned off the TV and sat down opposite him. Clasping her hands in her lap, she began, "Things have been ugly between us for a while now, and we're both unhappy. It doesn't make sense to draw it out any longer."

He stared at her blankly, forcing her to look away. After a long moment of silence, he asked her, "What do you want from me?"

"Well, just admit that we've reached the end...."

He didn't let her continue. "The end of what, Sidra? The end of marriage... or the end of love? And in either case, how did we get here?"

The accusation in his tone was intended to cut, but it had no effect on her. "Ugh! Farris, I don't know why you're always so difficult. Why can't you just let it go?!" She got up angrily and started walking around the room.

"Let what go, Sidra? Let you go? You want me to let you go?"

She grabbed her head in a show of frustration. "Yes, Farris! What have I been saying?!"

"Fine. I'll let you go. But I just want to know why? Why do you want to go?"

"I'm not happy, Farris," she replied bluntly, looking away from him.

"You're not happy with me?"

"No, I'm not." She looked down as she spoke, but her voice was steady.

"What did I do... or didn't I do? In all the years we've been together, I have always... *always*... put you first! From the smallest things – like just where to go for dinner or which movie to watch – to the larger things – like which state to live in! I always put you first. And I was always happy to do it – your happiness was more important to me than anything. So what did I do wrong?"

She looked him directly in the eyes now, and she responded, "You and I both know that no matter how hard you try, you can't control who you fall in love with. And well... I just think we've gone as far as we can."

"So..." Farris said, "What you're saying is you've fallen out of love with me?"

She paced away from him, thinking of the best way to word it. Sidra did not want to deepen his wounds, but he deserved an answer. "I've found someone else," she blurted.

He had known that eventually he would hear that phrase. Nevertheless, there he sat, openmouthed, eyes wide with disbelief, unable to breathe. He was devastated and confused at his own surprise. A moment later, he exhaled heavily and leaned forward, putting his head in his hands. Absorbing the shock, he tried to understand how and why his life had been turned upside down. He tried to recount how they had been before those late night secretive calls began. He tried to remember moments of anger or neglect or any kind of disagreement. But all he could see was warmth, laughter and love. None of it made sense. His head was spinning.

Her words had shattered his heart, his whole world. He lowered his arms clumsily and looked up at her. The pain was unmistakable in his sunken, half-opened eyes. "So you've been having an affair?" he asked, more to try to make it sink in than to actually elicit an answer.

Sidra saw no reason to lie, "I haven't slept with him, if that's your question. But he makes me happy."

Her first statement was meant to give him a feeling of relief, but the confusion generated by her latter statement destroyed any shred of solace.

His face seemed to drain of every speck of color as he looked up to ask despairingly, "When did *I* stop making you happy?"

Sidra sighed loudly in annoyance. "It doesn't matter when, Farris. The fact is, this is where we are now. Don't get me wrong, we made some great memories together. But now, it's just time we go our separate ways. I'm going to be happy with James. And I know you'll find someone to make you happy, too." Her tone was neither harsh nor tender; she was just trying to put it to him as honestly as she could.

She sat quietly, giving him a few minutes to digest her words, and waiting for a verbal response. When he didn't provide one, she said, "I'll pack some things and leave tonight. I'll come back for the rest later.

"I'm sure your firm can take care of the paperwork. I'll let you know where I'm staying so you can send it to me." Sidra didn't say it outright, feeling it would only cause him more pain, but the message was clear that she wanted the divorce finalized as soon as possible.

She walked up the stairs briskly and wasted no time in packing. She didn't want to prolong the awkwardness and discomfort that they had been living for the past several months. She just wanted it all over with.

Along with the things she packed were two photos which had been hiding at the bottom of one of her drawers. She put them in her bag without even glancing at them.

More than twenty minutes had passed, but when Sidra reached the bottom of the stairs, suitcase in hand, Farris was still sitting in the same desperate position, with his elbows propped up on his knees and his head resting in his hands. Sidra hated that he was hurting, but she simply did not have the ability to console him. She no longer had anything to offer.

"I'm leaving now, Farris. Like I said, I'll let you know where you can send me the papers. I wish you well." She walked away and did not look back.

As though she were guided by autopilot, Sidra drove through the streets with tears filling her eyes and streaking her cheeks. Her car came to a stop in front of the church. Kneeling in the pew with her hands clasped, her head bowed, and sobs shaking her shoulders, she felt too disturbed to even know what she should be praying for. Was she hoping for serenity? Forgiveness? Further guidance? *Oh Lord, You know my heart more than myself. I pray to You.*

About an hour later, with the same heavy heart and tears still glistening in her eyes, she headed toward the only friend she could confide in; she went to James.

CHAPTER 21: Irreparable Breaks

"Morgan, I think it's time we tell the kids what's going on and take the next step. Our living together but not living together already has them asking questions." Mariam stood in the doorway, arms crossed, as he sat on his makeshift bed in the living room.

"I'm not going to tell the kids anything," Morgan grumbled. "This is your idea; you're the one who wants a separation, I don't. So if you want to explain our situation to them, you're on your own."

Mariam sighed heavily, walked into the room, and closed the door behind her. "Please don't be difficult. I just told you they are already asking questions. We can't just leave things like this. It's too confusing for everyone."

"And I'm the most confused!" Morgan exclaimed. "You tell me you want a separation just because I asked you to wash my pants!"

"Oh!" Mariam couldn't help but laugh. "Is that what happened?! Okay."

"Yes, that's exactly what happened. I told you that you're falling behind with some of the housework, and you told me you want to separate."

Morgan's defensiveness and seriousness shocked her. She stood with her hands on her hips, eyebrows furrowed and jaw wide open for some seconds. "Are you... is that really what you think?"

"Yes!" Morgan nodded, punctuating his affirmation.

"You don't think it has anything to do with the fact that you were making up excuses to get me to quit my job? Or the fact that you treat me condescendingly every chance you get? Or the fact that you get *angry* when good things happen to me at work... that you were unhappy when I got a promotion? You don't think that those blatant acts of disrespect had anything to do with why I said we need to separate?"

"Mariam, you're blowing everything out of proportion. I don't treat you condescendingly, I just... correct you when you're wrong. What's wrong with that? And I wasn't upset that you got a promotion... I was upset that you didn't discuss it with me before you accepted it. And I got over it." He walked over and placed his hands on her shoulders gently. "And now I think you just need to take a few deep breaths. Calm down, and you'll see that we can just forget about these past few months, and go back to the way things were before."

Mariam, standing in shock once more, could not believe his audacity; even now he continued to patronize her! She pushed his hands off her shoulders, took a few steps back, crossed her arms, and said, "To the way things were before what? Before I started working?"

"Yes." The answer was obvious to Morgan; his baffled expression indicated that he simply could not understand why it wasn't equally obvious to Mariam.

"So... you think if I stop working, that will solve our problems?"

"Well... yes. Your home needs you more."

"My home was only affected positively by my working... but let's not get into that now. I just need to know what you plan on doing about our financial situation if I stop working. I mean... that was why I started work to begin with. So what'll happen when I stop again? We still owe your brother thousands of dollars for the money he lent us when the house flooded... how are we going to repay him?"

Morgan looked down at his feet. "We'll figure it out," he said in a low voice.

"That's what we're doing now... figuring it out. So, what have you come up with?"

"God, Mariam! It's not something we have to figure out right now!"

"I disagree, Morgan, because we already had this same discussion months ago, and just like my working was the only solution then, it remains to be the only solution. I don't understand how you can't see that!"

"What I can see is that it's causing more problems than good!"

"It's causing more problems because you're creating the problems! You are the only one who sees this as being a bad thing for our family. And quite frankly, it's shown how unbelievably selfish and envious you are!"

Her hand automatically rose to cover her mouth. The regret she felt at having spoken the words was painted all over her; she knew that no matter how true they were, those words would cause yet another break in her marriage.

Morgan let out an inaudible gasp and stood, eyebrows raised in disbelief. But his speechlessness lasted only seconds. "Envious?! I'm envious?! Of what... of you?! That's the most ridiculous thing you've ever said. You are mediocre at your job – at best. I don't envy mediocrity."

They stared at each other in silence; neither one speaking the truth which had just erupted. The ill feelings had simply become too strong to maintain a healthy marriage, and they both knew that it was over.

Mariam breathed deeply, trying to calm herself. Her arms fell to her sides. Some minutes later she finally broke the silence, "Please try to be out in two weeks. Otherwise I'm taking the kids to my parents."

She opened the door to walk out, but was instead startled to see Adam standing before her, crying.

It broke her heart to see him, but she had no comforting words for him. All she could do was hold him close.

Morgan, seeing his son so emotional, also wanted to comfort him.

"Adam, don't worry buddy. Mom and dad are just disagreeing about some things, but everything's going to be fine."

Mariam looked over her shoulder and shot him a look of death for lying to their son. Morgan didn't notice; his eyes were focused on Adam.

"Come on back to bed, sweetie." Mariam kept her arm around her son's shoulders as she led him back to his room and into his bed.

Adam wiped his nose and tried to stop sniffling. "Your voices were really loud, mom."

"I'm sorry we woke you, honey." She sat down on his bed, ready to answer the questions she knew were running through his head.

But to her surprise, he didn't ask any questions. He just looked at his mom and said, "Please don't fight like that again."

It took all her willpower to hold back her own tears. She sniffled and swallowed, trying to keep it together. How could she explain to her son that all the fighting had been done, and now there was nothing left to fight for? How could she tell him that after she had been with his father for a lifetime, after all the births and birthdays and holidays they had celebrated together, they had come to a dead end? How, after all that love, could there be nothing left to fight for? The knot in her throat grew, leaving her with nothing more than the ability to nod her head.

After she had tucked Adam into bed, Mariam retreated to her own bedroom where she couldn't help but replay all the scenes of her life starting from the moment she had decided to work. Everything had become better; she was happier because she was able to get out and interact with other adults. Her youngest kids, although it took them some time to get used to pre-school, had made friends and loved going to school every morning. Their financial situation had become more secure. Her working had improved all aspects of her life – except her marriage. The distance and awkwardness between herself and Morgan had begun that day. Thinking back on all those moments, she saw that he never encouraged her or said anything positive about her work. He was mad when she did well and was promoted. He even put on a preposterous show about her lagging in her domestic responsibilities just to get her to quit.

If it had just been about a job, she would have chosen her marriage over that position no matter how prestigious or rewarding it was. But she knew that quitting her job would solve nothing; it was not the root of their problem. She made the decision to separate after much thought and self-deliberation. It weighed heavily on her. The issues Morgan had with her work were simply the manifestations of a much greater problem, so taking work out of the picture would simply leave room for those manifestations to appear elsewhere. He would find other ways to be condescending to her and would continue to find fault with everything she said or did. The inferiority complex he had developed would continue to make him disregard her, and, although she hated to put her family in the ranks of a broken home, she knew that it would be impossible to live with a man who continually disrespected her.

Her heart broke at the realization that the man she had fallen in love with – the man she continued to love for over eleven years and whom she still loved – could be so self-centered, so vain, as to put his own ego before his respect for her. His awful treatment made her wonder if he had ever truly loved her. It seemed to Mariam that what he loved was the idea of her – a loving, supportive wife who carried the full load and burden of their family without ever complaining. She smiled through it all and pleased him in all aspects of his life. And because she loved him, she also loved doing that.

If he had loved her, he would not have begrudged her the promotion. He would not have accused her of faults she did not make. If he had loved her the way she loved him, he would have understood that they were one unit, and would have been as proud of her success as if it were his own. The reality of his feelings for her, after all those years, left her with an empty feeling in her chest and a heavy knot in the pit of her stomach. Curled up on her side, she smothered her cries into a pillow and hoped that after the ocean of tears there would be some feeling of reprieve.

Morgan, now alone in the living room, was angered by how their conversation had gone. He paced back and forth quickly, breathing heavily, clenching his fists as he rehashed in his mind all the scenes which had led them to this point. He thought the solution to their problems was evident and couldn't get over Mariam's hardheadedness. If she would just focus on her home and put aside her job, they could go back to the way things were before all of their problems, before all of the hurtful words that could not be taken back.

Somewhere in his gut he knew that their problems had less to do with Mariam's work than he let on, but his pride would not let him admit it. Somewhere in his gut he knew that the only way for them to remain out of debt was for Mariam to work. But admitting that, letting that happen, being happy for it, meant he had failed his family... and he had failed himself as a man. There was no way he could admit that he needed her help. The ball of frustration that had grown within him was too strong to contain; he grabbed the lamp and threw it against the wall. He watched as the glass shattered, envious of its immediate death.

CHAPTER 22:
Hint of Hope

It had been a couple of months since Porter had left the house. For the first time in years, Summer was independent. She had been yearning for this independence for months, but instead of providing her with a sense of freedom, all it brought her was increased loneliness and fear. She wanted to turn back the clock and undo the meaningless transgression which had torn her from the one person who meant more to her than anything. Only now, now that Porter was out of her reach, did she realize how great a blessing her marriage had been. Her once radiant smile was replaced by a droopy-eyed somber expression, and every night her pillow soaked up its fill of tears. Her heart broke at the possibility that she may never again feel the warmth of Porter's love.

The arrival of the utility bill one day opened Summer's eyes to a cruel reality of life: that it pauses for no one.

"It's all too much for me to handle," she confessed to her therapist, embracing herself and swaying slightly back and forth. "I've been... the past few months... I haven't told you... but...."

She paused, unable to continue.

"I'm here to help you, Summer. But I can't help if you don't talk to me."

A few quiet minutes passed, then Summer inhaled audibly, stopped moving, and looked her therapist straight in the eyes. "I haven't been taking the meds."

"I know that." The therapist's voice was comforting as was her thin smile.

"But I've kept them." She rocking again, nervously.

"Why have you kept them if you don't intend to take them?"

"Just in case. Just in case I needed them."

"You still don't think you need them?"

"I kept them in case I finally got up the guts to end it all," Summer blurted.

"I see." The therapist looked over her notes, then she put the notebook down on the coffee table beside her.

"Summer, you've taken a big step in coming to me. We've been working together for a while now, and I know that you still feel desperate and alone sometimes, and I can't tell you the road ahead will be easy. But if you can put your trust in me – truly – then we can work through this together. So, my question is... have I gained your trust?"

Summer and her therapist spent the remainder of the session mapping out a treatment plan. Unlike treatment plans she'd seen before, this one wasn't simply a list of medications: it included spending time outdoors, getting a job, and various phone numbers to keep handy in case her thoughts of suicide increased. Nothing had been fixed, but Summer left the office clutching the paper, hopeful that at least now she would be better prepared to handle the obstacles of her life.

Feeling an urgent need to get started with the treatment right away, Summer updated her resume and sent it out to various places. She understood that she was in no position to be selective, so along with a few art teaching positions, she also applied for secretarial work and sales.

A local half-way house for at risk adolescents provided her with the best option: they hired her as a full time secretary with an agreement that during her lunch hour she could teach an art class to any interested students. Even though technically that meant she didn't have any breaks during the day, the secretarial work was minimal, and she found herself looking forward to the class every day. It was also, ironically, therapeutic: spending time with youth who suffered some of the same emotional and mental struggles as herself gave her an increased awareness of her own condition.

Although it took some time for her to get used to the daily routine required of any full time job, she quickly learned that being out of the house from eight in the morning till four in the afternoon meant that errands and grocery shopping had to be done on the weekends, and the best dinners were those which could be eaten as she finished up projects at the easel or while she made calls in her continued efforts to sell her work.

To her surprise, that daily hour of teaching offered her a sense of fulfillment. The feeling she got when she saw one of her students complete a project was almost as satisfying as if she had completed it herself. And working with them inspired her own work; she was finishing her pieces much more efficiently than before, and they were coming out much more to her liking.

Every weekend she called Porter. She wanted to call him every day, every minute. She wanted to spend the rest of her life asking for forgiveness. But she knew she had to at least appear put- together.

"How have you been?" she asked.

"Fine, thank you."

"I hope work is good?"

"The business is alright. I'll be sending you some money at the end of the week."

"Thanks, Porter. But that's not why I called. I'm getting by okay with what I'm making from work."

"Good."

"It makes me wish I had listened to you before, when you told me to work."

Porter sighed heavily. *What good is it now that I had been right?* Nevertheless, he acknowledged her attempt to show regret. "I'm glad you are happy."

"I'm not happy. I won't be happy until you forgive me. And I know that might not come now... or ever, but I need you to know that."

How am I supposed to respond to that? Luckily, Summer didn't let the silence last long.

"I'll let you go. I would really like it if you came by sometime for dinner. I understand if you don't want to, but I need you to know that I want you to." Summer tried not to sound desperate. But even if she did, she decided, it didn't matter. She wanted her husband to know how sorry she was for what she had done and to know how much she needed him. She had grown to believe that there is no such thing as 'saving face' between a married couple; dignity was something they shared, so neither should repress feelings or words simply to appear resilient. Whatever needed to be done to fix the problem was what she would do.

Every week, Porter wanted to say, "Sure. How about tonight?" But every week, he managed to control himself. He was scared of how he may react when he saw her. He needed to make sure he had already decided before spending any time with her. And now, all these weeks after learning of her betrayal, after all this time he'd had to calm down and decide which course of action to take, his heart and head continued their quarrel. Despite that ongoing argument, this time when she asked him over for dinner, he didn't say 'we'll see.' This time an uncontrollable force from within him made him answer, "What about tonight?"

Summer's stomach flipped the same way it had when Porter had asked her to marry him. She tried not to get her hopes up, but she could not contain her smile. She even did a little hop. "Tonight's perfect. Around six?"

"Six is good. I'll see you then."

Porter hung the receiver up slowly, trying to figure out what he had just done. *Am I really ready to see her?* he thought. *What will I say? What have I decided? Oh God! Am I just making a bigger mess out of things this way?* He was worried that perhaps he had acted rashly in agreeing to see her, but he needed a second opinion. He wanted to see things from the perspective of a woman.

He called his sister, but she didn't answer. Then without realizing it, he found himself calling Kara.

"Hello?"

Hearing her voice made him suddenly aware that he was asking advice from the same woman who had offered to be more than just a shoulder to lean on. *This is wrong*, he thought. But just as he was about to hang up, he heard her say, "Mr. Lawson, is that you?"

Startled by the sound of his name, he felt obliged to answer. "Yes, Kara. Uh... I just... sorry... I dialed your number by mistake."

"Oh? Who did you mean to call?"

His silence affirmed her suspicion. "I'm not busy. If you need someone to talk to... I can come over. Or, if you would prefer, you're welcome to come over here?"

Porter became nervous and searched all around him for some sort of answer. He didn't know what he wanted.

"Look, Porter. I like to believe that we're friends outside of the office. And it sounds like you need a friend. So, I'm going to come over. I'll see you soon."

By the time he had digested her words and was about to object, he heard the click on the other end of the line and knew Kara would be knocking on his door in a matter of minutes.

As soon as Summer hung up with Porter, she made a quick phone call to a perspective buyer who had an appointment for that evening. Explaining that an emergency had come up, he agreed to reschedule for the following day. Although her art was important to her, Porter was decidedly more important; she was prepared to reschedule her entire life if it meant she could save her marriage.

Summer only had a few hours before Porter would be over, and she wanted everything to be perfect. She moved all her painting materials from the living room to the studio and quickly dusted and vacuumed. The rest of the house was already tidy and clean, so she put dinner on the stove and made a salad. Once all the preparations and cooking had been done, she picked out a simple black cocktail dress and jumped in the shower.

By the time she had showered, dressed, done her hair and make-up, it was already five past six. She ran down the stairs and lit the candles, knowing Porter would arrive at any minute.

At quarter past six, she had plated the meal and poured the drinks. Everything was ready. She sat looking out the living room window, expecting Porter's car to pull in at any minute. She could not contain her smile and the butterflies were threatening to fly straight out of her stomach.

At half past six she began to get worried, but told herself to give him fifteen more minutes. "His will be the next car around the turn," she assured herself. But the passing of more than a few cars and fifteen minutes made her unable to wait any longer. She dialed his number once, with no answer. She hung up and dialed again immediately. The second time, there was an answer.

"Hello?" the woman's voice said.

The words Summer had been ready to speak got lodged in her throat and she stood there, barely breathing.

"Hello?" the voice repeated, a little louder this time.

Summer's hand began to shake and a moment later she let the phone drop from her weak fingers. Her breathing became labored and she raised her hand to her chest to soothe the jabbing, but the pain would not cease. Rather, it spread from her heart and ran all through her body. Her legs suddenly became too weak to hold her and she fell seated to the floor.

What a cruel way to tell me, Porter, she thought as the tears streamed down her face. *So cruel.*

The guilt in her told her she deserved it. She had deceived him in the worst way possible and broken his heart; why wouldn't he seek comfort in the arms of someone else?

But then why had he agreed to dinner? Simply to get revenge? To make me feel the pain that I had put him through? Really? Why did I let myself get my hopes up? Why did I think he could forgive me? Why did I not expect him to turn to another woman? All the questions ran through her mind as her heavy breathing turned to sobs and she cradled herself, rocking back and forth. Porter had just shattered the last bit of hope she had been clinging to, and broken any remaining pieces of her heart.

The tears flowed for what felt like hours. When they finally stopped, she stood up feeling drained and jaded. Summer cleaned up the kitchen, her body unable to move at its usual pace. She threw the food directly into the garbage instead of putting it away in the fridge; she wanted no reminders of the evening she had expected to have. Carefully, she walked to her bedroom and stepped out of her dress and into a pair of sweat pants and a tank top. Pulling her hair into a tight pony tail, she turned off all the lights in the house, and paused just outside the bathroom. The medicine cabinet seemed to whisper her name.

CHAPTER 23:
Life in the Sun

It had taken Hasan a few days to overcome the grief that had showered him when the doctors announced that nothing more could be done for May. He had spent those days angry at everyone, adding tension to an already somber house. Then one early morning, as he opened his eyes against the rays shining in through the window, it occurred to him that his anger would lead nowhere. Actually, it was only causing harm; his anger was making him immobile. But now, in this new light, he needed to end the waiting. He refused to sit by and simply watch the days and hours go by, waiting for something he hated to happen. "We won't just sit and wait," he said aloud.

He got up carefully and went to the bathroom. As he rinsed his face during ablution, he made a silent invocation that the anger which had been fueling him be washed away with the water. Spreading out the prayer rug in his bedroom, he prayed with a renewed sense of humility. On his last prostration he asked God to forgive his ungrateful behavior. He asked God to bless his family, and to cure his wife. He asked God to give them all the strength to withstand the trials ahead. "Oh God, bless us with Your Mercy, in this life, and in the hereafter."

Once he had finished, he leaned against the bedside table and watched his wife as she slept peacefully. Her once curvy figure had shriveled into almost nothingness. Her light brown complexion was now yellow and pale. Although he ached to see her healthy again, there was no other person on earth he would have rather been with.

Wanting to wake her, he gave her a prolonged kiss on the forehead. When she opened her eyes, she found him smiling down at her. "What do you want to do today?" he asked.

Not quite sure if she had heard him correctly, May rubbed her eyes awake and sat up a bit. "Huh?"

"What do you want to do today?" he repeated with a warm smile.

"Hasan, I can't really *do* much of anything. I'm too weak...."

"So 'do' is the wrong word. Where do you want to go? What do you want to see?"

Ever since the night of the accident, May had been wanting to speak to Hasan about their last quarrel. It seemed to her that her chance had finally arrived.

"Hasan, I want to talk to you about the fight we had the night of the accident. I just want you to know that...."

Hasan cut her off, "Shhh. May, it's over. No need for this now. I get it. You didn't want to disappoint Noor. I mean, even though I do wish we could rewind and make that night end differently, I understand why you went. I think I probably would have, too." He kissed her lips softly and gently stroked her cheek.

"So you weren't mad?"

"No, I was. I was furious. But you are my love; I forgave you the second you walked out the door, just like I know you forgave me."

They held each other tightly for some moments, then Hasan cleared his throat and asked her again, "So... like I was saying, what do you want to see?"

She had been stuck in her house for more weeks than she could remember. But she doubted she had the strength to venture an outing.

"I don't think that's a good idea, Hasan. I'm too weak. I appreciate what you're trying to do...."

"Not a good idea, why? I'll carry you... don't worry about it. We'll manage. Now, where do you want to go?"

"I need to be here, beside all of you. This is...."

"This is *not* where you want to be. You've been home for too long. And we're all going to be with you. I want us to go out... just say where."

May heard something in his voice. It was more than mere desperation. Was it hope? She couldn't tell exactly, but she knew he wouldn't back down. She thought for a moment, then replied, "I want to eat chocolate covered strawberries in the park."

Hasan jumped out of bed and called down the hall to his mother as he pulled on his jeans.

"Mama, I have a quick errand to run. I'll be home in about half-an-hour. Can you have May ready by then?"

Hanaan furrowed her eyebrows in confusion. She looked back and forth, from Hasan to May. "Ready for what?"

"To go to the park. And you, too, mama."

He pulled his shirt on over his head, and left the room. Realizing that he had forgotten something, he came back almost immediately. Hasan walked straight over to May and kissed her forehead. "I'm going to go pick up the kids and inform the school that we're going away for a week. We'll go grab the strawberries from the supermarket and come right back. Is there anything else you want?"

There were lots of things she wanted, but only God had that kind of power.

"No, *habibi*. I'm good."

He kissed her smiling lips quickly. "I won't be long."

Fumbling with his shoes by the front door, he felt his mother standing directly behind him. "Do you need anything from the store, mama?"

"This is not a good idea, Hasan. She's too weak. You even have to help her to use the bathroom. This is not a good idea. This outing could make her sick."

And even though he hated the truth, he said it, "She's already sick, mama. She can't get any more sick. I won't just sit and watch and wait for her to go. As long as we still have her, we're going to enjoy our time together. Now... do you need anything?"

With tears filling her eyes, Hanaan shook her head. She watched as her son grabbed his keys and walked out the door. "God, be merciful on us all. Be merciful on us all."

An hour later they arrived at the park. Hasan carried his wife from the car to the sunny spot they had chosen and helped her to get comfortable. "Before we play let's pray *dhuhr* together; by the time we get home, the time for the *asr* will have already begun."

A few moments later they all stood together in prayer. Deen stood to the right of his father while Hanaan and Noor stood just behind them. May remained seated beside her daughter, but she, too, prayed with them. When they had finished praying, before anyone had the chance to get up, Hasan raised his hands in supplication, and they all followed suit: "Oh God, we Praise and Thank You for the innumerable blessings you have bestowed on us. We ask that you continue to bestow us with Your Generosity, Your Mercy, Your Forgiveness. Forgive us, Oh God, when we stray from Your path and lead us always back to You and to the Path of Righteousness.

"Grant us goodness in this life and in the hereafter. Grant us happiness and health. Oh God, bless our family. Bless my mother with good health always. Show her Mercy in this life and in the hereafter. Grant her the highest level of Paradise.

"Bless my children, Oh God. Let them be of the most successful in this world, and of those whom You grant the highest level of Paradise in the hereafter.

"Bless us with Your Bounty, bless us all with health. Oh God, cure May of her disease. God, Only You are able to cure, so cure her. Cure her, and bless her with a long, healthy life. Grant us the highest level of Paradise in the hereafter, oh God. Ameen."

After their father's supplication, Noor and Deen weren't sure if they should spend time with their parents, or get up and play. Hasan sensed their reluctance. "What? We came to the park so you could just sit there? Go on, you two. Go off and play. Let's see which one of you can kick the ball the farthest."

Once the kids had run off, Hasan sat behind May, acting as her cushion, loving having her in his embrace as they watched their kids chase the ball around the field. Hanaan wanted to give them some time alone, so she eventually got up to play with the kids.

"Is this spot too sunny for you? Do you want to move to the shade?"

"Hasan," May said, ignoring his questions. "For the children's sake... for the children's sake," she reiterated, stressing her words, "don't grieve me for too long. They're going to need to see you...."

"Shhhh. This is not the time...."

But May cut him off. "Yes, it is. I need you to hear this, so just listen. It's already taking more out of me than I can handle... don't make it harder on me."

He sat quietly, following her orders, waiting for her to catch her breath.

"You have to try to be strong for the kids," she began again. "They're going to need you more than you can imagine." She paused. Not because she needed to catch her breath, but because she knew that he would not easily listen to what she needed to say next; she paused to word it so that he would hear it. "But eventually – and it may come sooner than you think – they will smile and laugh and realize that they have to enjoy their lives. And that goes the same for you. I need you to enjoy your life... and that means you will have to remarry."

Her words both saddened and angered him. "Be quiet, May." He could feel the tears begin to form.

"You need to hear this... and you need to hear it from me. I know how much you love me and how faithful you are, but living alone for the rest of your life is a stupid way to show it. You need to find a partner... someone who will share your happy moments and lift the sad ones. Someone to love you."

"You are my partner. I pick you. I will *always* pick you." He snuggled his head in her neck and willed the tears to flow silently.

While she knew that she should object, she felt blessed to have found a partner who loved her so much, that he, at least for now, rejected even the thought of someone else. She pulled his arms tightly around her, and made a silent prayer that God alleviate her husband's pain. She prayed for God to bless him with health and reward him with happiness for his loyalty, and for his love. May prayed for God to bless her husband with a wife to love him faithfully.

A good while later, Noor and Deen came running back to their parents, followed by Hanaan who was panting to catch her breath. Deen sat in his mother's lap and Noor sat right beside her.

Kissing her kids, one after the other, May smiled and said, "I need you kids to do something for me... can you?"

"Of course, mama," they said in unison.

"You have to promise," she taunted.

"We promise."

"I need you to always be good to each other. And to listen to baba. Do you promise?"

"We promise, mama."

"And I need you to always remember that your first devotion is to God. With anything and everything you do, make the intention that it is for God. That way He will bless you always. Can you remember that?"

"Yes, mama."

"*Alhamdu lillah*. I love you both very much."

They each hugged their mom and showered her face with loving kisses.

"I think we should go back home now."

"You're sick of the sun? We can move to the shade." Hasan suggested.

"No, I'm not sick of the sun, but the shade is calling me. We should leave."

CHAPTER 24:
Pushing Through

"Sidra? Sidra, what's wrong? What happened?" The woman took Sidra's suitcase and led her inside the house.

"I'm sorry. I just... I didn't know where else to go. I ended it tonight. You're the only one I can turn to."

"Oh, Sidra. You are so stubborn." The woman clenched her empty fist momentarily and shook her head.

"It's for his own good," Sidra replied gently, trying to convince herself as well. "He'll realize that one day."

The tears flowed silently as Sidra sat with her head propped in her hands, her friend beside her. The smell of hot chocolate from the mug placed before her tried to offer its comfort, but Sidra was beyond its reach. Even the gentle strokes on her back were not making it to her soul.

Footsteps on the stairs behind them interrupted their silence. "Honey, is everything okay? Is that you, Sidra?"

Sidra didn't look at him. She just nodded slightly and waved.

"We're okay. Sidra's going to stay with us for a while until she sorts some things out."

"She's always welcome," the man said sincerely, in a tone too cheery for the situation. Without stopping or entering the room, he went quickly to the kitchen and a few moments later walked back up the stairs.

As though something had just pricked her, Sidra jolted, sitting up straighter. "Oh, God... I didn't even think. Is this... if my being here is going to cause you any problems...."

The woman cut her off, "Don't be ridiculous, Sidra. Jeff knows all about your situation. I tell him everything. He thinks what you're doing is very noble and self-less. I, on the other hand, think it's the stupidest idea I've ever heard!"

"Please don't start with me again." She rested her back against the couch and crossed her arms, as if embracing herself. "He'll be thankful one day."

"I don't think so, Sidra. You've crushed him. You betrayed him with what you did. That will weigh more with him than anything. You didn't have the right to do that."

"Are you finished?" Sidra glared at her friend with bloodshot eyes.

Holding her gaze, she placed one arm around Sidra. When she spoke, her tone was gentle, "Yes, I'm done."

Back in his big empty home, Farris knew that although his world had just crumbled, he needed to continue with his routine. He went on with the motions, but without any small talk, without any laughter, without a smile. His unshaven, much thinner face prompted his firm to give him a week-long vacation.

Faruq decided to stay with his brother during that time to ease his loneliness. When he finished unpacking his bag, he came out of the guest room holding a towel.

"Good thing they gave you some time off. You need a break," Faruq said encouragingly.

"I'm already broken," Farris replied, sitting motionless and in a trance on the couch.

"Come on, Farris. I know this is hard on you, but it is not the end of the world."

"I just don't understand! I don't understand any of it!" He got up and started pacing around the room, his arms waving around as he continued. "And if you weren't so incompetent, and had kept an eye on them, we would know exactly where he lives and we wouldn't be in this predicament!"

Faruq understood that Farris was speaking from behind an

emotional blaze, so he tried not to take his brother's words too much to heart. Still, he felt like he had to defend himself. "Farris, man, I'm sorry I messed up. But like I told you before, I didn't even know there was a back exit. I totally expected to see them get up and just go out the front door." His tone was low and apologetic.

Farris grunted loudly and rubbed his eyes with the palms of his hands. "I know, I know. I'm just... I'm so pissed!"

Faruq looked down at the towel in his hand for a second, then threw it at his brother. "Go take a shower. And shave. It'll make you feel better."

Farris did as he was told. Not because he wanted to, but because he seemed only to have the ability to obey. The confusion about Sidra had garbled his mind, making him unable to make any decisions on his own.

Faruq was determined to help his brother cope through the difficult situation he now faced. He made sure Farris did his laundry, could prepare at least two meals a day for himself, and cleaned up around the house. He tried to get him to go out and meet new people, but Farris refused.

"You've been stuck in the house for more than two weeks. You've gone back to work. Why not go out and have some fun on the weekends?"

"I go to work because I need to... I don't need to go out on the weekends. I'm fine at home."

"You can't live in this depression forever, Farris. I know it's hard. But you have to force yourself to push through it."

"I force myself out of bed every morning. That's enough for now."

Faruq shook his head, but recognized that his brother needed time. When Farris was still not up to going out the following weekend, however, Faruq forced the issue.

"It will be good for you to get out, Farris. You need a change of scenery."

"But I'm not in the mood, Faruq."

Laughing, the younger brother said, "Quite frankly, Farris, I don't care. You can either come willingly, or I'll have to hoist you over my shoulder. You know I'd do it, too. And I'll love seeing how people in the street react to your old man pajamas."

Farris cocked one eyebrow and stared his brother in the eyes. "You annoy me."

Faruq shot back his widest smile. "I love you, too, bro. Now go get dressed. And don't forget your jacket."

They had burgers at a local restaurant then went to the movies. While they stood in line waiting to buy their tickets, a couple of women in their late twenties tried flirting with the brothers.

"We're trying to decide which movie to watch. Which are you guys gonna see?" the brunette asked Farris as she twirled a strand of hair around her finger. Her almond-shaped brown eyes framed in lush lashes could hold the attention of any man she chose... any man but Farris. He simply wasn't interested. It was too much effort to even feign civility, and Farris didn't really care how he came off. He just looked away.

Faruq's quick response covered up a possibly awkward silence. "Whichever movie you ladies decide on."

The women giggled and Faruq continued to flirt with them as they purchased their tickets and took their seats. Faruq and the blond whispered and joked throughout the movie, making Farris wish he had just stayed home. *This is the last time I let him drag me out with him*, he thought. *Hoist me over his shoulder? What was I thinking? I'd have him pinned to the ground in no time! You're in for it when we get home, little brother.*

As they exited the cinema, Faruq charmingly asked, "So where would you ladies like to go now?"

"Actually," Farris interrupted, "I'm just going to call it a night." Farris began to walk away without saying goodbye or even recognizing the women. Faruq stood there for a second, jaw open, utterly embarrassed by his brother's anti-social behavior. "I'll be right back, ladies. Don't go anywhere."

He ran after his brother and quickly caught up with him. "Man, what are you doing?! This is the best thing for you right now."

"I don't want this. This has never been my scene, Faruq, and you know that. I'm just going to...."

But the sight of something beyond Farris made his brother interrupt, grabbing him by the shoulder. "That's him! Farris, man, that's him!" Faruq shouted, pointing in the direction he was looking.

Turning around so he could see what Faruq was pointing to, Farris narrowed his eyes. "What are you talking about, Faruq? That's who?"

"That's him!" Faruq repeated, excitedly grabbing Farris' shirt at the shoulder. "That's the man I saw with Sidra!"

The words forced Farris' eyes into focus. He saw the tall, brown haired white man so vividly, as if he were the only one in the parking lot. He didn't hesitate for even a split second; Faruq barely blinked, and suddenly Farris was sprinting toward James. He lunged at him, punching him square in the face. The man fell to the ground as the woman who was with him let out a gasp and crouched to the floor beside him.

Looking up at the attacker she screamed, "What the hell is wrong with you?! Why did you punch my husband?!"

Farris hovered over the couple, breathing heavily, rubbing his throbbing knuckles. Faruq, now standing beside his brother, held Farris' arm back and spoke out, "Your husband is having an affair with his wife. Isn't that right, James?"

"James?!" the woman yelled. "He's not James!"

Farris unclenched his fists as the woman helped her husband to his feet. Both Farris and Faruq knitted their foreheads in confusion. They stared at each other for a second, then Faruq looked back to the couple. "Yes, he is. I saw him with Sidra." His voice was noticeably defensive.

The woman pulled a tissue from her purse and blotted away at the spot of blood on her husband's cheek. He continued to hold it to his face as she zipped up her purse and stood before the two strange men, arms crossed in defiance. "You saw him," she finally spoke, "but you don't remember seeing me?"

Farris looked in confusion between his brother and this woman. Faruq squinted his eyes and stared at her. A moment later he said, "Yes, I remember now. You were with Sidra sometimes. But so what? He's having an affair with your friend."

The woman's pose did not change. "But you said she was having an affair with someone named James?"

Faruq nodded and let out a half-shrug.

The woman nodded in the direction of her husband. "His name's Jeff."

She paused for a moment, looked up at the sky, and let out a heavy sigh. "I'm James."

CHAPTER 25:
Different Kinds of Love

Morgan hadn't taken Mariam up on the two weeks she had offered him; the day after their confrontation he packed a suitcase and left. Before he did, though, he sat down with his four kids to explain what was going on.

"I think I should be there with you. We should do this together," Mariam stated.

In a soft voice Morgan replied, "We're not together anymore. There's no need to pretend."

"But I think it'll be best if I'm there, too."

Morgan clenched his jaw in an effort to remain calm. But when he spoke, his tone was noticeably sharp. "Let it go, Mariam. I'm going to speak to them alone."

When he entered the room, she stood out of sight just outside the door, leaning against the wall, listening to the explanation he gave his kids. Morgan held the youngest two, one on each knee, while Dina and Adam sat across from him. He knew the little ones wouldn't really understand what he said, but he wanted them to hear it nonetheless. He needed to feel as though he had done his part in warning them.

"Your mom and I have been... upset with each other lately. And we've tried to work it out, but we can't seem to come to a compromise. So we're going to take a little break from each other and I'm going to be going away for a while."

While Dina stared at her father, Adam looked down at his feet and closed his eyes tight, willing the tears back. "What do you mean a break, dad? Do you mean you're getting a divorce?" Fear was all over Dina's face as she spoke, but the cry escaped Adam's lips, and his tears began to roll down his cheeks uncontrollably.

"Well...." Seeing their pain intensified his own. A lump formed in his throat, and it took several seconds before Morgan felt he could speak without breaking down. He hugged his two eldest more to soothe himself than to comfort them.

From where she stood, Mariam covered her mouth and held her breath. She knew the reality would crush the kids, but she didn't want him to lie to them either.

Finally, he continued, "We don't know if we'll end up getting a divorce. For now, it's just some time apart."

Mariam breathed a silent sigh of relief.

Morgan tried to comfort his kids, telling them that he would visit them every day and they would be able to spend entire weekends together. He tried to laugh and joke, and even though the kids smiled through their tears, they did so only to please their dad. He hugged and kissed them each then walked out.

Mariam followed him to his car. "Thank you for not lying to them."

"They're going to find out sooner or later."

"Take care of yourself, Morgan." Mariam spoke the words with full sincerity. But Morgan simply nodded, got in the car, and drove away.

Mariam knew the kids would have a million questions for her so she went right to them. The two youngest were playing on the floor, and Dina and Adam were hugging each other. The sight of them almost brought her to tears. She sat down quietly across from them and decided she shouldn't wait for the questions.

"I know this isn't easy on you guys, and it might be a little bit confusing, but there's something very important that I need you to know.

"Both your father and I love you very much. And whatever happens between the two of us will never affect that. You will continue to be the most important thing in both my life and dad's.

Never doubt that."

The older kids nodded their heads as they wiped away their tears.

With puffy, red eyes and newly dried cheeks, Adam said, "We know you guys love us. But does this mean you don't love each other?"

Mariam let out a sigh and succumbed to the sadness which she had been repressing. She had never expected that her marriage would end up here. She and Morgan had been more in love than anyone she knew. And their marriage had always been solid. Up until the recent past, she could remember not one moment of resentment she had toward him. Of course they had their share of ups and downs, but the difference with them was... the good had outweighed the bad so significantly, that the bad was nothing but a hazy dream, never really having any weight. All of that had changed in what seemed like a second, and it was killing her inside. Her eyelids drooped, her smile vanished, and her shoulders sank.

She stared at her children, trying to find the words to explain feelings she herself couldn't grasp. "I can't speak for dad," she said in a low voice, "but I know that I will always want the best for him. And, in a way that may be different from before, I will always love him. But loving someone doesn't always mean you can deal with them. And I think that's where we are now. I do love your dad, but I just can't live with him anymore. It's gotten to be too hurtful."

She let only a few tears escape her eyes. Then she wiped them away and sat up straight. "And, of course, you guys can call dad whenever you want. He'll be staying at your uncle's for at least a little while."

They sat in silence for a few moments, then Mariam enveloped them in a loving hug. "Okay," she said, gently pulling away and brightening up her tone, "you two have homework to do. Go on so you can finish up quickly."

Adam and Dina left the room with faces still sad and arms wrapped around each other's shoulders.

~

Morgan turned into his brother's driveway and switched off the ignition. He sat there for a while, trying to figure out how his life path had led him here. His world had been turned on its side, and he couldn't understand why.

Despite his brother's offer that he could stay with him as long as he liked, even simply move in with him, Morgan felt like he would be more comfortable in a place of his own. Within a few weeks, he found a small apartment that was close enough to the kids so that he could stop by whenever he wanted. Even though the rent was reasonable, Morgan worried about this new added expense, and wondered how things would work financially now that they were split between two households.

Mariam tried to put his mind at ease during one of his visits to the kids. "Morgan, I've spent the last few weeks applying for jobs at other schools in the area. Working at the same school was fine before, but now it may be too uncomfortable for both of us, not to mention the other teachers. Anyway, so I've been offered a position at a private school nearby, and my salary will be slightly more than I was making before, so I'll be able to cover the kids' daycare along with what I've been putting toward our regular living expenses. That'll only leave one or two hundred to pay your brother back, but I think we've made significant headway with that already, so it's just a matter of time."

He understood exactly what she meant, and, despite himself, it put his mind at ease regarding the financial responsibilities he felt weighing him down. But admitting that relief would again mean he fell short towards his family. "Whatever. I can deal with it."

Mariam decided to just let it go. He wanted to save face; she didn't care... she had done what was right by her conscience and that was all she wanted.

For Morgan, this new position of Mariam's was more than just news; it meant that his family didn't have to rely on him, or couldn't rely on him, financially. It meant his family felt that he couldn't provide, and this sent him into a state of misery. It was bad enough that he had lost the only woman he had ever hoped to share his life with, and in the rare, fleeting moments of self-honesty, he recognized that his behavior was the only thing to blame for that. But now he felt like his kids, too, would be distanced from him because he could not give them what they needed. His failures suffocated him.

His depression began with just changes in his overall attitude; he went from being the 'cool' teacher at school, to being the grouch. He lost interest in his appearance, showing up unshaven and disheveled. After a few weeks, he lost interest in going to work altogether, and simply stopped showing up. The school, knowing their family situation, called Mariam more to let her know of his quick deterioration than to ask if she knew why he had stopped attending.

Mariam, however, had already noticed the change in Morgan. Just as he had stopped going to work, he had also stopped visiting the kids. For the past two weeks he had just been calling them on the phone, claiming he couldn't see them because of an increased load at work. Mariam knew he was making excuses, but she never could have pictured what he had become. One day after work, she decided a surprise visit might do him well.

When he answered the door, he was shocked to see who it was. But she was even more shocked.

"Morgan! Is that you?!" His features were barely visible through his unkempt facial hair. The state of his apartment was no better; there were clothes all over the place, mixed in with old pizza boxes and various half-filled bags of chips. He left the door open and went back to the old, smelly couch.

"Morgan," Mariam said gently as she sat down across from him. "I know that all of this is hard on you... it's hard on all of us. But this is no way to face it. This has never been your style. And the kids won't be able to handle seeing you like this."

"They don't need me."

"What are you talking about, Morgan?! You are their father... of course they need you! You have to teach them right and wrong, and show them how to play ball, and the right way to eat Frosted Mini Wheats. Who else can teach them all of that? And that's only for now. Before you know it there'll be driving lessons and high school basketball games to coach. They need you for all that stuff, and all the stuff in between."

"You can do all of that."

"I most certainly cannot! I'm not the dad... I'm the mom. I'm the boring one, who gets to give them medicine, and make sure they've finished their science project, and drive them to piano lessons every week even though they hate it.

"Who told you they don't need you? Because all I got all week was 'Where's dad, mom?' 'I miss dad.' 'When is dad coming over?' I lied to them, saying you called and said you weren't feeling well and you would be by as soon as you felt better. But I'm not sure they bought it."

"They asked about me?" Morgan's tone showed more than a hint of hope.

"Of course, Morgan," Mariam said reassuringly. "You are a part of them. God chose to bless us both with those kids, so they are our responsibility together. Just because our marriage didn't work out, doesn't mean we can bail on our kids."

A part of him was affected by her words, but another part of him was sick of her advice. "What do you care, anyway? You just said it, 'our marriage didn't work.' So what are you doing here? You don't care what happens to me."

The words didn't surprise her, but she chose to pause for a few seconds, to let him cool down, so that when she spoke, he would hear her clearly.

"I loved you for eleven years. It's not likely that kind of love can simply disappear. We've come to the end of our marriage, but I will continue to want only the best for you, Morgan. Our kids, despite where we are with respect to each other, have made us a team forever. For their sakes, we have to learn how to be good to each other, and to work toward their benefit."

Her tone became slightly sharper, "And what's going on here..." she waved her hand around the room, "is unhealthy for both you and them. I'm going to drop them off tomorrow after school. I'm sure this is not how you want them to see you."

She got up and walked out of the door, hoping that her words had had the right effect, worried that with his stubbornness, they may very well backfire.

CHAPTER 26:
Faithful

Clutching the list of emergency phone numbers her therapist had given her, Summer slammed the bathroom door closed. "That's not the answer, Summer," she told herself out loud. "That will never be the answer."

In her studio, she stood before the piece on the easel and held the brush loosely in her hand. Despite her strongest efforts, she could not get her mind to stop replaying the events of the night. The voice of the woman who had answered Porter's phone kept echoing in her ears, and the tears began to re-emerge. Immersing herself in the sorrow, she turned on the radio and let the saxophone wash over her body. She remained motionless, with her eyes closed, taking in the music... until the creak of the steps made her eyes jump open. She stared blankly as Porter walked down the stairs in silence.

"I wasn't coming," he began once he had gotten to the base of the steps. "Well, actually, I was coming, then I wasn't coming, and now... I'm here." His hands alternated between rubbing his forehead and getting shoved into his pockets. Part of him still didn't know why he had decided to go.

Summer's emotions were at war with each other. On the one hand, she was elated that Porter had shown up, it didn't matter that he was more than a couple of hours late. But on the other hand, she felt betrayed; he had been with another woman, and made a point of rubbing it in her face. The guilt in her kept reminding her that she had no right to feel betrayed since she had been unfaithful first. All three feelings washed over her, making her unsure of how she should react to seeing her husband. Unable to get a clear sense of her emotions, she took a step backwards without turning her head, sat on the couch and stared at him with a blank expression.

"After I hung up with you earlier," Porter continued, "I began to think that maybe I had rushed to accept your dinner invitation. I needed to hear someone else's opinion… but after I got that opinion, I realized it didn't really matter to me."

"Who did you ask?"

"Kara. She came over to help me… figure things out."

She nodded, his words not really bringing her any comfort. Porter was pacing back and forth in front of her.

"I felt like you had stabbed me in the back with a wooden spoon and were trying, as slowly and painfully as possible, to remove my heart in pieces. I had never imagined there could be such a distance between us, that we could become so disconnected that one of us could turn to someone else. The only thing in this world that I'd ever been sure of was our marriage. You destroyed all of that with your affair! And I couldn't even begin to try to see beyond it."

He paused, but continued pacing. Porter himself was unsure of where he was going with this speech. He was still confused, but felt like voicing his feelings may help him outline a course of action.

"I never showed you one ounce of disrespect… how could you betray me? How could you do that to us?" He stopped pacing and stood facing her. He wasn't really expecting an answer, just needed to make sure his words were sinking in. She raised her head slightly, shook it and shrugged embarrassingly. She had no words to speak.

"I don't know if I can do what I came here to do." Porter sat on the steps. "I couldn't get past feeling betrayed to see far enough ahead, to figure out how I feel about us. I didn't know if I still loved you… I didn't know if I still wanted us."

Summer held her breath, sensing he was about to give his decision.

"But I remembered something I had said to Kara about you once. We were talking about our families and I said, 'Summer is not my family, she is my life.' And I meant it. You were my air."

Summer bowed her head, knowing what must be coming next.

Porter continued, "But when I told Kara that tonight, she said that air gives life, and what you had done was killing me. She said that trust is one of those things that doesn't mend. Once it breaks, that's it.

"So I said, 'What about forgiveness? Don't those we love... or loved... or those who have shared our lives, don't they deserve to be forgiven for their mistakes? We're all human, we can all make mistakes.'

"She said, 'A mistake happens when you don't mean to do something, not when you are fully aware of your actions and, thus, willing to bear the consequences.'" He sighed loudly and rubbed his temples with his fingertips. He paused for so long that Summer thought maybe he was done, that maybe he didn't have anything more to add. Knowing this was the end, she could almost feel the final shreds of her heart fall apart. She did not have the energy to even attempt to stop the tears from running down her cheeks. He shook his head slightly and lowered his hands to his lap.

Looking down, Porter whispered with desperation, "I've been suffocating these past few weeks... you are still my air."

It took a moment for her to comprehend his words. She stared at him vacantly with her bloodshot eyes for a moment, then as soon as his words finally registered, she sat beside her husband and took both of his hands in hers. Before she could speak, he said, "But I don't know how I can trust you."

Summer swallowed the lump in her throat and begged, "I will spend the rest of my life loving you, and trying to gain your forgiveness and trust. Just give us a second chance."

When he lifted his head so his eyes finally met hers, he saw her sincerity, and couldn't help but wrap his arms around her.

"We'll get past this, Porter. I swear, I will live my life to make it up to you."

His embrace grew stronger as he whispered, "I've missed you so much."

CHAPTER 27:
Tender End

May spent the next few days watching her kids play in the yard and trying to enjoy the warm company of her family. Hasan left her side only for the bathroom and to pray. Although his mother offered, Hasan insisted that he help May with her showers and getting dressed. Unable to stand for long periods of time, she had been praying from a reclined position for months, and Hasan always helped her face the correct direction. As soon as she had turned her head to the left and made the closing prayer, he would approach her, kiss her hands and say, "May God accept your prayer."

In her weak voice, she managed, "From both me and you."

"Where do you want to sit?"

He had been asking her the same question, and she had been replying with the same answer – "Wherever you are, *habibi*" – for months. But on that Friday, she said, "Bring me to the bed, Hasan. And have the kids come in."

It was the first time she had replied without a smile. Hasan saw that her pain had increased, and her breathing was irregular. He hated that he understood.

Moments later she lay on her bed, surrounded by her husband, kids, and mother-in-law.

"I'm getting weaker every minute, and I don't think I have much time left. I want to tell you all that I love you very much. And I will miss you all.

"Noor... don't settle for less than you deserve. In anything... Ever. You will face lots of injustice; stand up always for the truth, no matter how hard that may be. *In sha' Allah*, you will marry a good man, who respects you, loves you and treats you like a queen. But if he ever stops treating you well, God forbid, have the strength to stand up and say to everyone, that you deserve better.

"Deen... being a man doesn't mean being the loudest, or the one who can lift more or run the fastest. It means being kind and gentle without being soft. It means being just... standing up for what's right, and not being afraid to admit your mistakes. Watch your father and learn from him and you will grow to be the best man... strong enough to fulfill all your responsibilities and sensitive enough to show your love.

"I want you both to remember that God is always watching... *always*. So you have to always do what will make Him proud of you. Do what's right, no matter how hard it is, and He will reward you in the end.

"Mama... please forgive me if I've ever been short with you. I never meant to be disrespectful. And I know you've carried so much already, but Hasan and the kids will continue to need you for some time still. God reward you for all you've done for me and for all of us. God bless you with good health always. I'm counting on you to be their loving rock.

"I'm going to miss you all. Now give me kisses and leave me with your father."

She had only been getting out a few words at a time. What should have only taken her a few minutes to say had taken more than half-an-hour.

The kids hugged and kissed their mother in turn, trying to get in as many 'I love yous' as they could, with tears streaking all of their cheeks. Hanaan kissed her daughter-in-law's forehead and whispered in her ear, "You have never disrespected me. My heart has only ever loved you, May. You are my daughter. I promise I will take care of them."

Alone with his wife, Hasan wiped his eyes, then snuggled in bed with her. He kissed her head a few times and whispered softly, "I love you. I love you."

"You are everything that I wanted from this world, Hasan. I'll be waiting for you."

He knew this was the end. He could not control his tears, but he knew that she still needed something from him; her last rites as a Muslim. He tried to steady his voice enough for the words to come out, "I bear witness that there is no god but God, and that Mohamed is His prophet."

"I bear witness," May began to repeat the Muslim testament of faith that she had said thousands of times in her prayers... that she knew better than her own name. But her breathing was too weak.

"That there is no god but God," Hasan encouraged.

"That there... is no god... but God," May managed.

Hasan waited some seconds so she could catch her breath.

"And that Mohamed is His prophet."

"And that... Mohamed... is His prophet," she said.

And as soon as she had spoken those sacred words, Hasan felt the full weight of her body against his chest. He held her body tighter, knowing she was no longer there.

Rocking back and forth, unable to control his sobs, Hasan cried, "Oh God, how am I supposed to live without her? Oh God... oh God... I can't live without her."

Hanaan knew that for the next few weeks, she would be responsible for everything. And that moment began as soon as she heard her son's sobs echoing throughout the house. She had promised May that she would be their loving rock, so despite her heartbreak and overwhelming grief for losing the mother of her grandkids, the woman she considered her daughter, she began to fulfill that promise immediately.

She got on the phone and called the sheikh of their mosque, who kindly took on the responsibility of the funeral arrangements. Next she called all their relatives and Muslim friends. Within two hours, May's body had been cleansed, wrapped in the burial shroud, and taken to the mosque.

After the *Asr* prayer, hundreds of the mosque's attendees – mostly strangers who did not know May personally – prayed for God to be merciful on her and to help her family endure this difficult time.

On the drive from the mosque to the cemetery, Hanaan said to her son, "God is sending us many signs to assure us of her place in heaven, *in sha' Allah*. Have you ever seen so many people at the mosque for *Asr*? For *Dhuhr* on Friday, maybe... but not for *Asr*. God sent all those people to pray for her. *In sha' Allah*, He will accept their prayers and grant her entrance to heaven, a much better place than this trying life."

Hasan's red eyes were dry now. He heard his mother, but he did not reply. His mind was contemplating the cruelty of life. Here, for example, was the ugliest day of his life... but the sun didn't have the decency to remain hidden. It shone brightly in the cloudless sky, as if to mock him in his remorse.

Just then he caught a glimpse of his children. The sun was warming their faces as they rested their heads on their grandmother's shoulders. Despite their tear streaked faces, they looked at peace. And immediately Hasan felt guilty for his ungratefulness at God's blessing.

"God forgive me, God forgive me, God forgive me... and give me patience," he repeated to himself. And although he knew it was of no use, he tried to let the sun comfort him as well.

After his wife's body had been laid to rest, with only the mound of dirt atop it as a marker, and all the people had paid their respects and left, Hasan stood at the site with his mother and children. He knew that he had to be strong for them, so he tried hard to hold back the tears. But how could he stop crying for the woman who had been his support, his partner, his love for so many years?

Hanaan wiped her eyes and placed her hand on her son's

shoulder, "Recite Qur'an, Hasan. Recite Qur'an. It will help her and us."

His voice shook through the words, but they stood there for almost another hour, reciting Qur'an together, and praying that God shower them all with His mercy.

CHAPTER 28:
Finalities

When Mariam saw the long string of cars lined up outside of May and Hasan's house, her heart sank knowing that she would never again see the smiling woman who had been her neighbor for so many years. She didn't let her sadness, or the uneasiness of not fitting in – which she knew she would feel – discourage her from her neighborly duties; she called Summer and they agreed to pay their respects to the family together. They tried to call Sidra, but no one answered.

Both women wore black and stood drying their eyes, trying to collect themselves before ringing the doorbell. An unfamiliar woman wearing a black head scarf and a loose black gown answered the door and simply nodded them in. A moment later, Hanaan appeared.

"Oh, ladies. How kind of you to come. Come in." Although her words were welcoming, Hanaan's tone was solemn.

Again, Mariam was the spokeswoman. "We're very sorry for your loss, Hanaan. May she rest in peace."

"God have mercy on her... and on us all," Hanaan said as she wiped away her tears.

"We know the house is filled with family and friends, but we wanted to pay our respects to Hasan and the kids."

"Of course. Come on this way."

The living room was packed with people. There were not enough chairs for everyone, so many of the condolers were sitting on the floor. The men sat on one side of the room and the women on the other, and they were all listening to one of the men as he read from what Mariam assumed was their holy book. She and Summer, having entered straight to the women's side, sat silently on the floor beside a woman who tried to inch over to make room for them.

They couldn't understand anything the man was saying, but for some reason they felt a calm wash over them; both women assumed it was due to the reader's melodious recitation. Mariam let her eyes scan the room quickly. It was enough for her to catch a glimpse of Hasan and the kids. They were all pale and looked exhausted. Seeing them made her eyes burn with fresh tears.

They waited till the end of the recitation, then got up along with many of the people who had been seated. Making their way through the crowd, the women finally reached Hasan. He was still sitting on the couch.

"Hasan, we're very sorry for your loss."

He had been looking down, but adjusted his gaze to see who was speaking to him. His glazed eyes gave Mariam the feeling that he didn't recognize them, but he managed to say, "Thank you."

"If you need anything, please let us know."

"Thanks," he said, nodding. Then he let his head fall back against the couch and closed his eyes. He had his arms crossed against his chest, in a self-embrace. His sadness and loneliness overpowered all his features. Mariam stared at him, puzzled by the face before her. She was sure that the last time she had seen him, just weeks before, his face hadn't had so many wrinkles, nor did he have so many gray hairs. She wrapped her arms around her waist and lowered her gaze. It broke her heart, but she believed that that's exactly how the loss of true love should be – life altering and hammering.

Mariam and Summer made their way again through the crowd so they could pay their respects to the kids. "Noor," Mariam took the young girl in her arms. "I'm so sorry."

Summer hugged her next, unable to get the words out through the lump in her throat.

"If there is anything you or anyone in your family needs, please let me know," Mariam said.

"Thank you," the girl barely whispered.

"I'm making a couple of casseroles for you guys. I'll bring them over tomorrow so I can check up on you again."

"Sure. Thanks."

The women gathered themselves to leave, but Summer turned right back around. Breathing deeply, she blinked rapidly and fanned her face with her hand. But nothing would work; the tears would not stop. Shrugging at her own weakness, she said, "Noor, your mom was a very special, kind woman. I wish I had known her better. If you ever feel like talking, I would love to listen to your stories about her." Noor nodded softly and looked down at her feet. As the tears welled up in her eyes again, she sat back down on the couch and curled up next to her sleeping brother.

As they walked out of the house, the women continued to wipe their tears.

"Porter isn't back from work, yet, but I'm sure he'll want to pay his respects. Do you think Morgan will want to go with him?"

"Ah..." Mariam paused for a moment to think, sniffled and wiped her nose. "I'm not sure, Summer. Actually, Morgan and I are separated. He's not living at home anymore. I don't know when... or if, even, he'll want to go."

Summer's raised eyebrows and opened mouth revealed her shock. "Wow, I would have never guessed that the two of you were having problems. I'm so sorry."

"It's for the best," Mariam said, letting out a sigh.

They stood in silence for a few moments at the end of Hasan's driveway. Pointing to her home next door, Summer offered, "Would you like to come in for some coffee?"

"I would love to, but I have to go pick up the kids from Morgan's. He takes them every day after school for a couple of hours. I guess I need to tell him about May, too. Thanks, though."

They waved to each other as Mariam crossed the street and Summer walked up her driveway.

A short while later, Mariam stood in Morgan's apartment, which was now organized and neat, with the exception of the few toys the kids had sprawled all over the floor.

"Morgan," Mariam scorned, "You know they need to get their homework done first."

"They did," he answered defensively. "They all finished their homework, then we played together. I was about to order pizza."

"We'll just have dinner when we get home."

"Aw, mom! We wanted to have pizza with dad!" Adam yelled.

"Next time. Come on... everyone get your things and let's go."

Through much huffing and puffing, the kids cleaned up. Mariam took the opportunity to tell Morgan about May.

"That's too bad," he replied. "Well, I get the kids tomorrow night, right? So when I come to pick them up, I'll stop by and pay my respects then."

"Good idea," Mariam nodded. "I can stay with the little ones, and you can take Dina and Adam with you."

"What? Why? They're too young for that."

"What do you mean, 'why'? Noor and Deen are their friends; they should at least tell their friends that they feel sad for their loss."

"Not now. Not when the house still smells like death."

"What?!"

"All I mean is, they're too young to deal with this. It's bad enough they're dealing with divorce. They don't need to deal with divorce and death."

"Whatever, Morgan. Fine, not now. But as soon as I notice that less and less people are stopping by to pay their respects, I'm taking them over there."

"Fine." He rolled his eyes at her controlling behavior which seemed never ending.

Morgan left the room while Mariam helped the kids gather a couple of toys they had missed. A few moments later Morgan reappeared, holding some papers in his hand. "These are for you," he said, handing them to Mariam.

Suspicion had her stare him in the eyes as she took the small stack, as though in his eyes she might find more answers than simply reading the papers. Her eyes grew wide, but she managed to suppress her gasp as she read what they were. "I didn't realize you wanted things finalized so quickly. You didn't even tell me you were filing."

"I just figured... there was no reason to put it off." Partly he was testing her, wanting to see if she was willing, one last time, to fight for their marriage. But mostly, he was just telling the truth.

Mariam nodded and placed the papers in her purse. "I'll look them over and get them back to you, or the lawyer, whichever you prefer."

"It doesn't matter," he shrugged.

And that was true – none of it mattered anymore.

CHAPTER 29:
The Straight Story

Since the day he had bumped into James at the movies, Farris couldn't stop replaying their encounter over and over in his mind.

"What do you mean you're James?" was as coherent as he could get when he heard her introduce herself.

"Jamie. But my nickname's been James since junior high."

Farris looked at the man whom he had assaulted with confusion. Then he and Faruq exchanged questioning glances.

"So... what you're saying is... Sidra's gay?"

"What?! No! Sidra's not gay!" She rolled her eyes and shook her head at the whole situation. Looking back at her injured husband, she said out-loud, "See, Sidra... and this is just the icing!

"Farris," her tone became less hostile as she took a step toward him and looked him in the eyes, "I'm James. I'm Sidra's friend... totally straight, totally platonic friend. We got close these past few months and she's been confiding in me the problems that you guys have been having."

James saw that her explanation was not making any sense to Farris; confusion was still painted all over his face. His wrinkled forehead and the upturned corner of his mouth reminded her that she had always put Sidra in the wrong and sympathized with Farris' situation. Torn between feeling sorry for him and hating that he had just punched her husband, she let out a heavy sigh and threw up her arms. "Urggh!"

A moment later, she began again, "Look, Farris, I know that you're *generally* a good guy, so let me just tell you that Sidra made up the affair. She has never cheated on you... and she loves you very much. And she knows that you love her."

Farris stood silent for a few seconds, but his eyebrows remained furrowed. "Why in the world would a sane person say they're having an affair if they're not? She specifically said, 'I'm going to be happy with James.' That's what she said!"

"I know. She just used my name as a... cop-out. She made it all up. I'm not totally convinced she is sane!"

"Why? Why would she make it all up?"

"Farris, I know this is all very hard on you, and knowing the truth, things seem even weirder. But I think you need to hear the 'why' from her."

But Farris couldn't wait for an explanation, "She wanted an excuse to leave me? Was that it? She wasn't happy anymore and she wanted to leave?"

James rubbed her husband's arm as she spoke, "She never wanted to leave you, Farris. I just told you, she loves you very much. She's a mess without you.

"But, like I said, I can't tell you any more. She's staying with us for a while. When you feel up to talking, swing by."

James took a small scrap piece of paper from her purse and wrote her address.

As he took it from her, Farris asked hesitantly, "You're sure there isn't anyone else? I mean, you're sure no part of it was real?"

"I'm sure," James reassured him. "None of it was real."

A moment later, Farris held his hand out to Jeff and said, "Um... I'm really sorry, man. I totally misunderstood the situation. I thought you were the reason.... Anyway, I'm really sorry." Jeff let out a weak nod as he shook Farris' hand.

After they had spoken, Farris hadn't known what to think... or what to feel. Was he relieved that Sidra hadn't cheated on him? Or was he angry that she had tricked him in such a cruel way? His emotions were in a tug-of-war. Even now, days later as Farris pulled into his driveway, he still couldn't tell which emotion was greater. But he couldn't put it off anymore... tonight he would go to Sidra and demand an explanation.

As he got out of his car, immersed in thought of how their meeting would go, he almost didn't see Mariam as she waved and came running over.

"Farris. Farris, hold on a sec," she called from across the lawn. "We tried calling you before, but no one answered," she said as she approached.

"We were out," he said, not wanting to go into even the slightest explanation. "What's up?"

"I just thought you should know that May passed away."

Farris let out a sigh. *Life doesn't give anyone a break*, he thought. "When's the funeral?"

"It's all done. She was buried earlier. From the look of their driveway, people are still coming by to pay their respects."

"You guys have already gone, I assume?"

"Yeah, I went a little while ago."

"I guess there's no reason to put it off. Thank you for telling me."

As he headed off toward Hasan's house, Mariam said, "Won't Sidra want to go with you?"

"She's still out. I'm sure she'll go when she gets back."

As he watched Mariam nod and walk back toward her house, he corrected himself, *If she gets back*.

CHAPTER 30:
Back Together

Since Porter had moved back home, Summer had been making an extra effort to include him in her work as much as possible. She figured their original problem had been a disconnect and she didn't want to leave any possibility of that happening again. She organized her days so that she took care of most of her networking as soon as she got back from work, just before Porter returned home. After dinner, she set up her easel in the living room where she could work while he read or watched TV.

For his part, Porter tried to show interest in her work without forcing his ideas on her. "How's work coming along? Are your students interested in learning, or are they just there to waste time?"

"No, they're all there by choice, so they're all interested. But some are more talented than others. And some just feel too jaded... they don't really put in the effort. I have one student in particular... I can see such potential in her. If she would just apply herself and focus, she would be great. But she's just too uninspired.

"I'm trying to think of ways to remedy that. I was thinking maybe a contest... and I could give prizes to the top three. But the prizes would have to be really great to motivate them."

Porter flipped through the television channels silently for some moments. "What about a laptop, or a cell phone?"

Summer had refocused on her piece and couldn't understand Porter's suggestion. "Laptop or cell phone?"

"As the prizes."

"Oh. Well, I'll be buying the prizes myself, so even though I'm sure my students would love to win a laptop or cell, I'll need to think of something more affordable."

"What if we sponsor the contest... through the business, I mean. We could use the publicity. 'Local business sponsors art contest.' We can even invite the press on the day of the judging. What do you think?"

Summer was speechless. "Would you really do that?"

"Sure. It'll be good for the community, and for the business. It's a win-win."

She stood there for a moment, unable to word her appreciation, then went over and kissed her husband lovingly, gently. With his hands at her waist, he pulled her toward him firmly until she sat on his lap. They hadn't yet made love since he had returned; he wanted to be sure he had truly forgiven her before being so intimate. Now, on the couch, gazing into her eyes, he could finally see her again. He held her close and kissed her passionately, and let his body take over.

Something about this time was different, though. His hands didn't caress Summer as they had done thousands of times before; they seemed more to be groping her. His movements were rougher than ever before. She realized he was trying to prove something, to them both, and she went along with it.

Disheveled and out of breath, they lay on the floor covered by the throw blanket. She knew he needed to hear it, "Wow... That was... amazing."

She had been anxious about how their first time would go. She had been yearning to be with him, knowing that their physical connection was the best symbol for their emotional attachment. And although he hadn't been as gentle as he usually was, she lay smiling in his arms, knowing that his making love to her was the best proof of his forgiveness.

Porter felt fulfilled as he pulled her to him, snuggling his face against her neck. For the first time since he had moved back home, he knew for certain that he had made the right decision. *Yes,* he thought, pulling her tighter, *this is how it's meant to be. That guy had nothing over me... she's never been this satisfied before. I'm so glad he's finally out of our lives and we can go back to normal.*

The next couple of weeks had Summer busy preparing for the art contest. Her students were excited at the opportunity to win the high tech prizes being offered as rewards, but they were more excited at the possibility of having their pieces on display in one of the local galleries.

"Are you sure, Summer? Do you believe these guys will follow through?" At first her students were hesitant, not believing that any gallery would allow their amateur pieces to be on display.

"They're not doing it to be good Samaritans, guys. It's going to be in the papers... and that means publicity. And that means money. They said they would; they have no choice but to follow through."

She contacted all the artists and art connoisseurs she had ever met, some just to invite to the event, others she wanted as judges. But Porter insisted that she leave the publicity to him.

"I'm sponsoring it... so let me take care of it. We'll contact all the papers, local television and radio channels. Don't worry... we'll make sure that everyone hears about it."

The weeks passed quickly and before she knew it the day of the judging had finally arrived. She stood nervously in front of the mirror fixing her hair and makeup.

"What if no one shows up? They'll be crushed. Oh, God. You know how sometimes I get queasy just before something bad happens? I have that feeling. Uh... this is going to be a disaster."

"Don't be silly, Summer," Porter comforted her with a warm embrace. "You've contacted the entire art world, and I've made sure everyone in the state knows about this. It's going to be great."

She held onto him for a moment, letting his arms encompass her. He had been so supportive on this project and their working toward the same goal had made them closer than ever. "Thank you," she whispered.

Porter laughed gently, "For what? You did all the work."

"Your support. None of this would have been possible without you."

"You are my life, Summer. This is nothing."

A short while later they arrived at the half-way house to find that her students had already set up their pieces. "Everything looks great, guys. People will start arriving soon, so you should be going over your explanations so that you can answer any questions without hesitation." As she continued to speak with her students, she didn't notice that Porter had left her side to help Kara, who had just arrived with the prizes.

"Thanks, Kara. Just place them on that table there. When she finishes we'll see where Summer wants them," Porter said.

"I've got all the food and stuff in the car. Where should we set that up?"

"Hey, Kara. Thank you for coming," Summer said walking over to greet her.

"Where do you want the food?" Kara asked coldly.

"We've set two tables up in the other room for that stuff. Guys," she called over to her students, "please help Kara bring in the refreshments and set them up in the other room." Kara turned and left abruptly, not waiting for the people who were following her.

Alone with Porter, Summer lowered her voice, "I didn't know that you had asked Kara to take care of all the stuff for the contest."

"I ask Kara to take care of everything. That's her job."

"I just thought..." Summer wanted to word it correctly so that he wouldn't get offended. "I just thought you might have had her transferred... you know... after everything."

"Transferred? What? Why?"

Why? Summer thought. *Because the two of you had become close while we were separated. Because she thought you should leave me. And because obviously she had someone else in mind for you!* "I don't think she's happy to be here, Porter. I mean, I don't think she wants to be a part of this."

Porter laughed out loud, "She's getting paid overtime to be here,

Summer. She's fine."

Summer was too concerned with the contest to continue with the conversation. She made a mental note to remember to speak with Porter about it later.

Within an hour the place was set up and swarming with people. Summer gave a short speech in which she thanked Porter for sponsoring the event and making it possible. She introduced the judges and gave them another hour to decide on the top three winners.

All the attendees were enjoying the art and the atmosphere. It seemed that the night would be a success after all. Summer and Porter chatted with many of the guests as they stood waiting their turn at the snack table. A few moments later, as Summer passed her husband a plate, she casually looked over his shoulder. Her eyes grew wide with disbelief; the man she saw standing a few feet back would surely turn the evening into a nightmare.

CHAPTER 31:
New Friends

The kids had been going to their father's every day after school, but as summer was quickly approaching, Mariam figured they had to set a schedule for the vacation. Instead of just waiting for the kids in the car as usual, she went up to Morgan's apartment.

Before she even had a chance to greet the kids or her ex, an overwhelming smell of cigarette smoke smacked her right in the face. She muffled her cough and put her hand up to block her nose. When the kids appeared, Mariam pushed her hands to her sides and tried to hide the disgust which had appeared on her face. She kissed the kids and asked them to go gather their things. She motioned to Morgan that she wanted to speak with him outside.

"What is going on, Morgan? Have you started smoking? It smells disgusting in there."

"I don't do it in front of the kids. They don't know," Morgan said, trying to blow it off.

"They may not have seen you smoking, but that doesn't mean they don't know. I didn't see you and I figured it out in less than a second. You can't...."

Morgan cut her off, "Get off my case, Mariam. You're not my wife anymore so stop telling me what to do."

"I am not your wife, Morgan, but that doesn't mean I don't care about you. And even if you don't believe that, then I'm sure you'll believe that I care about my kids. And I don't want them to see their dad taking up something that they've been taught all their lives is a fatal, disgusting habit. You can't do it... for them."

"Whatever," Morgan muttered as he waved her words away with

his hand. He then turned to go back inside.

Mariam rolled her eyes and shook her head, realizing she wasn't going to get anywhere with him on the cigarette issue. "We need to discuss the summer. How are we going to work out their vacation?"

Morgan turned back around, "Whatever, Mariam."

"No, not 'whatever,' Morgan. We need to set a schedule so that they get to see us both as much as they need and so that we can each plan around it."

Morgan let out a loud, annoyed sigh. "We have to do this right now?"

"It won't take five minutes, Morgan!" She was beginning to get annoyed by his immature behavior. "What are you so anxious to get back to, anyway?! They're just picking up their stuff and then we'll be gone."

Just then she heard a stranger's voice coming from inside. She wasn't sure, but it sounded like it may have been a female voice.

"What's that?" she asked, taken aback. "Is that the TV, or do you have someone over?" She squinted and strained her eyes to try to see into the apartment over Morgan's shoulder, but the tint of the glass was too dark.

Before he could answer, Mariam heard the voice again, and this time she was sure it was not the television, and it definitely belonged to a woman.

His expression seemed to alternate between smugness and embarrassment; her furrowed eyebrows and upturned lip revealed stark repulsion. They stood there staring at each other for a moment. The door opened behind Morgan and the kids came out, bags on their backs, and kissed their father goodbye. Racing off to the car, Adam called back to his mother, "Come on, mom. We have to leave!"

"Yeah, we definitely have to leave," she muttered just loud enough for Morgan to hear. Then, without having accomplished what she had intended to, and without saying goodbye, she turned and walked to the car. Morgan watched them drive away, knowing that

Mariam would not keep quiet about what she had learned.

Mariam was fuming on their short drive home. She was unable to respond to anything the kids said. Her mind was fixed on one thing: *He's not even responsible enough to hide his lewd behavior from the kids! He wants to act like a teenager – fine! But not in front of the kids! As though I don't have enough things to deal with... now I have to worry about what my children are breathing, hearing and seeing at THEIR FATHER'S! This is ridiculous!*

Once at home she told the kids to wash up and change into their pajamas as she prepared dinner. She figured by the time everyone was ready she would be calm enough to conduct herself as she did normally. As she stood in the kitchen she took deep breaths and counted to ten. A few times. But every time she started over, the scene at Morgan's would replay in her mind, and her anger would rise again.

"Mom... what are you doing?" Adam could hear her muttering something to herself, but he couldn't quite make out what she was saying.

Hoping that if he knew what she was doing he would stop asking questions, Mariam said, "I'm counting."

"Oh, mom. I'm learning at school," Gabe said. "It's really not that hard. See: one, twwwwoooo, threeeeeee, fouuuuuur, fiiiiiiive. Do you want me to keep going? How high do you have to count to?"

Her young son's words, spoken with such authority, forced the anger out of her and made her giggle.

"Ah... you guys," she said smiling at them as she served them each their plates. "So..." she placed her own plate on the table, adjusted her chair and sat down. "How was everyone's day?"

"Good," they all said in unison.

"What did you do today?"

The next half hour was filled with news about which child in preschool had cried because he couldn't answer the teacher's question, which one had peed on himself during recess, why math was now Adam's favorite subject and not English, and how Dina wasn't talking to so-and-so because he had called her ugly.

Then finally, Mariam heard the news she had been waiting for. "We met dad's new friend, Rebecca."

"Oh, yeah?"

"Yeah, she's nice," Dina said.

"Did she come over while you guys were there?"

"She was already there when we got there. It looked like she was in her pajamas." The four kids laughed as they remembered. "Her shorts were so short that her bum was showing!" The kids' laughter escalated, as did Mariam's rage.

She could feel the blood shoot to her face and her blood pressure rising, but, taking in deep breaths, she tried to control her emotions. She strained to think of a way to ask all the questions she needed to without rousing her kids suspicions.

"In her pajamas?" she managed. "That's kind of weird, huh?"

"I think maybe she and dad were taking a nap, because he was in his pajamas, too. Well, you know... a t-shirt and his underwear."

She couldn't control herself anymore. She slammed her hand on the table and got up suddenly. She leaned against the sink so that her back was to the kids.

"Mom... are you okay?"

Taking a few more deep breaths, she managed to control her voice. "Yeah... I just remembered that I forgot to do something really important at work."

"Can you just do it tomorrow? Or will they get mad at you?" Dina asked concerned.

The anxiety she heard in her daughter's voice made Mariam realize that she didn't have the luxury of reacting at will. She would have to be much more careful.

"No, sweetie," she said, forcing her breathing to slow and her voice to soften. "They won't get mad." Rubbing her daughter's head, she vowed, "I'll just take care of it tomorrow."

CHAPTER 32:
Guilty

She wasn't expecting any visitors, so when the doorbell rang, James looked outside her bedroom window to see who it was. When she recognized the car parked in the driveway, she called down the stairs, "Sidra... could you get that, please?"

Unsuspecting, Sidra opened the door and stood for a moment in disbelief, unable to speak. "What.... How did you find me?" she finally managed.

"A little birdy told me where you were," Farris replied with a serious expression on his face.

Racking her brain to think of how she should deal with this situation, she turned and walked into the living room. Farris closed the door behind him and followed her.

They sat on opposite couches in the living room. Sidra's eyes were fixed on the floor. Farris stared at his wife, waiting silently for any explanation.

Sidra decided that the best thing to do was to keep up the act. With a heavy sigh she looked straight into Farris' eyes and said, "I don't know why you can't just accept that we're over. I told you, I've found someone else."

"Why are you still lying to me?! I found you, didn't I? Don't you think that means I've also discovered the whole thing was a lie? Why are you still lying?!"

"Look, Farris. Maybe there isn't really anyone else...."

He cut her off, "No, shit?!"

Reflecting his anger, she responded in the same tone, "But what does it even matter? Don't you hate me now?!"

He paused for a brief moment, staring forcefully into her eyes. "Just about."

"Good, so then just go. None of the reasons matter."

"The reasons matter to me. I need to understand. Then I'll go."

She looked down as she spoke, some of the fire from her attitude quelled. "The truth remains that I'm no good for you anymore. You're better off without me. And I hate that you've surrendered to this life simply out of a sense of obligation towards me. So just go. Go live your life."

"When exactly did you stop being good for me? And what life have I surrendered to? I have no idea what you're talking about!"

"Yes, you do."

"No, Sidra, I don't. All I know is that you made up a cruel lie to end a perfectly happy marriage. You destroyed me with what you did... and for the life of me, I can't figure out why!

"Were you just bored with me? You needed a change?"

"No, Farris. Of course not."

"Of course not?! How can you say 'of course not,' when from where I stand that's the only logical explanation! And I never knew you could be so vicious."

She waited a few moments so he could calm down. "I was never bored with you. I can't even remember a moment of unhappiness in our marriage. And that's exactly why I had to be vicious. Otherwise, you wouldn't have let me leave."

He had calmed down some, but the contradictions she was throwing at him had his head spinning. "Sidra, you're making less and less sense. How can you say you never saw a moment of unhappiness and then say you wanted to leave?"

"I didn't want to leave, Farris. I needed to leave. I needed to leave because I can't give you what you want... what you deserve."

"You have never disappointed me, Sidra. I don't understand," he stressed.

Now clearly beaten, she let out a loud sigh, admitting there was no use. She had been trying her hardest not to say it aloud, knowing that the words themselves had the power to crush her.

"I can't give you the family you've always dreamed of. I can't give you children." She placed her hand over her mouth, as though somehow that could take the words back, or at least make them less real.

A few moments passed in silence, then she stood slowly and continued, forcing her voice to steady. "During our first couple of years of marriage, how many times did I hear you say that you wanted to fill our home with lots of little girls and boys to run around spreading laughter and mischief? You wanted it so badly that you made me want it, too. But when the doctor told me last year that I couldn't have kids, I wasn't crushed by that news; I was crushed because I knew how utterly disheartened it made you.

"I tried to ease your pain by pointing out some of the positives of not having kids. I told you we'd get to travel and live our lives and the only commitments we'd have to keep were to each other. But I knew that my words were empty, and they wouldn't be enough to soothe your pain."

She sat back down, and in a soft whisper managed, "You deserve the family you've always wanted. Please just go."

Farris straightened his back against the couch and tilted his head up. Staring at the ceiling, he tried to soak in all that Sidra had said. A few minutes passed in silence, then Farris began, "So, let me see if I have this straight: You pretended to have an affair in hopes of ruining our marriage because you thought I wanted kids and you can't have them. Is that right?"

"But I *know* you want kids, Farris."

"Sorry... so, you pretended to have an affair in hopes of ruining our marriage because you *knew* that I want kids and you can't have them. Right this time?"

Sidra nodded, apprehensive of what his calm voice was hiding.

He went on, "So you wanted to ruin our marriage so that I could find another woman, marry her, and she could give me children. Is that right?"

Sidra sat quietly with her hands in her lap, sure his question was rhetorical. But when she didn't answer he repeated, "Is that right?"

Without raising her gaze from the floor, she raised her eyebrows and again, she nodded.

He got up and walked around the living room a few times, trying to organize his thoughts. "Now," he continued, "have you ever, in all the years we've been together, heard me say that I want kids *at any cost*?"

"No, but...."

"Just answer the questions," Farris snapped, having subconsciously entered his lawyer mode. She had seen him at a few trials, interrogating witnesses, but he had never been this formal or cold with her.

"If I had wanted kids at any cost, don't you think I would have pushed the adoption issue more? Don't you think that maybe I would have tried incessantly to get you to accept that adoption would be a good solution to our 'problem'?"

"I thought you didn't want to push adoption because you agreed with me about *why* it's not the best solution. I thought you agreed that all children have the right to know where they come from, their ancestry, their culture."

"But I could have tried to convince you that adoptive parents can provide that for their kids, especially these days with open adoptions. I could have tried to persuade you that we could teach those adopted children what they had a right to know about their heritage. But I didn't even try, did I?"

"I just thought...."

"Did I try?" he cut her off again.

"No, but...."

"And had I ever said anything to you along the lines that you were the most important thing in my life and I would choose you over anything else? Had you ever heard me say anything like that?"

"Yes, but...."

"No buts," he put his hand up to stop her from continuing. "Now, did you not understand those words, or did you not believe them?" He stopped pacing and stood across from her, staring directly into her eyes.

"I guess I..." she stuttered. "I guess... I guess I didn't believe them."

"I see," he said, breathing in heavily and nodding. "I guess that makes me the guilty son of a bitch, then." He glared at her in silence for a few moments more, fire spitting from his eyes. When he finally turned and stormed out of the house, Sidra was left swimming in a pool of regret. She remained on the couch for some time feeling drained and unable to move.

Finally mustering up the energy, she walked up the stairs to her room and closed the door. From the top drawer, she pulled out the two pictures she had packed all those weeks before. Seeing Farris' brilliant smile broke her heart, making her want to cry. But her alternate personality had destroyed that ability. Sidra sat on the bed, and between tearless sobs, she spoke to her husband in their wedding picture, "I never wanted to hurt you. I never meant to." She looked over to the other picture, the one taken at their last vacation, and let her fingers trace his cap and his wide smile. Their happiness was so palpable, it only intensified her guilt. Holding the picture in both of her hands, she held it to her chest. "I just wanted what's best for you. Oh God, I just wanted what's best for him. Please, Lord. Please. Let him see that. Please, Lord, forgive me for being so cruel to him."

The flashes of Farris' anger from just moments before had finally convinced her that despite her intentions, her actions had been unnecessarily brutal.

CHAPTER 33:
Time Passes

The first couple of weeks after May passed away, Hasan spent most of the time alone, in his bed, trying to avoid the emptiness that filled his house and his heart. He could still smell her on the pillows and in her closet. He wanted to hold on to anything of hers for as long as possible, afraid that the black hole of loneliness would envelop him if he let go.

Having decided that he'd had enough time to be selfish in his grieving, his mother came to him one afternoon. "Hasan, your behavior is not good for the kids. They need to mourn with you... and you need to go on together. Yesterday Noor came to me with tears in her eyes, asking if you would be mad at them if they went back to school. After she asked me that, she asked me if she thought her mom would be upset... *after*. That was her *second* thought; they are more worried about your reaction because they don't know if there are rules to mourning. They need you to let them move on."

Hasan knew she was right, but he also knew that moving on would take more effort and energy than he had. And even though he knew his kids needed him, he just didn't know how to be there for them.

"You don't have to do anything more than spend time with them," Hanaan comforted him. "You all need that. And from right now. Go wash up... we'll wait to eat dinner with you."

Hanaan got up and left before he had a chance to object. A few moments later, he forced himself out of bed and into the shower.

The kids were relieved to finally see their dad out of his room. "*As salaamu alaikum*, baba," they both said as he entered the room.

He forced a smile, "*Wa alaikum as salaam.*" He sat down in his chair. "*Sitto* tells me you guys went back to school today?"

Both kids nodded, and he could tell by the way they avoided his eyes that they were worried about his reaction. "Good," he said, "That's good."

They were all quiet for a few moments while Hanaan served dinner. "Did you have a good day? Did anyone bother you?"

"No," Noor answered. "All our friends gave us hugs and said they were sorry for our loss. No one bothered us."

"Good. That's good. Sometimes kids can be real mean about stuff like this, so that's good that no one was," he said as he poked his food with his fork.

This reserved behavior was not the norm for his kids and he knew that they were being extra cautious with their words because of how he might react. He needed a way of assuring them that they could just be themselves, but as he could think of nothing, he simply asked, "Did anything fun happen at school today?"

Noor shook her head, but Deen began, "We're having field day next week. So we were talking about the races, and one of the kids said that I would probably win. He meant to say that I'm the fastest, but he said the 'fartest.' It was so funny." His laugh lasted no more than a second, then he threw his hand over his mouth and Hasan saw the tears well up in his son's eyes. Hasan got up and went over to Deen and put his arms around him. "Why are you crying, *habibi*?"

"Because I laughed. I'm not allowed to laugh."

"Who says you're not allowed to laugh? Of course you are, Deen." Hasan drew his son close to him.

"But how can I laugh when... when mama's up in heaven and we won't see her again?"

It took all of Hasan's willpower to keep his tears at bay. "Your laughter doesn't mean that you don't love mama or you don't miss her, Deen. You, too, Noor. It is one of God's great blessings on us that the one thing that is born big and gets smaller with time, is sorrow. So this is normal... this is life. And you have to live it; you have to laugh and have fun. None of that means you don't love mama. She is a part of you, now and forever, but that doesn't mean that because her life ended, yours should, too."

"She won't get mad that we're laughing when she's not here?"

"When she was with us, did she ever want you to be unhappy?"

"No," Deen said, shaking his head.

"She always wanted us happy and smiling. So that's how she wants it now."

The kids nodded and dried their eyes.

"But, baba," Deen said. "I'm still sad. I laugh sometimes, but I'm still really sad."

"Of course, *habibi*. And that's okay. Whatever you're feeling, then that's how you should be feeling. Don't feel guilty about it. If you want to laugh, then laugh. If you get sad, that's okay, too. There will be a part of you that will be sad about mama forever. But as time goes by, that part will get smaller and smaller. And that's the way God wants it so that we can enjoy life."

Hasan hugged his kids and as he got up to go back to his chair, he knocked over a glass of water. "Oh... I'll get it," he said, directing his comment to his mother.

"I know," she said as she continued eating. "And you'll get the dishes, too, when we're done."

He smiled and nodded, knowing that his loving rock would no longer baby her little boy.

Over the next couple of weeks, Hasan went back to work, and every day he would come home to various chores Hanaan left for him to do; some days it was laundry, others it was the dishes or cooking. She walked him through each step the first few times, until she was sure he would get it right on his own. His biggest problem was knowing that his mom was preparing him for when he would have to deal with everything without her. It was bad enough having to deal with the enormous void May had left; thinking of how it would be with neither May nor his mother made his chest ache.

One night after the kids had gone to bed, Hanaan and Hasan sat at the kitchen table drinking tea. "It's time for me to go, Hasan," she said.

He wanted to object, but the words would not come out. He knew that she needed to be back in her own home, and that it was selfish to ask her to stay any longer. He simply nodded.

"You are all set here. You can take care of it all. The kids are back into their routine, so *in sha' Allah*, everything will go smoothly.

"But before I leave, there's one last thing I need to talk to you about." She paused only long enough to gulp, knowing that he would not let her get through this easily, not wanting to give him any room to object before she finished all she had to say. "You are still very young. And one day – and that day arrives like the blink of an eye – your kids will be all grown up... away to college, then married. Where will you be?

"When your father died I was already an old woman. I didn't want to marry someone and end up being nothing more than his nurse and maid. And I know that my time is limited, so the moments I have left, I can share them with my family and my friends. But you still have your whole life ahead of you. You need a companion. God created us in pairs so we could share this life together... you shouldn't live the rest of yours alone."

Hasan was quiet for a moment, not wanting to be rude to the mother who had done so much for him. "May was my companion, mama. I don't want anyone else."

"Think of the future, Hasan. How alone you will be when the kids...."

"Mama," he put his hand up and shook his head as he cut her off.

"Fine. You don't want to do it for yourself, then do it for the kids. They are still babies. They should have a mother figure in their lives. I'm not saying you should go right out and start looking around... I'm just saying it's something you should keep in mind."

She quickly finished her tea, then got up and kissed her son on the forehead. "I'm going to go pack."

Hasan sat there alone, with a million thoughts racing through his mind. He wondered how life had turned and spun and landed him where he was. It seemed like only yesterday he was in college. Not just college, but he could actually remember being as young as his son. How had he lived all those years and come to be a widower sitting alone at his kitchen table? *The years do fly by like the blink of an eye*, he thought. And somehow, that gave him comfort; if the rest of his life could go by as quickly... before long, he would be with his love again.

CHAPTER 34:
Between Us

It took Summer a moment to internalize the shock at seeing Roberto. She didn't know how he had heard about it, or what his motives were for showing up, but she knew that his presence put her marriage at risk. Would Porter believe that Roberto had shown up coincidentally? She doubted it.

As they stood in a corner, munching on the snacks Summer had served them, she thought of how to best deal with the situation. There were less than two hours left of the night. *Maybe I can just avoid him,* she thought. *But there aren't enough people here to just get lost in the crowd, and I'm horrible at being secretive.... Porter will definitely figure out that something's wrong. And if he finds out then that Roberto's here,* she thought, *he'll misunderstand for sure.* That truth left her no alternative.

"Porter," she said in an alarmed tone, "I just saw Roberto."

Hearing that name again made Porter cringe. His whole face turned blood red. "Where is he?"

"Over there," she pointed, "smoking a cigar and flirting with that girl."

"Oh... it's just in his genes! I'm going to kill him."

"Please... please don't make a scene here." The desperation in her voice made him calm down slightly.

A moment later he asked her, "What do you want to do?"

"I don't know," Summer replied, almost in tears. "I'm worried that if we tell him to leave, we'll draw too much attention. What do you think?"

Porter placed his dish on a nearby coffee table. "I won't draw too much attention."

Holding her breath, Summer watched her husband go up to Roberto and put his arm around him. Porter wore a fake smile, and although she could see that he was saying something to Roberto as he led him out of the building, they were too far away for her to make out the words.

She continued to watch out the window as the two men walked over to Roberto's car. Before Roberto had a chance to put his key in the door, Porter kneed him fiercely in the groin. Roberto fell to the ground, incapacitated for more than a few moments. Porter fixed his tie, straightened his suit, and began walking back.

"You don't deserve him," a familiar voice said over her shoulder.

Summer turned to find Kara standing in front of her. "Excuse me?" she said, doubtful that she had heard correctly.

"Oh, don't play all innocent with me. I know your type. Nothing in your life satisfies you, so you look for new things to excite you. And when you get bored with that, you go back to the old. And the cycle repeats.

"Porter is too good for you," she continued. "Here he's sponsored your art contest, and you go and invite your ex-lover?! I'll bet *that* was the first time he's ever hit anyone! Look what you've turned him into. He deserves so much better than this. He should have never taken you back."

Summer's face turned red and her eyes bulged at the insults she had just been subjected to. As she watched Kara walk away, she heard Porter say, "Don't look so surprised. He deserved worse." He picked up his plate and began eating again, unaware that there had been any exchange between Kara and Summer.

Forcing away the embarrassment and the anger, Summer looked at her husband a moment later and said, "Thank you."

Her eyes were thanking him for so much more than just getting rid of Roberto and avoiding a potentially dangerous situation. In response to her genuineness, he kissed her forehead and whispered,

"Nothing comes between us."

After the winners had been announced and the prizes distributed, Summer and Porter started to clean up as the students celebrated. Luckily, Porter told Kara she could take off. As she was dismantling the pieces, one of the winners came up to Summer and said, "Thank you for this, Summer. This is as high as I've ever been... and I'm clean!"

She giggled at the girl's excitement, "Remember this feeling the next time you're tempted... and remember that it was your work that gave you this high."

The student squeezed Summer abruptly... and for the first time she understood what it meant to make a difference in someone's life.

"I mean," she said to Porter later that night as they got into bed, "I know that this doesn't guarantee they'll be able to stay clean, but at least it gives them something positive to invest themselves in. And it gives me... a lot of hope, too."

Porter held her close, "You did a great thing for those kids tonight. I'm really proud of you. I hope this will help you see things from a positive perspective all the time."

A few moments passed in silence, then Summer said, "Speaking of seeing things from a different perspective... I wanted to talk to you about Kara."

"What about her?" Porter said casually.

"She said some really inappropriate things to me today, and I just don't think it's a good idea to keep her."

"What?! Kara is... like... one of my best employees; she's responsible, diligent, professional...."

"She's not really professional, Porter."

"What are you talking about?" Porter unwrapped his arms from around her and sat up in bed.

Summer sat up beside him. "After saying some things that were... let's just say unacceptable for a secretary to say, she said that you should never have taken me back."

Porter was silent for a moment, hating to be reminded about something that he wanted to forget forever. As he lay back, turning on his side, away from his wife, he simply said, "She has a right to her opinion, Summer. I can't fire her... or even transfer her for having an opinion that's different from mine."

"She has a right to her opinion... but when that opinion is related to your personal life, she damn well better *keep that opinion to herself.*"

"She considers herself a friend. She's just looking out for me."

Summer hated his naivety. "She's not *looking out* for you... she's looking to get *with you.*"

Porter sighed heavily, "Just let it go, Summer. I can't transfer her. She's too valuable to the business, and I don't see that she did anything wrong, anyway."

Summer had expected that it would be difficult to convince him, but she had been confident that in the end he would see things as she did.

Before turning off the light, she tried one more time. "Tonight you said that 'nothing comes between us.' If she stays, I'm certain that won't be true."

CHAPTER 35:
Ground Rules

Mariam already knew who it was when she answered the phone. "Hello?"

"What's going on, Mariam? I went to get the kids from school and they weren't there. It was my day to pick them up, right? You drove them over yesterday."

"It was your day to pick them up, but you remember that summer schedule I told you we had to decide on? Well I figured it out myself: You don't get to see the kids again until you can guarantee that they won't see, hear, or smell anything inappropriate at your place. Just to be safe, let me add taste or touch to that list, too. Okay? Bye."

"Wait! Mariam, don't be ridiculous! You said yourself that I'm their father and I need to be part of their lives... you can't keep them from me!"

"No, I can't. But if I file for sole custody, and explain to the judge what kind of environment your apartment has become, he will. Trust me."

"Mariam!"

"Morgan," she said calming down. "I don't want to do that. What I want is for the kids to have their dad back. You're not a bachelor, Morgan... you're a father. I get that you want to enjoy your newfound freedom... I totally get it. But there have to be limits."

Morgan was sick of her controlling behavior. "I can't believe that even now... now that we're divorced, you still want to control my life!"

It took all her energy, but Mariam managed to remain calm. "I never wanted to control your life, Morgan. What I *need* is to raise my kids in an environment which supports the morals I'm trying to instill in them."

"I still have the same morals, Mariam!" he yelled defensively.

"Ah... when your kids go over to a smoke filled apartment and see you in your underwear at a time when you should have just gotten home from work, and you have a female friend over..." she paused, clenched her teeth and lowered her voice to a hiss, "*and her ass is sticking out of her pajamas, then I'd have to say you don't have the same morals*!"

Mariam slammed the phone down just before the kids came in from outside. She was sure they hadn't heard anything through all the commotion they were making.

At dinner that evening, Adam asked, "Why didn't we go over to Dad's today?"

She didn't want to lie to them, but what truth could she possibly say? "Ah... Dad's got a lot of stuff going on these days, so you'll be seeing him again when he sorts everything out."

"So we won't see him tomorrow, either?"

"No," Mariam replied softly.

"Or the next day?"

She sighed. "Like I said guys, you'll see him as soon as he works out his schedule."

Knowing full well that her answer had been insufficient and they would keep nagging until they got one that was reasonable, Mariam quickly distracted them by asking about school.

Lying awake in her bed that night, Mariam tried to think of how she could possibly trust her kids to be at Morgan's again. At the same time, the last thing she wanted was to deprive them of their father, or even limit their contact with him. She had no intention of filing for sole custody, but she had hoped that the idea of it would be enough to make him wake up. In either case, she knew that no matter which way things turned out, he would find a way to make *her* look like the bad guy.

Hoping that he would simply come to his senses and start acting like a responsible parent again, Mariam decided not to take any action for a few days. Several times she fought the urge to call him so they could discuss the situation, but she knew that he would consider that another control tactic.

A few days later, he finally called.

"When can I see my kids?"

"And hello to you, too, Morgan."

"We don't have to be nice to each other, Mariam. Just tell me when I can see the kids."

"You're welcome to see them *here* whenever you like."

He sighed angrily, but before he could speak, she began, "Morgan, there's no need for us to be mean to each other. We have to think about what's best for the kids, and what's best for them will always be that we are at least civil with one another. So even though you can't stand me, it makes more sense to just be polite.

"Now, I know you need to see the kids and on a regular basis. What we need is...."

"What *I* need is for you to stop telling us all what to do!"

Knowing that she would get nowhere with him, she let him have his way. "Fine, Morgan. What do you want to do? What should the visiting schedules be like and what are the rules?"

"Now that's more like it!"

He waited for a response, but she simply rolled her eyes, grunted silently, and proceeded to wring his invisible neck. "We can do a weekly schedule. So they'll spend a week with me, and a week with you."

"Sounds fair."

She waited for him to go on, but when he didn't, she asked, "And what about the ground rules?"

"They're the same as they've always been: no swearing, no fighting, when they do, they get time out...."

Mariam rolled her eyes at how determined he was to avoid the real issue. She listened to the rules that she had been raising her kids by for years, and when he was finished, she said, "Good. Sounds good. But what I meant was, what are the ground rules for us... the parents?"

"We're the parents, Mariam... we don't need rules."

"Oh, I disagree, Morgan. There are at least two rules I can think of off the top of my head: no smoking in the house while the children are with us, and no members of the opposite sex spending the nights while we have the kids, either."

She could almost hear him roll his eyes. With another heavy sigh he said, "Fine, Mariam, whatever."

"And... what about if those rules get broken? What are the consequences?"

"Are you threatening me, Mariam?!"

"Absolutely not, Morgan! I just think that we have to be absolutely clear about this. We have rules, so we need to know what happens if those rules get broken."

"They won't."

"I'm glad they won't, that's good to hear. But we still need to spell it out."

"What do you want? You want to file for sole custody if the kids accidentally see me smoking a cigarette?!"

"No, Morgan, I don't. Really." She tried to calm her voice. "Honest. I don't. But like I said, everything needs to be spelled out."

"Then... the offending party will lose visiting privileges for a week."

"Fair enough. And also the offending party will explain to the children why he or she lost those privileges."

"What?!"

"What do you mean, 'what'?" Her tone was as sarcastic as she could make it. "Let's just assume for a minute – and this is a pretty long stretch, but just for the sake of argument – that you find out that I had a guy over one night. The kids will be with you for two weeks in a row... you don't think they'll ask why they're not with me?"

"I'll just make something up."

"Oh, no. We just got ourselves rule number three: no lying to the kids. They have to know the truth. Maybe not in detail, but they have to know the truth. It's only fair that whatever parent screws up, has to explain his or her screw up to them."

"Fine." He paused for a moment. "What did you tell them about the past few days?"

"I just said you had to work your schedule out, but that's the last time I cover for you. If it happens again – like we just decided – you'll be telling them they can't be with you because you broke the rules."

"Fine."

Mariam knew that although he had been acting out of character lately, when it came down to it, he was a good dad. He loved his kids, and she was sure that he had missed them immensely over the past few days. "So when do you want to pick them up?"

CHAPTER 36:
Love is Enough

It had taken Farris a few days to calm down. He was still hurt by what Sidra had put him through, but a small part of him knew that she had done it out of love. He still didn't know what that would mean about their future, but he knew that they had to figure it out together.

This time Jeff answered the door. "Farris. Come in."

"Thanks, man. Sorry to disturb you, but I just need to speak with Sidra," he said as he walked into the living room.

"Sidra left. She's not staying with us anymore."

"She left? Where did she go?"

"I heard her tell James that she'll be staying at a hotel for a little while until her transfer goes through. She's taking this week off to pack and get herself ready."

"Transfer?"

"She asked to be relocated near her parents."

Farris felt like everything in his life was spinning out of control. He sat down and placed his head between his knees. He couldn't understand how she could continue to make all these decisions on her own and keep pulling further and further away from him when he had already discovered that her original premise for pulling away had been a lie.

He took a step toward the door. "I don't suppose you know which hotel?"

Jeff shrugged, "She didn't say."

"Of course she didn't," Farris muttered to himself. "Why would she? So that my life would be just slightly less complicated? Of course not."

Letting himself out the front door, he called out, "Thanks, Jeff."

Sitting at his kitchen table, he grabbed the phone book and began calling the local hotels in order. He said he wanted to leave a message for a guest, and every time, the reply was the same: "There is no guest here by that name, sir."

A short while later he found himself frustrated and discouraged. Slamming the phone book closed, he got up and went to take a shower. As the water washed over his body, calming him, he realized what he needed to do.

A couple of days later he sat reading in the living room when the front door opened. Sidra walked in quietly, closed the door behind her, then without realizing that Farris was there, walked past the living room and up to the bedroom.

"Finally," he whispered to himself, closing the book and setting it down carefully.

He waited for a few seconds, then climbed the stairs after her.

Sidra jumped at the squeak of the door.

"Farris! You scared the crap out of me! I thought you would be at work."

He walked in and sat on the bed without saying anything. When he didn't respond, she became anxious and started to rush. She pulled all the clothes she had left in the closet out in one big bunch and laid them on the bed. "I've just come for the rest of my stuff. I'll be gone in a few minutes."

"I called 23 different hotels looking for you."

She paused, looking at him intensely for a moment, trying to read his eyes. Deciding they only held blame and anger, she continued to grab things from the dresser drawers and place them on the bed. "Look, Farris. Whether or not you believe me, I did what I did for your own good...."

"I think you've talked enough, Sidra. It's time for me to talk and you to listen."

He got up, took her by the hands, and led her back to the bed to sit beside him.

"I took this week off of work when I found out that you were packing and getting ready to move back near your parents. When I couldn't find you at the hotels, I figured the only way for me to see you again was to make sure that I was here whenever you decided to stop by for the rest of your stuff. If I had thought, even for a split second, that you pretended to have an affair simply to spite me, or because you just wanted to leave out of boredom, or because you had fallen out of love with me, then believe me, you would have never seen me again.

"I know what you did was out of love. But I just... I guess I thought you loved me more than that. I thought you loved me enough to hear me when I say things to you. Like when I said, over and over, that although I want kids, I want *you* more. I thought you loved me enough to hear that. But you didn't."

He paused for a few moments, trying to gather his thought, trying to figure out exactly what he wanted to say. He went on, "Your 'affair' destroyed me. And when I found out it wasn't true, it killed me that you had thought of something so cruel to put me through. It took me a while to get over that. But I kept telling myself you wanted more for me, you wanted what you thought was better for me, and that was your motive. And that's why I can move past it... that's why I'm here now."

"Farris, I did want better for you...."

"I know."

"And that hasn't changed. And I don't think it ever will. I love you too much to let you settle for less...."

"I'm not settling for anything. I have exactly what I want... all I want."

Sidra stood up frustrated, "Farris, when we're old and sick, and you look back on your life, you will wish that at this moment *right now*, you had...."

"I will look back and Praise the Lord for blessing me with you in my life, just as I do now... every night. I will be certain that the happiness I found with you couldn't have come with anyone else."

She stood in the middle of the room, a look of despair in her eyes, her resolution beginning to falter, "You're going to get bored with me sometime, Farris. Just let that break come now, when I'm prepared for it… when I can handle it."

He stared at her through squinted eyes. A moment later he asked, "Sidra, what if our situation had been reversed; what if I was the one who couldn't have kids? Would you have left me?"

"Never."

"Are you sure?"

"Of course I'm sure."

"So why would you think that I could leave you? What's the difference?"

"It's different, Farris. Men and women… they're just different that way."

"You're going to have to explain, Sidra, because I don't see that difference. Actually, if there is a difference, then it's the one about women feeling the yearning to bear kids and raise them… the yearning to fulfill their maternal instincts."

She started pacing, thinking of how to word it, and a few steps later she stopped. "I got over that yearning to be a mom a while ago. It took me a bit, but I've come to terms with it.

"What I mean is that, in general, it takes a lot less to fulfill a woman than it does a man. For us, a smile, a kind word… that's all we need to be happy… to feel love. We can sacrifice even our most desired wishes, as long as we have that love to compensate.

"But for guys, they need… they get bored easily. They need change, and things to occupy them. Love isn't always enough."

He stood up, took her hand in his and, without letting go, placed it on his chest, over his heart. "Love will always be enough for me. I promise."

She stared into his eyes, searching for some kind of verification of his words. And just like every time she stared into his eyes, she saw only sincerity and adoration. Letting herself melt into them, Sidra placed her head against her husband's chest and exhaled as his embrace began to build a bridge over the rift that she had forged between them.

CHAPTER 37:
New Beginnings

Summer ran cheerfully out of the bathroom, and jumped onto the bed, unable to wait to share the news with Porter.

"Porter, honey. Wake up. Wake up, come on. I have something I need to tell you." She shook him as she spoke.

"What time is it?" he mumbled, turning his head to look at the clock. "Six thirty? Isn't it Saturday? Why are you up so early?" He tried to open his eyes, but sleep kept overtaking him.

"Come on. I just told you I have something important I need to tell you!" Her smile was wide as she climbed on top of him and shook him by the shoulders.

"Ok, ok. I'm awake. What's up?" He stroked her bare arms gently and couldn't help but share her smile.

"This is big. Are you sure you're awake?"

"Yes, I'm fully awake. Go for it," he chuckled at her childlike behavior.

"I'm pregnant!" She clapped her hands together in excitement.

But Porter's face went from smiling, to confused.

"Pregnant?" He got up slowly, forcing Summer down off of him.

"Yeah." She couldn't pretend to not notice his disappointment, but she kept the smile on her face, hoping to convince herself that his reaction was simply shock at the news.

"When? I mean, how far along are you?"

"Probably less than 2 months. I didn't think anything when I missed my period last month, but this time I took a home test. I guess I'll go see an ob/gyn later this week."

He was quiet, sitting on the edge of the bed with his back to her.

His silence erased the smile from her face. A few moments later, Summer asked him, "Aren't you happy that you're going to be a dad?"

"What about your meds? I thought that... well, taking them during pregnancy isn't safe?"

"My therapist has been tapering them down anyway, but I have read that there are alternative meds for pregnancy. I'll check in with her this week."

He'd barely heard her; his anxiety wasn't really rooted in the medications. But there were too many thoughts running through his mind for him to sort through the confusion. He simply got up, and went into the bathroom.

When he returned, Summer stared at him with sullen eyes. "What's wrong?"

"Really, Summer? You don't know what's wrong? You just had an affair a few months ago, and now you're telling me you're pregnant, and you don't know what's wrong?!"

"No, Porter. No.... It was longer... I mean, there is no way that... I mean, *you* are this baby's father! There is absolutely no question about that."

"I disagree with you. I'll need more proof than just your words. You know, my brother told me... he told me this wasn't a good idea," he kept speaking excitedly as he pulled on a pair of sweats. "He said this type of thing remains in your past and you can never truly get past it. At the time, I didn't know what to think. I thought he didn't really understand marriage... or love, for that matter.

"But now... he was right. Everything had been fine between us these past few months, more than fine even. They've been better than ever! And news that should have made me happy and excited and nervous, just shot through me like a knife, all because of an affair that I had convinced myself I had forgiven."

Summer stared at him with wide eyes, unable to completely register what he was saying.

"But..." she let out hesitantly, "You did forgive me. And you can be sure that this is your baby."

"I don't know, Summer. I just need..." he finished getting dressed and looked around him, searching. "I need... I don't know what I need. I need some time to think. I mean, even if this is my kid, am I really ready to be a dad? I don't know anything about parenting. And there are still so many things I wanted to do before getting bogged down with children." He shook his head nervously. "I don't know. I don't know." He grabbed his keys and headed for the door. "I need to think. I'll see you later."

Summer was crushed by his reaction. She sat alone on their bed, unable to move. She had known that Porter wouldn't be immediately thrilled by the news, but she had anticipated a much less hostile reaction. Although it was his brother's hesitation that Porter claimed to be voicing, Summer had her own suspicions about who was behind his behavior; she knew that if Kara was still working closely with her husband, she would do and say anything to drive a wedge in her marriage.

Sitting there for a few minutes, an image of May crossed her mind. Remembering how strongly she had spoken of forgiveness, Summer thought that perhaps she was missing a step in the process of truly obtaining forgiveness. She sat up straight and, looking up at her ceiling, in the solitude of her home, made a prayer. She prayed to a God that she was only beginning to believe in, that He forgive her sins, and bless her marriage.

"And please, God... don't let anyone come between us."

She hoped that time would be kind to her, and quickly cause Porter to have a change of heart. In either case, she was determined to celebrate her good fortune. She showered and dressed then made her way over to Mariam's.

"Hey, Summer. How are you? Come in."

Stepping through the doorway, Summer realized something wasn't right. "This quiet isn't normal for you... is everything okay with the kids?"

Mariam couldn't help but laugh. "Wow, when even your neighbors can tell when the kids are away, that is a sure sign that everything they do is about one hundred decibels louder than normal!"

"Oh, they're away," Summer repeated. "No... they're not louder than normal, they just have more energy than most people. Their mere presence makes the air itself more alive," she joked.

Mariam chuckled, "That's a nice way to put it!"

"That's actually why I'm here."

"Oh, no," Mariam could tell what was coming. "What did they do?"

Summer chuckled. "No... no. They didn't do anything. I meant, if you wouldn't mind, I could use some advice... from a veteran mother to a mother-to-be."

"Oh my God! Summer, that's great! Congratulations!" She hugged her friend zealously.

"I figured... after four, you must be an expert."

"You would think," replied Mariam, throwing her hands up. "But they just keep adding new chapters to the book, and despite my best efforts, I just can't keep up!"

Summer sat at the kitchen table as Mariam poured them coffee.

"I'm only a couple of months so I know it's still early. But my biggest issue right now is Porter. I thought he would be excited. Well, maybe not excited. But not... alarmed. How did Morgan react to your first pregnancy?"

"He was actually more excited than I was. Morning sickness hit me pretty hard and very early on with Adam, so I remember being absolutely miserable the first few months. And that's not to mention the emotional roller coaster I kept us on. But he was very supportive and very excited. He bought me my first pair of maternity pants all by himself."

Mariam's words added to Summer's concern. "Oh."

Seeing the anxiety increase on her friend's face, she tried to appease it, "But I'm sure lots of people freak out about having kids. And it's not like it's happening tomorrow; if you're only a couple of months along then he still has seven months to prepare himself. Maybe he needs that time to do some things he feels he won't get to do once you have a baby."

Summer nodded, "Yeah, maybe. Maybe we can do some light traveling or something. I just hope that's enough." Her eyes betrayed that there was more to her concern than she was letting on.

But Mariam tried to bring her back to the celebratory mood she had arrived in, "I have to go buy some things for the kids tomorrow... would you like to come along? I mean, I know it's still very early, but it's never too early to just look around and see what's out there."

Summer's smile finally returned, "Oh, that would be great."

"Why don't we make a day of it? Lunch and all."

"Perfect."

As Summer started to get up to leave, Mariam asked, "Do you think Sidra would like to come along?"

Summer shrugged, still smiling.

"Come on."

The women found Sidra sitting on her front step having her morning cup of coffee.

"Good morning, ladies."

"Hey, Sidra. We're going out tomorrow – shopping and lunch – and we wanted you to come along. We're celebrating Summer being pregnant."

"Oh, my God! Summer, congratulations!" Sidra stood up and hugged her friend sincerely. Her heart ached slightly that Summer was experiencing the very thing that she could not... the only thing missing to make her life complete. But she wished only the best for Summer. *God bless you and your little one.*

"I would love to come with you guys, but tomorrow is our anniversary and Farris and I are spending the whole day together. But maybe next weekend we can do lunch together?"

"Sounds good. So what do you and Farris have planned?"

Sidra rolled her eyes, "He's making me go wall climbing! Can you picture me, strapped into one of those harnesses that always remind me of diapers, and hanging for dear life to a wall? Not a pretty sight."

The women's laughter was contagious; Sidra found herself laughing with them. "He said we each get to pick something to do and the other person can't refuse. So," Sidra cleared her throat, sat up straighter and asked teasingly, "you know what we're doing after wall climbing?"

"Uh oh! Sounds like a dangerous deal!" Summer joked.

"I tried telling him that it was in his best interest to have a compromise instead, but he refused." She shook her head sympathetically and shrugged her shoulders. "So... we're going to a spa! Can you picture six foot four Farris, wrapped up in towels from head to toe, like a pampered princess!" Their laughter could be heard all the way around the block. "He'll actually probably like the massage, but if the facial doesn't get to him, I'm sure the manicure-pedicure will make him think twice about taking me wall climbing again!"

The women chatted for a few more minutes, then Sidra excused herself. "I wish I could stay, but I have some important errands I need to run. But we're on for next weekend?"

"Of course. It's a date."

As Sidra drove away, Mariam and Summer finalized their plans for the following day, then each of them walked back toward her own house. Before getting to her driveway, Mariam spotted an unusual sign in her neighbor's yard.

"Sold? Sold when? When did it even go on sale?"

She needed to find out before going home.

"Hello, Mariam. Come in," Hasan said.

"Thanks, Hasan. I just... I just noticed the sign," she pointed out the door at the front yard. "Are you moving?"

"Yes. I decided it doesn't really make any sense for us to live here anymore. It's important to be near family. I tried desperately to convince my mom to live with us, but she's just too stubborn." Imitating his mother's voice he continued, "'I can't live anywhere but here. This is my home and it will be till the day I die.' I tried so many times, I even had the kids ask her, hoping to guilt her into it, but no luck. I found a job near where she lives. We'll be staying with her until I find a place, but the realtor already has some houses lined up for me to check out, so I don't think that should take too long."

"Oh." She was quiet for a minute. "And how are the kids handling that?"

"They hate that they'll be leaving their friends… but they need their grandmother now. She needs us, too. I mean, God bless her and give her health, but I have to be near her in case she needs taking care of. It's a good move." Hasan nodded to assure himself that moving the kids from the only home they had ever known, the one that held all the memories of their mother, was the right thing to do.

"Of course. Of course it'll be good for them to be near their grandmother." She paused for a minute. "It's just that… my kids are really going to miss Noor and Deen. I mean… I remember when we first moved here. I was pregnant with Adam, and May was already running around chasing Noor. I guess I just thought we would always be neighbors."

Hasan nodded in appreciation of her sentiment. But his short pause gave her the chance to say what he was thinking, "I guess nothing stays the same forever.

"Well," she continued, fighting back unexplainable tears and trying to sound more cheerful, "I'd like to have a last get together before you go, at least so the kids can say goodbye. When do you leave?"

"I'm afraid that won't be possible; we're all packed up." He waved his hand behind him, indicating all the closed boxes piled up. Mariam hadn't noticed them until just then.

"Tomorrow the movers will just put all these boxes and the furniture on the moving truck, and we'll be on our way."

"Tomorrow? Wow, that was quick. Wow."

For some reason Hasan moving his family away was affecting her more than she knew it should. But it just seemed that everything was changing all at once, and she had no control over any of it.

Wiping away the few tears that had escaped, she forced a smile and said jokingly, "Do you know who my new neighbors are? I mean, are they as loud and obnoxious as you guys?"

Hasan laughed. "If you thought we were loud and obnoxious, then you definitely won't appreciate the new neighbors. She sings, he plays the drums, and they have three dogs, each weighing about twice as much as me."

"Really?" Mariam asked with eyes bulging. She was hoping he would say, 'no, just kidding.' But he didn't.

"Really."

"Oh, that does *not* sound good."

Hasan handed her a tissue, and as she wiped her eyes and nose, trying to regain her composure, she asked if the kids were around so she could say goodbye. A moment later they both came running down the stairs.

"I wish I had known that you guys were leaving so soon... I would have made sure my kids were here so they could say goodbye. We are all going to miss you very much. I hope you enjoy being with your grandmother. I'm sure you guys will make friends right away with the neighbors and at school." She hugged the kids and as she turned to leave, Hasan held the door open for her.

"Good luck with everything, Hasan. I wish you the best."

He gave her one long nod with an appreciative smile. He watched her walk across the street and go into her house. Closing the door, he let out a soft sigh. He knew what he and the kids needed was to be near their family, but this had been his home for so many years. He could not help but feel sad at the thought of leaving.

"Is something wrong, baba?" Noor asked.

Ruffling her hair, he smiled and said, "No... *Alhamdu lillah*, everything is fine.

"Did you guys finish up? Do you need my help with anything?"

"No, baba. We're all done. You just have to move the boxes from our rooms down here."

"Good. I'll let the movers take care of that tomorrow. Right now we have one last errand to run. I don't want to leave it for tomorrow. You guys get your shoes on."

An hour later, Hasan and his two children stood at the foot of his wife's grave. They recited some passages from the Qur'an and Hasan led them in some brief supplications.

They stood there for a few minutes in silence, wiping away their tears. Then Hasan spoke, in a voice that the children could barely hear. "May, *habibti*, tomorrow we're moving to go live near my mother. That just makes more sense now. I found a good job there, and I'm sure that within a few weeks I'll be able to find us our own place.

"The kids..." he paused for a few seconds, "well, and even myself... part of us hate this move because it will take us away from the home that carries all of our memories of you. And because we won't get to visit you here."

Their crying intensified for a few moments. Hasan again wiped his tears and tried to control his voice. "But I don't really believe that I need to come here to pray for you or even speak to you. We can pray for you from anywhere in the world, and you'll get the benefit of those prayers. And we can talk to you from anywhere, and *in sha' Allah*, the angels will carry those messages to you.

"And all our memories... they aren't held in a two story building made of brick and wood... they are held in our hearts. We will have them... and treasure them forever, from any place on this earth."

He paused for a few moments. "I'm going to go wait in the car so the kids can have some privacy to say whatever they want to you. I miss you very much. And I will continue to love you until we meet again. *As salaamu alaikum, habibti.*"

From his car, Hasan watched as his kids sent their love to their mother through tears that refused to pause. A few minutes later he saw them both blow kisses toward the grave and say their final goodbyes.

As the sniffling subsided on their ride home, Hasan said, "I know you guys are sad about this move. But I think being with *Sitto* will be good for all of us. Even her. I'll bet she's missed Poopy since she left us."

"Baba! His name's Poppy," Deen corrected.

"Try telling that to *Sitto*!" his father replied.

And although they were faint smiles, coming from faces streaked with tears and crowned with bright red eyes, Hasan saw in them a hope that he prayed would be strong enough to get them through.

Glossary of Arabic Terms

- ***Asr*** is one of the five daily obligatory prayers for a Muslim.
- ***As salaamu alaikum*** is the proper Muslim greeting; it means 'may peace be upon you'.
- ***Alhamdu lillah*** means 'praise be to God'.
- ***Dhuhr*** is one of the five daily obligatory prayers for a Muslim. Friday Dhuhr is prayed in congregation, and therefore mosques tend to be more crowded during that prayer than any other.
- ***Habibi*** (m) [***habibti*** (f), ***habaybi*** (pl.)] is an Arabic term of endearment—used especially in the Egyptian dialect—that can be translated as 'sweetie', 'sweetheart', or 'my love.'
- ***In sha' Allah*** means 'God willing'.
- ***Ma sha' Allah*** literally means 'what God has willed.' By using this term, a person states that someone or something is awe inspiring while simultaneously protecting that person or thing from envy.
- ***Sitto*** is one of a few Arabic terms meaning Grandma.
- ***Wa alaikum as salaam*** is the response to *as salaamu alaikum*; it means 'and may peace be with you also'.
- ***Wudu*** is the ablution performed before prayer.

Made in the USA
San Bernardino, CA
02 December 2019

60733458R00131